The *Good* Mistress

Praise for

Amarie Avant

" I love a tall, dark and handsome man with a large bank account. But what I liked most about him was that he was a British aristocrat with a twisted mind. Dark is my favorite. He has everything in life and yet he chose a profession of danger. (I won't give away his trade) It wasn't because he was spoiled or bored; it was because of his warped mind stemming all the way back from childhood."

~Author Dormaine G. "Connor"

"All I am left saying is this was a good read that will keep you on the edge of your seat not wanting to put it down this read that had so much drama until the end and even then you will still be left wanting more.."

Arlena Dean Reviewer

"Fear was an interesting read, to say the very least. When I first began the story, I wasn't sure of what to expect. This is a new author to me, and I don't venture out much. With that being said, I'm glad I did. I found two very different main characters on the outside. But deep down inside, they were both dealing with the disappointments of life. ."

~Janice Ross "Jezebel Jones"

The *Good* Mistress

A Billionaire Romance

AMARIE AVANT

ALSO BY AMARIE AVANT

FEAR: Falling In love with an Alpha Billionaire 1-3

Publisher: Blu Savant Press
Cover Design: Anna Crosswell / Cover Couture, www.bookcovercouture.com
Photo Copyright: BeautyBlowFlow / Shutterstock
Photo Copyright: pisaphotography / Shutterstock
Photo Copyright: Kiselev Andrey Valerevich / Shutterstock

Library of Congress Cataloging-in-Publication Data
Avant, Amarie.
The Good Mistress/ Amarie Avant.
p. cm. – (A billionaire roomance. bk, 1)
ISBN-13:978-1523315550 (pbk.)
ISBN-10:1523315555

1. Contemporary–Fiction. 2. Interracial Romance–Fiction.

Printed in the United States of America

To Brandon, you are the best love story of my life.

JBug (Janice) and Dormaine, you two are loved (and on occasion) harassed by yours truly!

Patrice, I hope Mila has an abundance up depth.

Prologue
Mila Ali

I made a mistake... Mila exhaled. Notes of black maple bourbon coated her tongue with the raw taste of *him* as she backed against the marble ledge of an accent table. The room's embellishments were elaborate. Millions of dollars' worth of modern paintings graced the wall, but Mila was the centerpiece. Before his lips had touched the velvety dew of her rich, dark hazelnut complexion, Mila had been of sound mind. Mila knew how seductive she looked the instant she'd slipped on the lingerie he sent to her. The French couture olive green lace teddy graced her bodacious ass and hips, solidifying her place in his world. So she'd walked into his lair with confidence. Ready to go...making demands. Complete the deed. Just then, fire lit that bulbous ass of hers. "I made a mistake…"

Billionaire Blake Baldwin declared, "No. No, mistake made. You came into this motherfucker like you own it! Now own it. You voiced your stipulations, and I quote, 'No tying me up or *down*. No spankings. No gags. No debasing. Period'. Mila, a moment ago, *you* called the shots. Tell me, where the fuck is *that* Mila Ali? I want to fuck *that* Mila. The *bold, bossy* one."

"How unfortunate for you." Mila smiled, in the short time Mila had known Blake Baldwin, she'd taken on this snide stance that the usually good-natured Mila rarely had. He conjured her strongest emotions, even before they'd actually touched. However, having agreed to this position, she genuinely added, "I just changed my mind about this sexual tryst. My apologies."

Mila was shocked he didn't retort. She fought against that hypnotic emerald gaze, allowing her own to survey the taut planes of an eight pack stacked above a glorious V-shape. A raised scar traveled along those abs—courtesy of one of his daring mountain climbs in a far-off exotic place. Dressed in a pair of silk navy blue pajama pants, Blake stood. He was well over six feet.

Mila took a deep breath as he stepped over to her. Why had she stopped kissing him? The answer lay in the way that his full lips collided with hers, as if he could read her mind. But what she really *needed* was a quick fuck.

For an entire month, Mila formulated a game plan for this encounter. The golden god should have been a short-term fix. He became her first taste in months. Blake wasn't the real threat to her sanity, time was.

Six months' shy of thirty, Mila already knew one thing: she could never love again. It wasn't as if Internet communications mogul Blake Baldwin sought anything more than a fuck. This would be a win-win for him.

"Damn, Mila. You stepped into my house like you own it. *Own it.*"

"Ye...yes..." Halfheartedly listening, Mila searched the room for her coat and stilettos. She needed to be as calculating as Blake. Mila eyed her camel hair coat across the room.

"I *am* leaving." Mila smiled curtly. They were both highly educated people; however, she knew the sneaky bastard was stalling. Mila snatched up her coat that fell just past mid-thigh. A lump formed in her throat. "Look. I want to get over Warren, but..."

"But you'd rather leave?"

Nope. I'm not taking the bait. She'd only known Blake a few months. Mila refused to mention more about Warren. It's never in good taste to talk about your fiancé to another man. Not ever.

As she shoved one arm into the coat, Mila thought, *I'm beside myself with heartbreak. I'm hardly thinking straight.*

As soon as she began latching the buttons, Blake towered over her. For the first time in what felt like an eternity, the muscular organ that Mila believed to be her frozen heart, skipped a beat.

Blake took the peach silk scarf dangling from the back of a settee. "When will we try this again?"

Mila shrugged. "Maybe I'll fuck you next week. How about that?"

He looped the fine silk within his fingers. No longer the center of attention, but damn, Mila wanted to be. All the while he stroked the scarf, her pussy quivered. A deep, almost animalistic groan escaped his lips. "Next week, you say? I'm patient."

She tried not to scoff. *Damn, I've run from this man. Cussed him. And now I want to run again...* Blake slowly twined the scarf fashionably about her neck. Next, Blake reached down, his lips barely brushing her own. The gesture was warm, a friendly token, yet it was just enough to weaken her knees.

"Your wife..."

"We've already confirmed I'm in an open marriage."

"Yes, we have…" Mila turned away. *I'm almost to the home front.* Mila ambled toward the front doors, faltering as the scarf slowly unraveled and fell from Blake's fingertips. He moved behind her in one fluid motion and pressed against the soft side of Mila's round ass.

Blake's warm breath tickled all the way down her spine and struck a wild frenzy at her nether regions. "Mila, you're so fucking gorgeous." He nibbled her collar bone, his cock spearing her buttocks. "Do you know what you deserve? Diamonds to compliment the sparkle in those beautiful almond eyes. I could offer you so many things to showcase your beauty, Mila, but only on the condition that you become exactly who you were designed to become."

Mila. Ate. Every. Fucking. Word.

And then Blake stopped.

"What was I designed to become?" Her neck welcomed those nibbles that he bestowed with fervor. Her ass grinded against the rock hard beast.

"Blake, what do you want me to be?"

He shifted away, pushing down his pants. He slid on a condom like a pro, yet she still almost died waiting. Blake's hand slipped beneath her jacket, down to her hip and continued to the lace teddy. A ripple of desire escaped Mila's lips as Blake pushed the lace material to the side. His fingers glided over silky ebony coils. His heartbeat steadied against her back. That damn intoxicating cologne infused her nostrils with each breath she took. Blake allowed a finger to toy with her sweetness. “Blake, what is...”

He growled while his foot swiped the inside of both her feet, lengthening her stance. The act was sheer good cop, bad girl erotic. He smacked her ass so hard that her breath hitched, and still, she was lost; stuck on stupid as two fingers now delved inside her swollen petals. Mila's hips arched, needing more than this bit of satisfaction. “Blake... Tell meeee... Wh... What—”

“Mine. Mila. You and your beauty, *all of you,* were designed to belong to me.”

“Yesss...”

“Good fucking god!” Blake shouted as her long orgasm drenched down his fingers. He tore the camel jacket from her arms, pushed her body forward. Mila found leverage with the marble countertop as his cock eased teasingly into her wet core. A vase of orchids crashed to the floor. Each and every inch he had to offer filled her up and then some. Her hands braced against the table. With each thrust, Blake molded her walls to his cock.

It was a hard fuck: pure aggression and naughty spankings with no room for thought. Now that was exactly what she came for. Mila imagined her ass cheek had been branded by his handprint.

“Harder!”

Blake hit her g-spot a hundred times over. The table banged against the Venetian wallpaper over and over again. Sweat glistened across her burning skin. Mila thrusts her curvy ass back to meet Blake's dick.

Blake reached over as his fingers grasped her thick mahogany strands, pulling them back and making her ass arch even more.

Fireworks exploded as they came together long and hard. Something told Mila that there'd be no after-sex hugging— all good, because she didn't want love. His jagged breath felt like home to her bare back.

Mila, breasts rising and falling, did a one-two step, regaining her balance. Blake smiled at her. His voice, breathy as he caressed the dampness of her neck, advised, "Now that we've finished the business portion of this meeting-" He paused, large, barbarian-like hands grabbing her cheeks as his mouth bruised her own with a hard kiss. "At your wish Mila, I've consented to your request of no tying, no gags. No debasing... It's my turn. Go upstairs to the first set of double doors. Get in my bed. Lie back. Legs wide."

Mila fell speechless. They'd just fucked. And that was only the start, he reassured her with a kiss, but the look in Blake's eyes implied that the quick fuck ended. He planned on devouring her body, slowly and meticulously.

Now for him being the easy way out? Hmmm, if Mila had been grounded at this moment, she'd know that using Blake to help bring her back to life after losing her fiancé could never be an option. He'd pierce through the numbness, but there'd be a bigger price to pay.

CHAPTER 1

Blake Baldwin

Beverly Hills, Four Months Before

THE SORT OF man who lived life to the fullest, Blake's upbringing taught him how to toe the line, to primarily get what he wanted, then strike when needed.

This was not the time to strike.

He glanced at the scotch on the marble mantle of the 2,000 square foot master suite, but refused to hear Diane's fucking mouth about his drinking before noon, even if she had a point.

The feather duvet puffed around Diane's delicate frame as she climbed around the Cal King bed. She had already thrown the feather pillows at him for waking her up so early. Her white silk robe blended with her porcelain skin, haphazardly opened as the hasty knot slackened. Blake glared at his beautiful wife, and then her demure features transformed into an ice princess. All the while, Diane's pale gray eyes narrowed.

Blake snatched up his initialed *BB* diamond encrusted cufflinks They awoke hours ago, and he'd satisfied the greedy little witch before showering and asking her ever so nicely to get ready.

"I'm not in the mood for your shit today, Diane. We have a funeral to attend. Get dressed."

Diane pointed her cigarette at him as he put on a tie. "Sorry asshole, I don't like funerals. *Your* employee, *your* business, *you* attend the damn funeral."

"Oh, it's all *my* business now. That's right. Guess what?" Blake walked over to the bedside table. "These are *my* meds. Remember that every time you take one of these happy pills or buy one of these stupid knickknacks." He tossed a crystal figurine. It crashed against the French hand-painted wallpaper. "*I* bought it. *I* made you!"

"Oh yeah? Well you made me a material blonde." Diane flipped her hair. "But guess what, asshole?"

Blake smirked, not even wanting to know her mantra or how "asshole" became his nickname. They had attended Yale together. Diane's major had been undeclared for two years before dropping out. Her family's money allowed her a lifestyle of frivolity. He'd been a Computer Science major, and now his money dwarfed her inheritance.

> *Back then, Diane had a real body: a tight ass and certified tits. Okay the tits were a size B, maybe... But palming them was amazing, amazingly fucking real. Now Diane was a trophy. There was once a time when he'd give a few billion for them to go back in time. Now silicone saturated her pretty little "Prom Queen" genetic make-up. A*

fucking gorgeous zombie, since now only premium sedatives were her fancy.

"Warren just died." Blake attempted to appeal to any morsel of humanity in his wife.

Diane blinked in response.

Warren Jameson had. been on Blake's financial advisement team. Barely twenty, Blake had invented a cell phone application at the start of the new millennium, when apps at the time were, by societal standards, expensive. These days, most apps are free with the option to buy-in to various components after downloading. This had given Blake a foothold into the social media world. The entrepreneur, turned millionaire, continued his favorite past-time of writing codes, while dating Diane, who was still wealthier than he at the time.

"Let's bow off the funeral. Blake, fuck me, baby..." She sank into a seated position at the edge of the bed. Burlesque had nothing on Diane as her long, dramatic, willowy legs swept apart, allowing him a glimpse at her tight little pussy "C'mon baby, you've always had an appetite."

He licked his lips. Diane had waxed. Every contour within that cunt glistened, calling out to him. But the pink budded lips were of course plastic, too.

Instead of taking the bait, Blake stared deep into Diane's stormy gaze. Blake grabbed Diane's calves, dragging her over. She grinned. He would be late to the wake.

~~~

Gray skies and a flurry of clouds added to the somber mood as the Catholic Cathedral loomed before him. An Armani shoe planted on the curb as Blake stepped out of the backseat. He personified luxury, wearing a custom suit made of the finest vicuña wool. He extended a hand to his wife, to which she glared and flipped her wrist for him to move as she got out of the car.

"I can't believe you'd ruin my day," Diane grumbled as the Mercedes-Maybach swooped away from the curbside.

In one fluid motion, Blake looped his arm through hers and yanked her close. "Don't start, Diane."

He nodded to a black couple. The woman had to be Warren's family; the resemblance lay in her downcast, distraught eyes.

"Blake." Diane stopped in her tracks. "I can already *smell* his dead body."

Blake scolded himself for being the cause of this predicament. Nobody seemed to notice her dramatic display. They stepped into the sanctuary and noticed most of Warren's wealthy clients stood at the back and came to pay their respects.

There were hushed cries, except for one very loud woman whom he remembered as Warren's mother. He didn't know who took the fucking cake: Diane's furrowed nose and her silent argument, or Warren's mother's weeping.

Halfway down the aisle, Blake stopped in his tracks, his vision zoning in on a rare thing of beauty not fifty yards away. He watched
~~~

her offer tissues and hug others. She seemed entirely too altruistic, too helpful, too giving. Where was *her* shoulder to cry on?

Blake had seen her hair before—that thick, silky, lustrously long mane—in a photo Warren had had on his desk. She'd been wearing a coy smile in the image.

Shit, I would have had her already if I
had known how fucking gorgeous she is.

She flitted around, offering comfort to mourners, rubbing Warren's mother's back.

All sounds dissipated as Blake rubbed his fingertips together. Her long brown hair coiled into a thick braid over one shoulder, grazing a perky breast. Her natural beauty was a work of art he could study for hours. A smattering of gloss shone on her full, heart-shaped lips. She was the very thing that Diane pretended to be when they first met.

In this place, God's place, he wanted to fall to his knees in worship and hike up that black dress which hid a delight of curves. He wanted to palm her ass while placing one of those ample thighs over his shoulder and then he'd have a plentiful feast on the succulence between her thighs as Jesus held out his palms in the background.

Her moans would become a symphony throughout the cathedral. Maybe he'd lay her on one of the pews. No, better yet, the stage, where he would anoint her cunt with his cock until a deliriously erotic smile illuminated that melancholic face.

Then she turned in Blake's direction. Those chocolate brown eyes warmed through him, but the connection didn't last a nanosecond. Mila looked straight through him.

CHAPTER 2

IN A FRACTION of a second, she went from selecting wedding ceremony flowers—peonies or lilies? —to telling Warren how she had sent in a proposal for a grant to this or that organization, to her fiancé being no more. There'd be no more happiness, no more arguments. No more asking Warren to turn off the MacBook or the iPad or his iPhone, or any other worldly contraption. No candid, lazy days where they would chat about the names of their future children and how he'd say their son and daughter *had* to resemble *her*; no great debates since the two disagreed about political parties.

A large canvas picture of Warren shrouded by a plethora of roses perched on a stand beside his casket. Handsome, with dark brown skin, he had the sort of trustworthy smile that made you want to reciprocate. But Mila couldn't be capable of such a difficult feat then. His Cherrywood, top-of-the-line casket lay closed. Mila's last image of the man she'd planned to marry had come over FaceTime, before a business meeting in New York.

The final message was a missed call he made from the airport as he waited for his return flight.

"Mila, I haven't even started loving you like I should." Warren's voice had been somewhat muffled.

He paused.

She would give her life to see the expression on his face, because though thousands of miles away, his emotions were deep. Warren never groveled—most of the time, he gave her his full attention. However, the wedding planner did *say these would be trying times. "But I love you with all of me. When I get back, I want to spend every waking moment talking about ... peonies with you," he had scoffed. She could only imagine that he was smiling. "Look, if you want hot pink bridesmaid's dresses, I'm all in. I apologize for being so busy these past few weeks, and I know for a fact that the government grant you've been rewriting for months is already perfect. You really gotta stop second-guessing yourself. Send it in, beautiful."*

Then Warren, and a few others, boarded a company jet home…

Mila stifled a sob. He had wanted to make things right. And once he returned, they'd start over.

Her face was expressionless other than her turned down brow and a single tear at a time. She knew if she allowed herself to feel, she would break.

Warren's mother, Mrs. Jameson, had damn near passed out from seeing the closed casket.

Since Mila and Warren weren't married, her parents probably wouldn't show at the funeral. She didn't even know if they planned to make an appearance at her pending nuptials. Mila's Somalian family had spurned her western ways, just as she had refused the arranged marriage she was expected to honor.

As Mila turned around to continue ushering, her best friend, Clarissa, walked in. The beauty outshone her geeky counterpart, Todd, who dressed in a simple Armani suit. Clarissa's red hair had been brushed back into a chignon. She wore a flowing black number that, on anyone else, wouldn't seem appropriate for a funeral. But Clarissa being Clarissa, she evoked the somberness of the moment as she held out her slender hands.

"Hey, Mila. Why are you working so hard?" Clarissa pulled her into an embrace before Mila could answer, which sent tears burning into her almond eyes once more.

"Just keeping busy."

"Hello, Mila. How are you hanging in there?" Todd peered through his Clark Kent glasses.

"Alright, thank you. And you?" Todd had been one of Warren's closest friends and cohorts. She'd introduced him to Clarissa a few months ago.

Suddenly Clarissa gasped. "Mila, look over there..."

Mila's eyes landed on her friend's target as Clarissa said, "Everyone said he'd be too busy to come. I'm surprised."

"He?" Mila continued surveying the room, unsure who Clarissa spoke of. Though most of the non-family members flocked toward the back of the large cathedral, the room was filled with powerhouses. Warren, with his sharp wit and analytical capabilities, had helped build many empires.

"Blake. *Blake Baldwin...*"

Mila shrugged. The name was familiar because she heard Warren thank his boss on numerous occasions for those grand vacation packages that Mr. Baldwin provided each year. Mila only needed a quick trip to Vegas or a weekend in Napa Valley to clear her mind.

There would be no more closed-eyed, serendipitously pointing to a new destination on the globe with Warren. There is no more Warren...

"The one that is so unnecessarily hot. I'm creaming in my panties. Oh, his wife is hot as hell too."

Mila glanced through the sea of affluent men, and there amongst the muck stood a dominating force. His face was sculpted by the gods, with a sharp nose, chiseled jaw, and a brow bridge that appeared to take ages to construct. Unshaven, with a dash of stubble that had many women wanting to touch the soft bristles, even in the church. A tailored suit molded his broad shoulders and brawny biceps, with every sinew carved to perfection. Only Mila could see none of it through her blur of tears.

"I'll take you to meet Blake." Clarissa licked her lips. Even wearing prescription eyeglasses, Todd didn't seem to notice or care. He straggled along behind the two since Clarissa's eyes were for his boss, Blake Baldwin.

"Diane, you're looking gorgeous." Clarissa commenced the ass kissing while also kissing each side of Blake's wife's cheeks. "Blake..."

"Ms. Ali." Blake hugged Mila before *hello* could cross her lips. "As Warren's employer, I feel at fault."

Mila's throat constricted as she held a slender hand to her neck, shaking her head. "No, no..."

Clarissa came to Mila's rescue to make Blake feel less guilty. She began to paw at his lapel. Diana cut her eyes over. Todd, as usual, disregarded the flirtatious gesture. Mila was too numb to notice any of it.

Mila shook her head. Had he read her? *Yes, this was his fault!* "No. It... It's not..." The words clogged in Mila's throat. Warren died in a small jet crash. One of Baldwin's jets. Doing one of Baldwin's jobs. So, yes, Baldwin was at fault. But the reality of this fault, as Mila saw it, she had yet to utter. She could not even speak the words that her fiancé had died. As she'd helped Warren's mother prepare for the funeral, Mila could not fathom how she actually had never spoke of it.

Mila lifted her index finger, needing a moment. Diane rolled her eyes, causing Mila to turn and scurry toward the front of the church to greet the one family member who bothered to show up and support her.

Mila approached her sister Lido, the middle child. Mila was the baby. They were the black sheep of the three Ali girls.

"You okay?" Lido's cat eyes cut toward the back of the church. Be it the catwalk or the church, the international supermodel had no qualms about cussing someone out to protect her baby sister.

Mila nodded. It wasn't the right answer; hell, it wasn't an answer at all. She wasn't all right. She had estranged herself from family when Mila chose to attend UCLA. After obtaining an MBA, Mila was to return home to make good on an arranged marriage to a prominent Ethiopian. But Mila had been scouted by an elite, ruthless conglomerate. She'd lost herself climbing the corporate latter.

Mila sighed, remembering how Warren breathed life back into her soul. There was nothing like proving yourself in a man's world. Mila would miss Warren for a lifetime. She most certainly wasn't all right. She might never be.

CHAPTER 3

THREE MONTHS HAD passed since Blake had seen her. There was just something about a woman who nurtured in times of need. Blake had envied Mila's majestic and wavy mahogany hair as it tenderly swept over her shoulder, wishing it were him doing the touching and caressing instead. He felt any assistance of comfort on his part would have been premature at best, since the redhead had done most of the talking during their encounter at the funeral.

Blake had his assistant order two dozen white roses, and the strong, floral scent floated from the black leather passenger seat beside him. He had not inhaled such a sweet, angelic fragrance since the last time he'd seen *her.* Soon, and very soon, Blake would stake claim to his latest conquest. He dressed down for the occasion, wearing a crisp, white button down underneath a beige cashmere sweater that always brought attention to the golden flakes sprinkled throughout his green eyes. Premium distressed jeans and loafers completed Blake's laidback ensemble. He drove his new Tesla, the *smart* sports car that his social media company had helped branch out in the early 2000s. Blake drove toward Laguna Nigel, CA in the OC. Though the Jameson-Ali home wasn't a mansion, the home was still a jewel and on pristine Pacific Ocean front property.

The Tesla crept to a stop at the wrought iron gate. The window zipped down and Blake pressed the intercom.

"He..Hello?" Mila's sweet voice was hesitant through the speaker, enticing him even more. His hands tingled with anticipation. With every dollar he made, surrounding himself with good people was lost to him. He *needed* her.

"It's Blake."

"Blake…?"

"Blake Baldwin." Her lack of recognition left him dumbfounded.

The gates slowly opened, and the Tesla proceeded up the fragmented stone. He pulled in next to Mila's Honda Accord. Warren's Porche was gone. Mila leaned against the doorframe, casually dressed in a pair of jeans which clung to her womanly curves, but the oversized shirt swallowed up much of her silhouette. She stood straight, almost as if ready to flee, when Blake pulled the roses from the passenger seat.

"I thought Todd would be with you. For months he's offered to drop off a few of Warren's knickknacks from work." Mila, eyeing the roses, looked like she expected the billionaire to transform into an assistant.

"No knickknacks. Just me." Blake walked around the stone water fountain.

Even in her "ugly" garb, Mila couldn't keep him out. Blake extended a smile worthy of a toothpaste commercial. "Anyway, Warren didn't keep many personal effects at work." As he tried to hand Mila the flowers, she just stared.

"What are these for?"

"To brighten your mood." He felt giddy inside, like a fucking thirteen-year-old boy. The more of a challenge Mila became, the harder he would explode inside her. That is, once she succumbed to his irresistible charms.

"Warren didn't have at least one photo of me at work?"

Blake paused. "Oh, I see. You've never taken a visit to the office, Miss Ali."

"Mila."

"Mila." He tried not to smile. "Mila, Baldwin Corp isn't a conventional office in the least. There's only one conference room. Then there's the heated lap pool when it's too cold to surf outside. Everything's done as a team. Bouncing off ideas, learning about how other social network sites are strategizing. Star Wars is about as personal as it gets."

They just stared at each other for a moment, eyes lingering a little too long, and Blake noted that Mila had not rebuffed his gaze. Yet he could tell by her body language that she erected a thick wall around her soft-looking skin that he was eager to chip away.

Mila turned away. "Oh I'm so very sure you do. You have a very tight-knit corporate family. Company retreats for your employees, oh, and let's not forget the extravagant family vacation."

Blake had not even begun to prep for this challenge as evidenced by the tartness of her tone. "Miss ..."

"It's Mila!" she snapped, head held high but a dam of tears flooding her cheeks. "I've been *Miss Ali* for my entire life. I was just this close to living happily ever after. You stole my dream! *You're* the reason Warren is dead!"

You're the reason that Warren is dead...

Her words clanged in Blake's ear. Before guilt could gnaw at his gut, Blake watched her crumble to the floor in agony, as did the flowers he had forgotten he still held in hands. Before she could touch the ground, he caught her and took her in his arms. It pained him to see any woman cry like this, but Mila touched him inexplicably. In the three months since Warren's death, she lost weight, and her body looked frail. And what was even more astonishing than the heartbreak Mila Ali endured?

Blake's guilt.

CHAPTER 4

Warren and Mila's relationship didn't begin with love, or even lust. Mila was at his younger brother, Keith's, dorm room with friends. Keith always had some sort of get together after finals week. And Mila would hang out until it started to get to rowdy. Having shunned her father's intended, Mila's sole focus was education. She had been getting ready to leave before the laid-back When the older, intelligent Warren dropped by, wearing a suit. Clearly Keith hadn't versed him as to how his parties progressed. As Warren began to walk her to her dorm, Mila found out that he was an alumnus with the same degree. They belonged to the same honor society.

Instead of ending the night, Mila and Warren took a few bottles of import beer and went up to the roof to chat.

Sheepishly, and a tad tipsy, the conversation switched from "which professor to avoid in grad school" to everything under the sun. He was just that easy to talk to. Mila had told Warren the type of home she wanted to own one day.

When Warren and Mila reconnected seven years later, she was surprised that Warren actually remembered all the requirements she said that she wanted in a home. Mila wanted large rooms, enough for four children, when he hadn't even considered children at all.

The Jameson-Ali home was all rustic wood; towering wood pillars from floor to ceiling and distressed furniture that made a house a home. They purchased six months into their engagement, and it had every requirement she'd mindlessly and dreamily told Warren of so many years ago at the tender age of 20. At that dorm party, she'd been half tipsy, and half astonished at how dreamy Warren gazed at her. He'd tried to pursue Mila back then, but her mind had been set on education, romance not even in her realm of understanding. The living room embodied the highest level of tranquility, with panoramic floor to ceiling windows spanned the entire back of the home that framed the vast ocean and an unobstructed view of Catalina Island. Mila's only dream was that the home she resided in held enough comfort for her to read on her Kindle, or perhaps become even more adventurous and open up a paperback. And Warren had made that dream a reality, because he had been thoughtful enough to recall that lazy conversation.

And now, in the center of it all, Mila laid on a cobalt and white canvass couch. She swept the back of her hand across her eyebrow. Her temple throbbed as she shifted her position on the couch. How had she gotten here? Had she fallen asleep watching guilt-free afternoon talk shows? The flat screen was dark so she could not have possibly been watching TV. The four sliding glass doors spanning the entire living room were open. The blue sky mirrored the mellow waves in the distance, and there wasn't a cloud in sight.

Out of nowhere, the dreamiest baritone voice permeated the sound of the ocean lapping at the shore.

"Mila… good. You're awake," Blake said from the arch in the hallway. He held a glass in his hand and a bottle of aspirin.

But exactly why was he here? The few minutes leading to her mental breakdown flashed before her eyes, and warmth flooded her cheeks. She rose from the decorative pillow that had given her a crick in the neck. "I didn't mean..."

"Take these. Drink this."

Damn, she'd been an asshole. He'd come by with flowers. She'd *accused* him of causing Warren's death.

How hospitable. She didn't know one thing about Blake Baldwin, and not being a fan of gossip magazines, Mila never had the opportunity to form any star struck prejudices.

Wetting her parched lips with the tip of her tongue, Mila tried to catch Blake's gaze. That, however, proved difficult, with his being so tall and standing at full height. "Uh…"

"Blake."

The warmth radiating from Mila's cheeks traveled along her jaw and down her neck. Blake had an uncanny effect on her. It was as if they just met, and the funeral did not count. Even when he arrived at her door unannounced did not count. She'd spent innumerable nights drowning herself in cheap bottles of Merlot, so perhaps her mind was still in a toxic state of confusion, because at this moment, she could lose herself, and all the numbness she felt, just by glancing into those eyes.

"Blake, I'm just… not in the right frame of mind today. Not that going crazy is an excuse." Mila paused to shake her head. *I just called myself crazy? That's what I get for drinking so much wine and crying every night.*

"Rest for a while longer, then we can chat. Doctor's orders." Blake offered Mila a faint smile which made her believe he was more than a robot on a bunch of magazine covers.

Mila closed her eyes and leaned back. Moving alone added bass to the drumming in her head. Each night, she was unable to asleep without liquid persuasion. Now, she awoke daily with brain drumming—aka a massive hangover.

Mila fell fast asleep once again, worry-free of any stranger in her home. A dark abyss of nothingness welcomed her, banishing any memories, good or bad, of Warren.

A fragrant perfume awakened Mila from her blissful dream state. If the wooden beams hadn't been her focal point upon opening her eyes, she would have sworn she were back in Somalia or even Ethiopia, where her family fled to in 1990 at the spurt of the Somali civil war. She'd been no more than a toddler at the time. Feelings of being back "home" overwhelmed her as the aroma of cumin enveloped her senses. Then there was that one undeniable note that made it all different: The *Desi* spices. A few of her Indian friends always shared their dishes, and she could definitely detect the exotic spices in the familiar gravy she came to know so intimately. Mila stood up, and a cool evening sea-salted breeze caused the sheer curtains of the sliding glass doors to shimmy. The days seemed to pass quickly by unless she had to work, but Mila could have sworn she had a visitor.

Blake ... Blake Baldwin came over this afternoon.

As she glanced in the mirror propped against the bright yellow wall, Mila stifled a gasp. Blake once again appeared against the archway wall.

Mila remembered packing away Warren's things. Crying and boxing up clothing for Goodwill. Now another man stood before her, and he seemed to see right through her. She still knew nothing about Blake.

Should I apologize again?

"You must be hungry." There it was again, his ability to make statements that weren't a question, but a fact. As if he *knew* her. The look in his eyes, not entirely green at the moment, were a murky olive, full of angst.

Those damn eyes were trying to put her into a trance. It was the way he spoke the word: HUNGRY. Blake seemed hungry for her. The lips of Mila s pussy began to swell, quivering with desire. A milking within those sweet folds wetted her panties. "No, I'm not hungry."

Blake stepped closer, and Mila had nowhere to go but fall back onto the sofa with him on top of her.

Mila's heart pounded as another jolt took over her lady parts, but Blake didn't make a move. The intensely aromatic curry seemed non-existent as the masculine power of his cologne enthralled her nostrils. Strong notes of frankincense and the seduction of patchouli overwhelmed her senses, and Mila all but lost her mind.

"You have to be hungry, Mila. You've slept half the day. I got bored. I cooked."

"Thank you, Blake but nope, not really. These days I haven't had an appetite unless its grapes magically transformed into wine."

"Wine will go just right with dinner."

He is not *flirting. No, this is me being in the wrong mindset. His wife is drop dead gorgeous. I'm a blubbering mess.*

Why would he want her? Besides, Blake wasn't trying to prey on her emotions.

Blake grasped her elbow, his demeanor sympathetic. Through the muslin fabric of Mila's flowy black tunic, his warmth reminded her of… life. She didn't want to live in this current world without Warren, yet she couldn't slap his hand away. His thumb kneaded her skin. "Can't say that I understand what you're going through, Mila, but please allow me to be your friend."

"We don't know each other, Mr. Baldwin." With as much gumption as Mila could muster, she pulled away from his grasp. Though calming, and his touch, the first she'd had in months, reminded her of a wolf in sheep's clothing. Very expensive, organic sheep's clothing. That is, if her perceptions weren't driven by lack of sleep, and gallons of wine…

CHAPTER 5

DEMEANOR STIFF AND devoid of emotion, Blake sat in his office in his Los Angeles-based firm, located in Santa Monica. Though he had the large, corporate headquarters in Silicon Valley, like the other big social media outlets like Facebook and Twitter, this was home for Blake's most trusted workers. The building windows were tinted black. Inside, geeky electronics dotted royal blue glossy tables and chairs. The entire building was eco-friendly and open spaced, except for Blake's office.

Sitting behind the massive, custom-built desk, Blake brooded, his fingers steepled, and his handsome face expressionless. His assistant, Nina, stood before him in a tight pencil skirt, and a blouse struggling to contain the God-given caramel breasts that his face had played in and his cum had glossed many a time. Today, the sexy Puerto Rican would not suffice.

Nina's accent purred as she continued to pop the buttons of her white blouse. "Blake, baby… I can put a smile on that face."

Blake gave a blasé gesture for Nina to get on her knees, wondering when Mila would come to him. It had been two weeks since he'd last seen her, and by God, he'd thought of the best reason to force her to come to him after she'd all but kicked him out with mounds of Tupperware of Chicken Tikka Masala. It had been a very long time since Blake cooked a meal, let alone one he'd learned while touring India. The glimmer in her dark eyes had been hard, yet so fucking hot while she told him to share the meal with his wife.

This had been the longest that he desired a woman without being able to fulfill the erotic thoughts consuming him. *Fuck! Why am I even considering pursuing her?* Blake wrestled with the notion of chasing the intelligent, kindhearted, and gorgeous Mila Ali. Warren had actually been one of his good friends, even if they had dissimilar interests.

Nina, his Nina, crawled over, breasts spilling from her bra through the top. Those damn six inch heels that he once let climb all over him had been kicked to the side as she crept around the table.

Pissed off, Blake unbuttoned his belt. He leaned back in the matching custom-built chair, mind still muddled over Mila as her unknowing substitute unzipped his pants. A sensual bubble of laughter escaped those Chanel red-painted lips as Blake's cock shot upward, like the Eifel tower in Paris. His erection was that beautiful of a sight to behold. The woman before him had no clue of his motivation. The power he held over her made him hard in a flash. Nina's greedy lips slowly drew in his long, thick stiffness. She was damn good, with a gorgeous, full mouth. Nina gave ample attention to the thick veins soaring up and down his manhood as her tongue flicked at each one, heightening his pulse with each languorous swipe. The pleasure was so intense that it momentarily ebbed Blake's unyielding desire for Mila. Nina twirled her tongue around the tip of his dick. *That fucking moan.* It made her tonsils vibrate against his rod. Any thoughts he had were dashed when a primitive sigh swept over Blake as he dominated the chair.

"Does this feel good?" Nina kissed the tip of his manhood.

Blake stopped, gripping the armrest and shoving a hand into her silky hair. Once he maintained a decent grasp on her tresses, he gave her a thrust. No more words. All she was good for was swallowing his creamy cascade. The movement caused his cock to hit the back of her throat, eliciting an ecstatic moan from her. Wet, sweet lips glazed his dick, giving it a glossy off-white sheen.

There it was. At last. Blake exploded, and Nina took it all.

Nina guzzled down his seed to the very last drop. With his head back, Blake waited for her to lick up the last bit when the frosted double doors burst open. Nina froze beneath the desk. Though she hadn't completed the transaction, not in the fullest sense of their regimen, a smile illuminated Blake's face. He gave a gentle nudge, and Nina got down into place.

There stood Mila in a canary yellow, cable knit dress which stopped mid-thigh, complete with knee high boots. And damn it, she wore no make-up. So fucking glorious. He marveled at the sneer stretching across her lips. "How dare you!"

"Miss Ali, if you'd please…" Blake's assistant Barbara said from behind her as she and Todd scurried to catch up.

Todd's eyebrows furrowed with worry. "Mila, what's wrong?"

"Uh uhn, Todd. I don't need a peacekeeper," Mila cut in. Blake stared listlessly at one of his most valuable employees.

Another woman stood behind Todd as they all entered the room.

Mila said a few choice words to her, as well. Blake remembered her as the woman who'd brazenly flirted with him at the funeral. She had to be Todd's girlfriend. Either way, Blake was glad that his game plan got a rise out of Mila. Blake refocused as Mila cussed at him for paying her mortgage. All the while, Nina kept post underneath the desk.

"Mila and I were out for lunch. One of the diners across from us recognized Mila from a magazine cover," explained the redhead.

"What magazine? What are you talking about?" Blake feigned innocence. His strategy worked. He'd paid Mila's overdue mortgage, and had one of his assistants leak it to the press. With money being tossed around, the tabloids came to their own conclusions.

"*Us*!" Mila shouted. "Can everyone just leave?"

"Yes, everyone, please." Blake hid the smile on his face. Mila wanted to be alone with him.

Todd placed his hands in his khakis, he rubbed his thumb over the stubble on his chin then did an about face.

"Clarissa..." Mila addressed the redhead, who seemed more like a Chihuahua, wanting to protect Mila. He concluded that the two were good friends if they were out at lunch when one of Mila's coworkers accused him and Mila of having an illicit affair. Damn, the tabloids were usually correct. This was the first time they'd acted prematurely, but Blake had given them good reason.

Mila tossed the magazine on his table. It read: *Billionaire Pays Mistress's Back Mortgage.* The headline was among top billing on the front page of People magazine; however, once they actually *did* commence their fling, any candid photos of them together would garner a solo cover.

CHAPTER 6

AFTER CLARISSA LEFT, Mila turned back to her enemy. Head cocked, she waited for an apology. How dare he pay her mortgage? Warren had put down almost fifty percent of the Laguna Niguel beachfront property. They had already paid for the wedding venue, amongst other lavish details. Then Mrs. Jameson wanted the most expensive funeral, down to the minuscule detail.

Mila would never be able to pay the mortgage on her own. The Mila fresh out of college went straight to Hewitt Corporation. Instead of returning home and becoming the shadow of one of the most sought-after suitors in Ethiopia, Mila seized the golden opportunity. She helped Hewitt bulldoze small businesses. By the time she made associate she'd become exhausted, realizing she'd forgotten about her long-ago dream to open a resource center. Now she worked at Versa Home Improvements, a luxurious remolding company. As a sales manager, Mila didn't make a fraction of what she once did. And the only thing she had from Warren—*their* home—was in jeopardy.

Both of their names had been on the deed, and now she had

acquired the debt.

"They've left at your request, Miss Ali. What can I do for you?"

"Don't insult my intelligence, Baldwin. I want to speak with you in private."

Blake mumbled something under his breath; his chiseled face still held a glint of cockiness.

She watched the "bedhead" of an alluring Latina rise from between Blake's knees. The woman kept her back to Mila while buttoning her shirt. Chin up, Mila tried to keep her judgmental eyes from the homewrecker as the girl began the walk of shame. With a deep sigh, Mila closed the double doors behind her. When she turned around, Blake stood.

He undid the buttons of his linen shirt, and her eyes zeroed in on the perfect V as his undone pants fell. His waistline was stacked with muscle. The muscles in his arms chiseled like a Demi god. Then Mila's eyes landed on his shirt as it fell to the floor. Rationality returned.

"Wh... What are you doing?"

"Taking a shower, Miss Ali. Join me, if you'd like. Didn't you come to chew me out?" He shoved down his pants as if this were an Armani boxer brief commercial. He shoved off his underwear. "By all means, chew me the fuck out."

Her eyes popped. Flaccid. But so huge. Saliva liquefied her mouth. As he moved around the desk, Mila glared at a crescent-shaped, tanned ass. No boxer/brief lines. The sun adorned every inch of Blake's body.

"Ms. Ali, keep staring and I'll have to insist you join me."

She had no words. This type of shit did *not* happen in real life. Men didn't disrobe at work. He was playing a game of entrapment, as if she couldn't deny him. *Well, I'm a different breed than he's used to; I am Mila Ali. I've seen horrible inequality that many can't even imagine, even after my family moved to Ethiopia. With my MBA, I've helped fatten the pockets of rich men.* Mila placed her hands on her hips, knowing she had never been the type to lose herself over a man. Heck, she didn't even do it for the money when working for Hewitt. Becoming an associate was supposed to prove to the most important man in her world—her father—that she'd made it.

She took a deep breath, knowing that no matter how drop dead gorgeous Blake was, he had no hold on her. Fifteen was the last age where good looks blinded her.

Blake wants to play games?

Her heels resounded off the walls of Blake's office as she stepped toward what was presumably a bathroom. The entire area seemed to have been transported from one of those Million Dollar Listing San Francisco shows and placed in his office. Just the fixtures were even more expensive than that of all the bathroom displays at her job. Gray tile with mosaic glass splashes gave the room a sanctuary-like allure. Her eyes narrowed as he stepped into the shower that could hold half the sluts running around the office at any given time. There were rain sprouts over a section of shower that had seating for those lazy days, and waterfall style sprouts for those days when a refreshing pour was needed.

"Mila..." He twined her name, making it brand new after all the years of hearing it. Her eyes landed on him, trickling down his gloriously taut body as water caressed every inch of his muscles. "I'll take you complacent or aggressive." He grabbed a bottle of L'Occitane.

"I doubt that, Blake. You won't be taking me any damn way."

Translucent white liquid squirted onto his large hand. Cum. She hadn't had sex in 114 days, not that she was counting. He dropped the bottle onto the shower floor. Again, her eyes zeroed in as rain drenched every inch of his physique. Eyes connected with Mila's he rubbed the soap onto chiseled pectorals. Her pussy walls quivered. But she was stronger, so much stronger than the juices drenching her thong.

Mila stood, legs planted wide. Since there was no glass shower shield between them, nothing obscured their connection.

"My beautiful Mila—"

"*My*?" The man was infuriating. "I don't think so."

Though the constant drumming of the shower sounded, Blake's soothing low tone still compelled her. "That's exactly where you've gone wrong. Thinking. You're over thinking this." He let his hand travel down to his cock. Water was all around. In the shower, in her mouth, traveling down her throat, and most certainly pooling down below. Standing at the entrance of the shower, Mila wanted to lose herself in the moment. A craving took over as his dick, so magical and inviting, refused to stop growing. "*Desires*, now desires are primitive. No thought necessary. You want something. Go for it." He still stroked the strength of his cock.

With every caress from his large hand, her labia quivered. Coupled with the sound of his voice, an aged wine, bold, yet smooth, Mila was at a lost. "…Are you listening to me, Mila. You want something. You go after it."

Mila licked her lips. Thick and long, he had more erection than any woman should ever need. It stood to attention, saluting her. Then she remembered the last words he said. And now, they were at the part where the billionaire would lose his own childish game.

"Hmmm. Go after what I want you say?" She stepped closer, stopping just before the spray of water sprinkled on the tips of her stilettos.

He nodded.

"And you want me."

Blake grinned. His eyes hard, as if just the mere glance could singe the clothing right off of her. "Yeah. But, I'd rather you come to me, Mila. I want you to cum so fucking hard—"

"Stop." The gasp flew from her parted lips, both sets of lips swollen, aching with desire. But Mila gathered her dignity. "Now get this through your head, Mr. Baldwin."

He moved so close that her minty breath caught. The steam from his body enveloped her. Blake reached just past Mila and grabbed a plush navy blue towel from the counter.

"Baldwin, you'll have your 14 thousand dollars back within a week, and I won't be seeing you ever again. There will be no paying my mortgage or any other foolishness. Do I make myself clear?" As strength lifted her shoulders, and her spine stood rigid, Mila wondered where she'd get the money. With Warren's last paycheck, Mila had held the funeral, and she'd had to pay out of pocket for a few odds and ends such as floral arrangements to cover such a large church.

She'd paid half of a $4250 mortgage payment, but the bank returned it due to their inability to take partial payments. That was three months ago. They'd sent a pre-foreclosure letter when she became two months behind. The life insurance agent had yet to provide a date to pay out Warren's policy. None of the wedding venues cared of such tragedies, and Warren's mother wanted the funeral to rival a wedding she never got for her son.

"$14,000, what are you talking about?" He arched an eyebrow as the plush towel polished off taut muscles.

"I see that you like to fuck with people."

"Billionaires' trait perhaps." He shrugged, grabbing the L'Ocittane lotion. The psychotic man meant for her to go crazy as he rubbed a dime size worth on just one muscle. He had to be at least 36. Why act like such a prick?

"Well, you may be right, then." She nodded. "Billionaire's trait. So you micromanage too?"

He raised an eyebrow, then asked for her to lotion his back.

"Okay." She took the bottle with a coy smile and squirted cold lotion on his back. She dropped the bottle and stalked out of the bathroom. That asshole thought she would drop her panties?

CHAPTER 7

HE KNEW THAT paying her mortgage would blow up in his face. Risk verses reward implied that his desire just to be in her presence outweighed all ramifications. Blake was a patient man. He admired how well she clung to the thought of her dearly departed fiancé. Naivety, or perhaps loyalty, had the woman hell-bent on wallowing in melancholy. And he'd waited for the mortgage to elapse two times before paying it.

Dressed in a simple black Armani suit, Blake ambled down the staircase. He headed down the hall and toward the display room, where all his powerful, uber fast toys were kept. Blake told his chauffeur to take the day off and stepped toward the display of luxury cars. He'd grabbed one of the keys off the rack and clicked the unlock button. The Lamborghini lit up. Well, that could only mean that divine intervention wanted him to make a statement. He'd make that statement at Versa Home Improvements, Mila's job in Newport Beach. The powerful engine purred as he pulled out of the showcase area and down the U shaped driveway.

Diana's Benz coupe came through the entrance. Wisps of platinum streamed into the air, prompting Blake to turn away before her face came into view. He became deaf to her car honking as he zoomed away. Digging a hand into the inside pocket of his blazer,

Blake turned his phone off before his wife could call. She couldn't want anything, she rarely ever did…

On the drive from Beverly Hills to Newport Beach, Blake considered his investigator Lamb's words.

Mila and one of her other two older sisters were estranged from their Somalian parents. The three girls came to America together to attend college. All three completed graduate school—summa cum laude. The oldest, Yasmin returned home to a man of her parents choosing, married, and then they came back to America when the engineer husband began working at a Los Angeles Metrolink. The second oldest, Lido—who Blake realized was at the funeral, lived in Los Angeles with her lover. Lamb wasn't able to determine the reason for the familial falling out, but based on the correlation for both Mila and Lido's estrangement with their parents, cultural assimilation had to be the cause.

When GPS took Blake down PCH, he slowed his pace to practical—which was otherwise impractical for the beast at his fingertips. Pulling up the curb, he realized there wouldn't be a valet. He glanced in the mirror. Not one hair out of place. Diamond BB cuff links just right. Blake picked up the bouquet of roses and headed out of the car, mind on Mila's lips. He wanted the argument, a verbal debate to ensue while visualizing his semen glossed on her full lips.

Blake smiled. The image was clear as day. That gorgeous mouth of hers, polished by cum. This prompted flirtatious stares from the females, meandering in and out of the building, and gawks of acknowledgment from their counterparts of the social media mogul. Yet his calculating pace stayed steady, mind on the minx's mouth. Blake dominated the entrance of Versa Home Improvements, where a sign displayed: "Affordable prices, Affluent lifestyle…"

There were big posters along the beams and hanging from the colossal gray walls of the factory style warehouse. If he didn't look up, the various floor models of kitchens and bathrooms became more appealing. However, red-tag sale signs totally ruined the ambiance. Then his eyes landed on *her,* across the way at a kitchen display.

Like a wave skimming a crystal clear lake, Mila's hands swept over various focal points of the kitchen display she showed to a Latino couple with a child. Blake envied the toddler in his stroller as Mila paused to show him attention. Her bright smile was genuine, and the same look Blake remembered from his own childhood caregiver.

Then she stood, pink lips slightly parted, in the middle of a sentence. Her body stiffened as she looked Blake's way. She gave the young couple an apologetic smile then sauntered over.

Mile stopped short of any physical contact and glared at Blake. He waited for her wrath, welcoming it.

"I forgot to tell you, even as you showered last time we crossed paths, you still smelled like an asshole, Mr. Baldwin. A *married* asshole." She grabbed the roses and flung them straight into the trash can.

"Aren't we on a first name basis?"

She turned in heels that should have been walking all over him and moseyed away. Job well done. Job very well done, might he add, gawking at her ass. Everyone else gawked at him. Those rounded melons paused as a fat man in a double breasted suit hindered Mila's path back to the Latino couple.

He was as tall as he was wide, making it difficult to get around. He also carried himself with a lofty flare of … importance. The man latched his thumbs into the pockets of his suit asking, "Mrs. Ali, aren't you going to make introductions?"

"Sure, my current customers are this way." Mila gave a curt wave of her hand toward the kitchen department.

Fatso gave Baldwin a quick grin of apology. "Miss. Ali—"

Blake cut him off. "We're having a bit of a lover's quarrel."

The man's face flushed, but Blake had no care in the world. Mila's boss knew exactly who he was, the *very married billionaire*.

CHAPTER 8

FOR THREE YEARS, Mila worked at Versa Home Improvement. She'd started from the bottom, needing to humble herself after the very last business she'd helped Hewitt acquire. Mr. Versa knew her worth and wanted to make her manager of the company, but no, Mila sought to become the girl she once had been. The one who helped at her father's practice when their own Somali people fled to Ethiopia over the years. Since she no longer had her father's love, she delighted in helping people improve their surroundings. Besides, her childhood dream of a resource center would have the referrals for housing upgrades to meet codes and standards.

Slowly, Mila worked herself up as a sales rep until she became supervisor of sales. Occasionally she helped out on the floor, so here she was, during one of the biggest sales of the year.

They stood at a modernistic bathroom display, with gray walls, white porcelain block style vanity set. Her graceful hand swept over the various focal points, as Mila spoke.

"… At least pretend to be interested, Mr. Baldwin." Mila felt his smoldering gaze.

"You don't believe I'm interested?" Blake's warm breath tickled her earlobe and sent thrills of lust and horror down her spine.

"Blake, this is not a game. I'm sure you run through a slew of women, your status extended as your right. But unfortunately for you, I was raised to be much more than a married man's *side piece*."

There, she'd gotten it out. Asshole. In a blur, Mila bid Blake Baldwin farewell *forever*. As she walked away, she forced herself not to cross her fingers. This was too darn easy. A moment ago, his demeanor had been that of a tiger on the hunt. Mila decided to take a fifteen-minute break.

While striding to the rear of Versa Home Improvements, each step made Mila's resolve crumble.

She pushed against the revolving door that read EMPLOYEES ONLY with such haste that it whipped back, and Mila had to brace herself, forearms up. *Where is my small taste of serendipity?* Mila stalked into the room, empty except for a few discarded pressed-fruit bottles.

She'd snapped. Why had she given an irrelevant man like Blake Baldwin control? It was obvious that Blake lacked family values, and morals in general.

Mila took in a lung full of air and leaned back on her heels against the wall.

Before she could right herself, Blake stood before her. "What are you doing in here, Mr. Baldwin?"

The man had to have multi-personality disorder. One day he wore all black to a funeral, the next he stripped in front of her, then he seemed friendly and inviting in a cashmere sweater and … hell, Mila had a photogenic memory of every part of Blake. Today, his blazer was shoved up to his elbows as he dominated the space between them. It was as if the asshole had air-rights to *their* space. Ownership to… her. And with the few times Blake and her crossed paths, or even crashed into each other, he conquered her attention, sending her emotions in a whirlwind.

She'd lied. The. Man. Epitomized. Sex. Trying not to breathe Blake into her nostrils was a task made difficult, not wholly by his nearness. "Blake, you need to go." Mila tried to push at his arms.

Silently, Blake's hand sought the back of her neck and he leaned in. Heart booming in her ears, Mila lost all cognition. Deaf, dumb, and all wide open. Only two senses lingered. Taste. Touch. Smell. Oh yeah, that was three. His presence consumed her with desire.

Blake's lips locked onto hers. At first taste? Perception returned, giving her a plethora of thoughts, and branding itself along her brain. This moment was ingrained in her memory. The first taste she had in so very long. The softness of his lips, coupled by the tickle from his five o' clock shadow. The silk of his tongue was the paintbrush, her mouth a canvass. He sought to devour her. A deep moan, so feminine. The weakling. He ended the mouth-fucking with a nibble of her bottom lip. His ultra-white teeth grazed the soft pink fleshiness, giving a tender pull. The tingling flew from one nerve ending straight to the lips of her labia. The scent of him had been astounding in its own right. Now for the touch, Mila grasped the back of his neck and pulled him closer. Blake wanted to feast on her lips, so she'd help him with that. His hand blazed across her thigh, scorching her skin with desire. As she leaned back onto the wall, he hefted her leg around his narrowed waist and over the firmness of his perfectly contoured ass.

The mere act sent his dick piercing against her hip.

Eyes wide open, shock consumed the initial idiocy, reminding her she'd spend the rest of her life alone. No cock included. She knew love once. The moment was fleeting, and that was okay.

"No. *No*! We..."

Blake groaned into her neck, warm breath tickling her collarbone as he waited for her guidance. Mila wanted to say how readily accessible they were in the middle of the goddamn Employee's lounge. At any given time, someone could walk in. Her words came out as gibberish. Blake, the egotistical asshole, ignored her. All six foot two inches of him dropped to his knees. Idiocy returned as he hiked up her skirt.

"What the fuck are these?" he gasped between catching his breath. The hot pink thong was a gag gift from Veronica and Lido during one of their drunken girl nights. The material was thin, yet the metallic green punchline written on the triangle of the material spelled *you can eat my buffet*. The carpet snatcher's, aka Lido and Veronica, had jokingly promised they had the same panties in different colors.

"They... are... *clean*." Mila decided not to explain herself to a man who deserved nothing. "Stop."

Instead of pulling down her thong, to Mila's horror, Blake pulled them up! The harsh movement sparked a frenzy as the soft cotton rubbed against her clit.

The room grew silent as Blake continued his inspection, the

angles of his handsome face sharpening with delight. He parted her legs, and then his nose touched her thong. Warmth radiated into her center as Blake took a deep breath. A primeval growl escaped his mouth, making her clitoris tighten. His tongue dipped out, wide, pink, wet, pleasing and leisurely stroked upwards. Mila tried to push down her thong, but, he held it firmly against her hips. She cursed herself for not being the type of woman who went commando.

"You say I'm an asshole, right?" he smirked. "You're smart, Mila. So I believe in you. I believe in your goodness, Mila, I know you are trying to hold onto your wholesome ways but your eyes say 'fuck me now!' And that body, every sexy ass curve is begging for me to touch it." He paused to take a deliriously long scent of her nether region. "You can fucking tame me. Cleanse me. If only I can just pull down this thong and burry my face into your sweet, wet pussy."

"Just… just ppp…. pull my panties down."

Again his face glided back and forth over her thong. Blake hooked her leg over his shoulder, now Mila's left hand clutched into his hair while her right hand dug into the shoulder of his blazer.

Pleading on the tip of her tongue, Mila's eyes zapped to the door. High heels clipped down the hallway.

His masculine chest rose as he took another deep breath of her lady parts. His long tongue flicked out and prodded the cotton barrier of a drizzling sheath.

She wanted to help him take off her panties, but a man like him took no pressure in asking. He just... took. Yet, he continued to get a delicate taste of her honey through those cotton panties. The soft, warm, faint wetness of his mouth made Mila's eyes close and her head again fall back against the wall. At this very moment in life, nothing else mattered. If someone walked in, fuck it. She chuckled psychotically under her breath and waited for him to fully take her.

"Please fuck me," she begged. As usual the man only responded when he wanted to.

When Blake's tongue no longer sought solace through her cotton panties, Mila's eyes opened. The longing evident in the melancholic look on her face.

He stood.

She died.

Blake planted a hand on the wall behind the side of her ear. Pinning her to the spot.

"Now, we both know what I want, Mila. And this assessment has assured me that your sweet fragrance has the ability to cleanse me." His tone blanketed her with an unquenchable thirst. Blake made her want him. He need not even wait for her response.

He unrolled the sleeves of his blazer, and Mila's heart clenched. She caught her breath. He paused before turning around. She waited for him to give a time, a place, any order. However, he wanted her. She'd follow.

"Oh, one more thing." Blake thumbed his lip for a second. The fucker made her eat every intense second of waiting. She didn't know if running to the trashcan to dig out the flowers or apologizing for calling him an asshole would suffice, but she couldn't speak.

Couldn't move.

"My beautiful Mila, I'll be away for a month. Let's not operate under the guise that I don't have the means to take you with me. I refuse to. See, I've never been more insulted in my life." Blake's smile twitched. That unreadable, dark cloud phased before his radiant green eyes.

"In 30 days I'll return. You will be ready for me."

She nodded.

"Your flowers have been removed from the trashcan, Mr. Versa has personally ushered them to your desk. And your assistant has no doubt retrieved a vase and water so that you can take care of the gift that I've given you."

"But I don't have an assistant."

He shrugged. "I'll see you soon."

Mila took Blake Baldwin in from head to toe. His tie perfect, not a hair in disarray. No lint on his suit. He leaned in, his cool breath tickling her lips. Silently, Blake savored her mouth once more. No frenzy like before. Elegant, poetic. A farewell. And then he was gone.

She wanted to cry, only a whimper would escape. By God, she wanted this man now! In the middle of this employee room. She wanted to fuck Blake Baldwin on every kitchen model display counter and island, every shower and bathtub. Mila wanted to fuck him on the VERSA welcome mat right in front of the sliding glass doors. Then she wanted to lay in his strong arms take a break, take him home and fuck him until the numbness passed away...

~~~

Mila settled on a Mediterranean Lean Cuisine for dinner. With the sliding glass doors open, the cool sea breeze entered the house. She lit candles and even took out another magenta colored poppy plate, the same regimen she used while working for Hewitt Corporation. Those years of being young, cocky and wanting to show the world just how much she knew were filled with nights alone. Except, back then expensive organic take-out while researching the next big investment meant a good night. These days, after having known love, Mila just felt alone. Tears streamed down her cheeks as the incessant white-noise from the microwave reminded her just how alone she was.

Mila stopped at the quartz countertop and snatched up her cell phone. Even if she'd always cling to the guilt of not living up to her father's standards, Mila sought the voice that had soothed her for a lifetime.

"*Subax wanaagsan*—Good Morning," Mila's mother said, voice questioning. Though her mother was up before the sun arose, praying or cooking, Mila glanced at the clock on the wall. 8:37 here, and she calculated that it was just after 6 a.m. in Ethiopia.

"Ma, how are you?" Mila greeted in her native tongue, leaning both elbows against the counter, eyes captivated by the flicker of the candles on the dining table. The glow illuminated across the vast wood chairs, this place was her ghost town. A bolt constricted Mila's chest as a memory flashed through her mind. Their tiny box car packed to capacity, although only mementos were squeezed in the
~~~

back with the three sisters. Mila had watched a mother and child trekking across the wilderness. The woman's child clung to her back, legs dangling. The boy couldn't be but a few years younger than Mila. She couldn't fathom how Somalia, her home, had become a place to fear. A place to run from…

"*Wann fiicanahay*—I am fine." The soothing voice she needed to hear dashed away an image of the Somali mother's blistered feet, caked with blood and mud. It ceased the six-year-old Mila's frantic questioning as to why they couldn't stop to help, even as it was obvious there was no room in their car.

But, this soothing voice was hushed. It hurt to the core when her mother's tone lowered. Mila could just imagine Mrs. Ali's retreat to one of the darker areas in whatever room she currently stood in, in order to continue the conversation.

"How is da—"

"Mila," her mother cut in, just as the microwave beeped. It made Mila's heart tighten. The untold rule was that she didn't speak of the father. She was not to utter her father's name. It was too late to apologize. "How is everything going?"

"Great..."

"Oh my beautiful daughter, tell me. Tell me what's wrong," Ma chided, in the motherly tone that wrapped itself around Mila like a warm blanket on a frosty night.

Mila bit her tongue. *I've lost the man I was to spend my entire life with. The man that I've imagined having three children and growing old by my side as we debated everything under the sun.* As

Mila admitted to "just" missing Warren. Within her brain, she shouted: *I just want to ask how he's doing. More than that, I'm sure I'd be great if I could just say hello to dad.*

"Oh baby, I know you miss Warren." Her mother said all the wrong words in an attempt to soothe her soul.

Mr. Ali was a good father; While Yasmin always helped in the kitchen and followed their mother around, Lido did her own thing.

Mila, on the other hand, was once Mr. Ali's shadow. She'd been daddy's little girl.

"I might visit… the… country soon." Mila said after about ten minutes of feel-good conversation. They'd just talked about food, so the wrong part of her brain had sparked the mindless notion.

"*Laga Yabee*—Perhaps..." Ma paused for a second. Mila's breathing hitched. Would her mother invite her home? "Well, I will talk with you later, my beautiful daughter."

"All right, ma." After they hung up, Mila she dialed Lido. *I'll eat later...*

"Hello," Veronica answered the phone with her French accent. A drop dead gorgeous blonde, the two were fucking glorious together. They'd been hair and skin models for commercials, lithe body parts entwined in many haute couture magazines. All tangled up, tall, graceful limbs, and strikingly beautiful facial futures. It was no wonder the two had fallen... Just like Mila for snubbing the arranged marriage, Lido too was ostracized from their heritage. All because she noshed on photogenic pussy.

"Hey, Veronica." Mila smiled, leaning her elbows on the

counter. Though not the person she'd called, Veronica would do just fine.

"Oh Mila… baby, how are ya?" Veronica had this way of making every word sound orgasmic.

"I'm hanging in there. How are you?" They chatted for a while since Veronica and Lido were the only family that she had. She could hear pots banging in the background.

"The next time you call, please make sure I'm alive."

In the background, Lido went off. People fell head over heels for Lido Ali, who resembled Iman and rivaled the current beloved Somali, Fatima Siad, but she couldn't compel a blind person to eat her food. The back and forth bickering between the two supermodels was all fun and games, since the girl really couldn't cook.

"I'll do just that, Veronica." Mila joked. "But let's not wait on little ol' me. You have to place a baggy in one of those crystal vases, Veronica. Sneak that crap into the bag. Save yourself." Mila almost brought herself to tears for laughing, and not in a good way. Usually, she would joke along with them, but today any real laughter was followed by guilt. The guilt of coming so far to be independent, then ending up in the same predicament that she initially clung too. Like the Somalian woman and child, Mila didn't want to be alone.

"All right, Mila. We have to get together soon." Veronica had the ability to read Mila through the phone and know she still suffered from a broken heart. "Now here's the chef."

"Oh so I'm the chef now? We shall see, Veronica," Lido giggled. The phone static got louder as Lido put Mila on speaker, saying

"*Walaashay yar* —little sister—I'm cooking this dish that Ma use to make."

"Ma..." This call to her *walaashay weyn*—big sister—should have served as a Band-Aid, to temporarily mend her broken heart. Lido rarely, if ever, mentioned their parents. The father? Never. The mother? Well, this still shocked her. She confessed, "I just spoke with Ma."

"Why?" Lido said, and Mila could just imagine she was throwing daggers through the cell phone. "Look Ma can cook her ass off but, they left us to the wayside—"

"Lido stuff it," Veronica snapped in the background.

"But there are no cocks in this house to stuff this mouth with. So how should I stuff it?" Lido quipped, never one to allow her opponent to end the argument, even if she were the only one arguing. "Look, Mila. I wouldn't be surprised if Ma wanted you back into the fold."

Courage stacked the muscles in Mila's back. Come. Back. Home?

"No. Ma doesn't even let father know when I've spoken with her."

"Yup, the dutiful wife keeps mum." Lidos flamboyant accent had notes of a British tone, since the models had just returned from London. "Mark my words, *walaashay yar*, father knows that Warren is..." Lido's inflection softened for Mila's benefit "...has passed away. Father knows exactly where you are, what you're doing, and how to mend your broken heart. But he's just too damn smart to learn how to have a heart."

"Okay, Lido." Mila walked over to the dining room and blew out the tapered candles.

"Fuck it, Mila. I know you more than you know yourself. Every once in a while, you want a fairy tale romance. Hell, even when you were working 24/7 for those fucking 'suits'." Lido always referred to the head honchos at Hewitt Corp as suits. "You had a little bit of fun every now and then. So somewhere deep within that big, smart head of yours, you want fireworks. With Warren, you got to be that sweet little girl everyone loved and knew. You were no longer the analytical, business woman, Mila. You quit Hewitt, then went back to talking about that helping *poor* people crap. So right now, Ma might be feeling sorry for you–"

"Lido, I don't need anyone to feel sorry for me."

"Yeah, whatever. Play up the sympathy card, Mila. See if Ma opens her damn mouth to defy him; and he gives in. Lord knows you want to be daddy's little girl again. Our dearest mother will work in your favor then it will be me, the middle child at my lonesome *again*. You'll move to Ethiopia, or at the very least near *Yasmin*," Lido seethed, spitting out their sibling's name. They're eldest sister lived in a proximate neighborhood that had most Africans. "Either way, you'll have them all. That's a fairytale ending for you, huh?"

Mila doubted it. But Lido was molded by God to redirect any tragedy and gear it toward herself. "You know I'd never leave you, *walaashay weyn*. It's you that travel to these fashion events around the world, Lido. You leave me every season." Mila sighed. Damn, she'd called for a shoulder to lean on, but ever the middle sister, Lido made it seem like she was the one suffering.

"Listen ladies." Veronica became the glue that held the sisters together. "We all made mistakes. Granted, I'm considered Lido's worst mistake. Pretty little Mila, you've done things that won't get you back to your birthplace. But here, the three of us will not judge each other. We'll stick together. Okay, girlfriends?"

The sisters agreed in unison. Not fully placated, but feeling that the call had brought her closer to home than the discussion with her own mother, Mila hung up. The mother and child who fled Somalia on foot flooded Mila's mind again. She owed it to them, being able to climb the corporate ladder so swiftly… even if she would have lost her soul by making associate at Hewitt.

Every time Mila thought about the blood, blisters, and mud on that young mother's feet, she wondered where the two had ended up. Mila went back to the microwave to warm up her food, and consider what to make for dinner when her sister and Veronica came over. Thank heavens the two would bring the wine. The really good shit.

CHAPTER 9

A BLANK CANVAS. Those three words moved him. A blank canvas—the quintessence of the luscious Mila Ali. He stepped into the high-end lingerie store in Paris. It hadn't exactly been on the way from an invigorating climb of The Matterhorn in Switzerland, with a few of his adrenaline junkie buddies. But three weeks ago had been the last time Blake laid eyes on the woman who'd driven him mad.

An upbeat French song fused through hidden speakers in the airy store. Blake deciphered the language, and the melodic underscore was delightful. He reached over to caress the abdomen of a human mannequin. Though there were more mannequins dressed in every cut and style of corset, lingerie or panty set in the haute couture store, this particular one beckoned him with her resemblance of the one and only Miss Ali. Skin the color of unblemished coffee, ample hips and lips. As he palmed the fake breast, Blake perceived a shudder ripple through her body. Though the elite boutique made dreams come true, this one was not his dream. Just a replica of *her.* Mila Ali, the one whom saw through his bullshit.

"Bonjour, Monsieur Baldwin," Elle purred his name. She, the owner of the store, held power at the tip of her manicured fingertips. Not an inch over five feet, Elle's golden hair grazed the angle of her cheekbone in a blunt cut. The black leather corset made the milk of her silky skin touchable. However, unlike her fleet of flesh, nobody touched Elle. She licked her berry-matte lips. "It's been a while. Same sizes?"

"Non, Belle." He rubbed the silk hairs of his chin and took a gander of all the statuesque beauties gracing the display areas.

"Viviana's breast size, Elise's ass size, no—maybe a tad larger."

"Oh, very curvaceous. Let's see what goodies we can find for you." He'd always enjoyed returning here, and watching their asses as they moved around and did his bidding. Elle's slender hips swayed as she mentioned what she had in store for him

She stopped at one of the treasure trunks of unique pieces, digging through different silky or satiny material, and handed him a red lace number that was so fucking erotic. Blake's dick instantly rose as he imagined Mila in it. Ruffles in the panties were for those hardcore moments, where he gripped her bra strap, and fucked her ass up.

Though licking his lips, Blake said, "Have that gift wrapped. But it's not *the* one."

"All right, I'll satisfy you, yet. I remember the first time you came in here, Mr. Baldwin." She paused, turned, and leaned into him with a teasing smile. Those sweet dimples were the reason he allowed her to delay his goal. Elle's glossy talons rubbed up and down the lapel of his Italian suit. "You were buying something for your wife. You said nothing in here would rival, only enhance."

Exhibiting no emotion, Blake allowed the woman to dawdle over dreams of long ago. He recalled it, too. This place had been way out of his league back then. A rich man had told him that he'd bring every whore in here for goodies. Blake, on the other hand, came here to buy something for his *wife*. He'd been the anomaly, madly in love with the woman he'd vowed his life to. To make matters worse, it was his first business trip, and Blake could hardly afford a fucking *thong*, forget the matching bra.

Blake made that statement. It had been true. Diane had been beautiful.

He took the glass of champagne Miu handed over. The Asian swished back into the darkness until she was called again. Useless memories of a perfect past were dashed. Even Elle's faraway wishful look of lust disappeared. She already knew that he'd bought for hundreds of women after Diane. Why would she bring that up now?

The crisp taste of champagne went smoothly down Blake's throat. He followed Elle past another treasure chest and chose a few pieces, but none that would bedeck Mila the first time he had a taste.

Perhaps she smelled the earthiness of his return from the Swiss Alps, because those lusty blue eyes roamed over him. "Or shall I put something together for you?" Elle's two fingers walked across the muscles playing peek-a-boo in Blake's chest. The minx wanted to play, what a rarity.

A silence ensued, leaving them with the seductive track of another French songstress. Blake relied on the pulse of Elle's swan neck as his large hand clasped around the small of her back. He pulled her closer and leaned down. Though six inch heels had lengthened Elle's legs, she in return, rose to the occasion. Their lips met. The first touch of femininity that he'd taste in all of three weeks. His tongue dipped into a luscious mouth, but his mind was oceans away. Delving into the syrupy pond between Mila's thighs. He kissed the breath out of Elle's mouth. Elle in return began to tug at his belt.

His hand engulfed her tiny, cool ones. After three weeks, he'd wait one more for Mila. So there'd be no going there with Elle. Blake's mind conjured up exactly what Mila would wear. He whispered in Elle's ear, "I'll need it complete by the end of the week."

CHAPTER 10

A WEEK AFTER Blake left, Mila attempted to forward the funds back into his bank account, but nobody in all of CHASE could determine how the money had gotten into her account. After Lido loaned the cash, Mila had gotten a money order and scrawled Baldwin's name before transforming into one of those weak women who decided to keep it. The man had oodles of money.

It's the principle, Mila, dang, she inwardly fought with herself while calling Todd and asking him to meet her outside of his job.

The good guy stood on the curb, shuddering in the cold air as Mila's Honda pulled up. Todd hopped off the sidewalk and jogged around to her door.

"Can you make sure Bl… Mr. Baldwin gets this." Mila kept a firm grip on the envelope.

Todd reached for it with a nod of his head. As he tried to take it, Mila mentally prayed for sanity. *But this is chump change to Blake…*

"And don't tell anyone about this, namely Clarissa."

"All right, Mila," Todd assured, his bifocals foggy around the edges.

~~~

"I've lost my son, the least this woman can do is pick up her things and go!" The words jarred Mila, making her shoulders jump
~~~

as she started up the stairs with her umpteenth load of laundry. The voice could be none other than Warren's mother. Unbelievably, she'd had the motivation to separate the colors from the whites and physically begin to wash. Now, the clean clothes were thrown onto the guest beds in three different rooms. But Mila was proud of this little attempt.

She dropped the laundry basket at the top step and ambled back down.

"*Mary*," Mr. Jameson gave a testy tone to his tightly wound wife.

Biting her lip, Mila considered if she should just run and hide somewhere, but the two hadn't even rang the doorbell yet.

"I bet the entire house smells now! What if she did some sort of African mumbo—"

Mila whipped the door open so quickly that Mrs. Jameson choked on invisible dust. As shaky as her smile of greeting was, Mila was impressed she greeted Warren's mother cordially. "Hello Mrs. Jameson, hello Mr. Jameson."

"Oh you're... you're home…" Mrs. Jameson's hand zoomed behind her fat hip.

"Do you have a key to my house?" Mila blurted as soon as the thought popped into her head. Not intending to be rude, just surprised since Warren had never mentioned giving his parents the key.

"The key to *your* house, Mila, look around you. Girl, if it weren't for my son, you'd be somewhere hoofing it. Or … let me give you the benefit of the doubt, somewhere warm and cozy *in a hut*."

Mary Jameson didn't always hate Mila. Warren's mother regarded Mila as all of the other pretty young thangs, flocked around one of her sons. *Keith.*

The Jamesons' were neighbors of her uncle's family who not only fled Somalia, but didn't stop until they came to the states. At fifteen, Mila and her family came for vacation, and Keith had been her first kiss. She'd prayed long and hard after doing something so foolish. As a sophomore at UCLA, Mila and Keith crossed paths once again. Keith had this funny way of lifting her spirits, and going out with their group of friends after acing finals kept her sane. He flirted, but they never shared anything more than that one childhood fling.

Mila gulped back the lump in her throat.

"Mary..." The old man shuffled in his orthopedic loafers. The two wore t-shirts from The Grand Canyon, from which Mila guessed they had just returned. They had a Mercedes RV van, and Mrs. Jameson would always complain under her breath that she'd be traveling the entire US-of-A to find a woman worthy of her oldest son.

As his wife opened her mouth, wrath targeted on her husband, he launched himself toward Mila for a hug.

Awkward.

"How are things, Mila?"

"All right." Her heart percolated as if returning to life with the fatherly hug. For the moment, his evil wife disappeared. Mr.

Jameson reminded Mila of Warren. All around good, nerdy, sweet, with a dash of awkwardness.

"How about the two of you?"

"We're all—"

"I was worried that you needed help, Mila," Mrs. Jameson said, voice devoid of malice… It had to be a trick.

Mila's eyebrow arched.

The big woman pulled an envelope from her designer purse. "We came to see if we can help take this house off your hands."

"Mary, we're still standing at the front door." Mr. Jameson gestured for her to take a break with the guerrilla antics.

"Oh come in..." Mila stepped back and allowed them entrance.

"This is a rather large home." Mr. Jameson seemed to be winging it. He diluted the venom his wife exuded with his calming body language.

Mr. Jameson excused himself as his cell phone rang in the pocket of his cargo shorts.

Mrs. Jameson shrugged. "Yes, so big. After Warren furnished it, and y'all prepared for the wedding. Well, the house… and the mortgage I'm sure is expensive..."

Mila glared at her. The woman had never tried to be affable before, so this had gone too far. Mostly Mila avoided her soon-to-be mother-in-law, but Warren wasn't there for buffer. "I'm sure it is too much for me, in your opinion. And the home? It's too big for me, since where I'm from, a mud shack will do."

"Mud shack, *your* words. Not mine." Mrs. Jameson held up her hands, palms out, all innocent.

"Mrs. Jameson, your name is not on the mortgage, nor is it on the deed. My apologies that you had to be inconvenienced by opening this bit of mail."

"You know what, this tone of yours is atrocious. We're only trying to help you. That's the thing with you girls these days, running after a man with nothing to fall back on."

Keeping her mind trained on one goal, Mila reiterated, "My mortgage is paid, Mrs. Jameson." *Oh no, please don't bring on Keith. I'm not in the right mind frame to prove that I haven't fucked both brothers. When you're the one who always pimps them out, asking for this or that.*

The woman sucked her teeth. "Hmmm. Well, from the bottom of my heart, I hope all goes well with you here. I pray to God I never have to see your face again, Mila Ali. You know exactly what I mean."

Mila's body stiffened. As if Mrs. Jameson hadn't been taking shots before. This was a low blow, indicating Mila would now run after Keith, the beloved son. Mr. Jameson stepped back into the room, his ignorance cutting the tension, as he mumbled, "Well that was one of my old golfing buddies, who just found out I was back in town...."

"Let's go," Mrs. Jameson ordered.

Mr. Jameson said his farewells while his wife stepped out of the house. He promised that if she'd need anything he was a phone call away. Then he too left.

Mila sunk to the bottom step of the stairs. Knees pulled to her chest, hair draping over her body, she willed herself not to cry. Her back hurt like hell. Clarissa had offered a spa treatment, and to pay for it since they often took turns in the past. *But ... there will be no more luxury treatments, I'll survive this.*

About ten minutes later, crass shouting, carried by the sound of the wind, swept by. Grumbling at the thought of spending the night with a bottle of liquor store wine and another lean cuisine, Mila paused, assuming she'd left the television on. But the sounds carried loudly, tensely.

Lido!

Her sister and Veronica promised to come by for dinner. Though Mila had excuse after excuse for hanging out with Clarissa, these two had seen her at her worst. She clambered to her feet, grabbed both of the doorknobs, and swished the front double doors open.

"Oh you think I'm some sort of voodoo priestess." Lido shouted, conjuring up their natural dialect simply to fuck with Warren's mother.

As she rounded the large fountain, Lido popped into view, holding two fingers up, voodoo style. Mr. Jameson whispered in his wife's ear, but the words were written all over his face. He sought peace.

More crass and culturally insensitive words came from Mrs. Jameson. The type of words that normally rolled over Mila's shoulder. She regretted stooping to Mrs. Jameson's level a short while ago. But Lido?

"Okay, my love," Veronica tried to drag Lido toward the door.

"Oh, no. But I must hex this bitch!"

"*Bitch*?" Mrs. Jameson spat.

Mr. Jameson sighed. "C'mon, Miss Ali, let's all be —"

Mila's eyes widened as Lido began to bellow the hex. The gibberish brought Mrs. Jameson damn near tears.

Mila tightened her lips so as not to bust up laughing. "*Walaashay weyn, joogso!* Big sister, stop!"

"But I'm almost done!"

"Mila," Mrs. Jameson exploited a genial tone, similar to the one she used a while ago to get under Mila's skin. "What is she doing?"

Mila's eyes widened in mock concern. "Can you move?"

The dummy had been moving all around, rolling her neck, but now she demonstrated unquestionable obedience. Body stiff, she said, "I... I...

Mila gestured for her to run, and run she did. Mrs. Jameson hopped her fat ass into the driver side of their champagne S600.

Lido's slender frame doubled over, and she laughed her ass off.

Mr. Jameson, though not drinking the Koolaid, got into the passenger side right before she skidded back on the road.

"Hey, don't hit my Bentley!" Veronica shouted, baby blues almost popping out of their sockets as the car stopped inches away from the pearly white convertible. Then Mrs. Jameson shifted gears, the powerful car lurched forward as she made a U-turn.

If it weren't from the shock of the moment, Mila would enjoy the sun rays caress of her bare shoulder. Her hobo dress swayed in the salted wind.

"Oh Lido, you didn't have to do that." Mila reprimanded.

"Humph." Lido turned on pointed heels and stalked into the house, Veronica at her heels. By God, Mila ached for the back rub that Veronica gave to Lido in the grand entrance of her home.

"Ladies, I have to apologize."

"No you don't!" Lido snapped. "You've held your tongue since we've met that bitch—"

"Babe, the language..." Veronica interjected, voice soothing.

"*That fat ass bitch*," Lido enunciated every syllable, "better go stuff a Twinkie in that mouth. You, Mila, you're too fucking nice. That shit is for the birds, Mila. It's a new day, new age. Don't apologize for shit." Still not off the soap box, Lido shied away from her girlfriend's pawing, and stepped closer to her little sister. "Open that gorgeous mouth of yours and reign."

Head cocked to the side, Mila inquired, "Are you finished?"

"I could go on, I'm opinionated. I'm conceited, so doesn't that imply everyone should kiss my motherfucking ass while providing all ears?"

"Veronica is the only one that should kiss your ass, physically not literally." Mila smiled. "Now that you've calmed down, Lido. I wasn't implying that I needed to apologize to Mrs. Jameson."

"And *Mrs.*," Lido continued her rampage, "You still aren't on a first name basis with the bi—broad! Is *that* 'b' word okay?"

Mila huffed at her sarcasm.

"Listen, Pet, just listen," Veronica implored.

"As I've previously attempted to say, I wanted to apologize to the two of you. When the Jamesons arrived, I totally forgot about cooking. Honestly, today was a good day. I've washed clothes..." Mila shook her head, thinking about how she had even opened up Microsoft Word to reread her proposal for the government grant. "That's beside the point. But honestly, I felt my heart beat this morning, then they came. So, my apologies, I didn't prepare anything. And to make matters worse, hell, I can't even afford to buy the three of us Happy Meals from McDonald's."

As she simpered, the ebony and ivory models smiled.

"Well, before we were getting out of the car and that woman starting talking shit," Veronica said, "We were going to grab the groceries from the trunk."

"Groceries?" Mila's eyebrows rose.

"Yes, I can't cook." Veronica placed a delicate hand to her tiny bosom.

"Don't say it," Lido cut in still smiling.

"We all know she can't." Veronica laughed.

"How do I deserve you two?" Mila asked following them outside. "First, you pay my three months of mortgage, now this."

"It's nothing. We cleanse every morning and eat out every night." Lido shrugged as Veronica popped the trunk.

"Think of it along the same dynamics as one of our guilty 'You buy, We Fry' place off Crenshaw, in L.A." Veronica rubbed Mila's shoulder. "Except you will eat most of it and we don't have to purge."

minutes, he called incessantly.

Then a text popped up.

Mila, u need me. Pick up the phone.

The muscles in Mila's eyelid twitched. She didn't need him. In college, he was comedic relief after a long day. But more than that, a buffer for other guys when she wanted to go to the bar and hang out without being hit on. After the small get together that left Mila and Warren chatting, Keith, a man she considered as a best friend, disengaged from her.

Keith Jameson: *You don't need Lido to pay your mortgage.*

Keith Jameson: *Mila, you're family. Forget what my mom is harping about. I'll help.*

Something didn't seem right. Though he'd tried to get into her panties over the years—pre Warren—Keith was sneaky. She knew he'd bring home girl after girl, but never became fazed. If anything, Mila endeavored to welcome Keith's current flavor. Heck, she and the roommates gave Keith a gag-gift. A fake coupon for a lifetime supply of condoms.

As Mila switched her phone to Airplane mode, she put Keith out of her mind. Besides conjuring laughter after a long, hard day, Keith could be suffocating. She placed her cellphone on the nightstand and lay back in bed.

The vaulted ceiling became Mila's focal point. She wanted to keep this home. It reminded her of Warren. *He loved me before I even knew what love was...*

It had been almost three years since Mila resigned from Hewitt

Corp. One of the partners still kept in touch—she'd even listen to a few proposals from time to time. Returning to the fold would be easy and help her save this home. But that lifestyle, the cutthroat mentality, didn't sit right in the pit of her belly.

Somehow, the mysterious Blake Baldwin popped into Mila's thoughts. He was different. She wondered why he'd pushed away her desire to fuck him in the Employee Lounge. As an analyst for Hewitt, Mila understood certain behavior. Granted, she had called him an asshole one too many times and threw away his flowers, but Mila had been wet; ripe for the taking that day.

How had she lost her mind so easily? She'd never been an owner of those cutesy little contraptions for lady parts. No dildo collecting dust. No penis envy when fighting another ex-cohort at Hewitt for a campaign. Nada.

With the shake of her head, Mila tried to extract the desire from her mind. She'd gone from being the apple of her father's eye, to having a keen eye, and an acute sense for reshaping small businesses. Then she'd found love with Warren, only to have it snatched away.

I should have just stuck with the arranged marriage...

She held her pillow tight, not wanting to be alone. In three weeks, Mila would delight in the sweetest of sin. Blake had the ability to make her heart beat while she was in his presence. He summoned the hardest emotions, desire, anger, irritation, need...

This will be a business transaction. Just sex between two grown-ups. I am not a whore. Mila determined that a few rules might be in order. Blake seemed to have a large appetite. She'd whet his, and he would make the numbness go away, if only for a little while…

CHAPTER 11

MR. CLEAN, THAT is exactly what Mila concluded, eyes darting up and down the frame of such a large man. As he stood on her porch, with dim light glowing down, she took in those bushy eyebrows. Heck, even the fact that he was clean shaven made her feel dirty. Even in his stiff suit, that seemed to be tailored for his rather thick neck and build, he intimidated her. He'd called himself "Lamb" and said he would be her driver for the evening.

Driver? Hmmm.

Ex-Navy Seal or Homeland Security?

Lamb's mannerisms were stark, tone crisp and even more calculating than Blake's. Yet, Blake's guarded demeanor caused butterflies to take flight in her tummy.

Lamb held out a large box, shiny onyx in color and silk to the touch, and backed away.

Mila stood in her doorframe, unsure if she should grab her coat.

Lamb's icy stare glued on to hers. "Please get dressed."

"But..." The argument died on cherry red lips since his thick, suited frame paced back toward an awaiting Escalade. Mila turned, gripped the box under her arm, and went back upstairs.

In the bedroom, Mila chucked the box onto her bed and stood before the tall mirror that leaned against the wall.

"I look good," she told herself. That damn Blake, he had to have known she spent valuable time determining what to wear. A deep breath fizzled out of her as Mila stepped toward her tall canopy bed and picked up the gift. Her hands untwined the satin bow. Inside, bunches of tissue paper began to fall out. Then her hands grazed an olive green teddy. Lace, with such intricate design, it was one of a kind. Lido would riot for a sultry little number like it. Next, she pulled out perfume.

A quick spritz of the French concoction cast a spell around the room. The luxurious, smooth notes proffered Mila with a delicate floral façade.

The

Bastard.

Again, she dug into the box. Stiletto heels that she paused to take a photo of and text to Lido and Veronica. Seconds later, back to back PINGs sounded as her girls replied. A smile dug at the corners of her mouth.

Then the fucker had topped it all off with a camel coat. A moan escaped as she held it to her chest. It complemented her skin tone, as did the lingerie. Each item seemed to be specially selected to embellish. To adorn. To enhance her magnificence.

Almost an hour later, she stepped out of the house with the coat covering Blake's little specially selected treasures. Lamb got out of the driver's side as she sauntered by the fountain. Head held high, she got into the car.

Yasmin's gumption. Her *pre* marriage gumption encompassed

Mila.

Lido's sexy confidence.

After seven years, Veronica was her sister, too. So Mila took a dash of Veronica's demure seduction. She'd greet Blake in such a manner. He'd cum at the sound of her voice.

When the Escalade didn't take the exit for Beverly Hills, Mila glanced at Lamb.

As if he felt her stare through the rearview mirror, Lamb said, "Just a little while longer."

Dots of perspiration blanketed her top lip. Mila stopped herself from rubbing her palms on her bare legs. She again channeled her sisters.

The SUV pulled off the freeway and traveled into the mountains. Was there some sort of natural getaway in Southern California? The trees soared into the sky. Her stiletto tremored as Mila moved her crossed legs.

Then spears of yellow highlighted through the thick of the trees. A glass house came into view. She'd fallen for the natural views of the home Warren had bought; now Mila anticipated falling for this view too. Mother Nature was sublime.

I'll be the best fuck Blake has ever had. At that she took Lamb's callused, deadly hand...

~~~

There they were at the fork in the road once more. Seconds ago, Blake reiterated that the quick fuck across the accent table, their very first fuck, was just something to clear the air. He'd sent her off
~~~

without words. Legs filled with lead, she started for the hallway. *Go upstairs. The first set of double doors. Get in my bed. Lay back. Legs wide.*

Cool, glossy wood beneath her feet, with every step, Mila breathed in deep. *What the hell am I doing? The numbness is gone now.* His cock made her delirious. The raw roughness of the way he'd handled her body had inebriated her mind in all the right ways. Not one thought of Warren, no sadness, only primitive desire as her ass arched in the air. But if he wanted to seduce her slowly—she refused to think the words 'make love'—how would that end? The dynamics seemed too intimate.

Mila stepped into the room, where a Cal King seemed the only focal point. It was dark outside, but the glass windows displayed a wide range of forest.

I can do this, she told herself, yet those pretty little toes of hers stayed put.

"I told you to get in bed." Blake's measured tone reached out and wrapped around her.

She turned. Blake held the neck of a bottle of Cabernet Sauvignon, that cost more than a year's mortgage for Mila. He tipped the bottle back, drinking straight from it. The entire act, barbaric, yet enticing. In his other hand was a bowl of assorted fruit, strawberries, grapes, sliced kiwis. Before she could wonder about his intentions, Blake led her to the bed.

She tried to stand before him, but he commanded, "Hands and knees now, since you chose not to listen."

Her kitty took over. No need to respond. Mila climbed onto the tall bed, one hand and one knee after the other. The Egyptian cotton within her fingers made her moan.

"Now arch your back." She imagined his teeth were gritted. When he didn't do anything, Mila looked back to see his lofty gaze lowered to her jewel as he took another sip of wine. Without words, but so damn controlling, Blake gestured for her to turn forward.

Mila glared at the headboard that should already be knocking against the wall. They should already be within the throes of passion.

"You still want to leave?" He asked. It seemed his voice was lowered. He must have gotten on his knees.

"Stop taunting me, Blake." She arched her back more.

He groaned. "Look, what do we have here? Mila, I'm not even touching your pussy. But it's so wet… pink and glistening…"

Mila's head snapped back. "If you're going to fuck me—"

"If you don't turn around, I *will not* fuck you." His glare glued onto hers. "*Who* loses?"

Mila's eyelid twitched. Nobody in their right fucking mind said things like this. She'd had two flings during her powerhouse Hewitt days. One had been powerful, one was a coworker. But who said stuff like this? As if she lost because he decided to be stingy with his manhood. She sucked in her breath and turned around.

"Thank you, Mila," he replied sardonically, "Now my rules."

"Fuck your rules, Blake. I told you no spankings; Your handprint is all over—"

Mila braced herself for this newfound pleasure in pain. But his hands staked claim to her hips instead of hitting her ass again. *Damn, I shouldn't have made that a stipulation.* She had never been spanked during sex. Liquid lust wet her mouth as she remembered him taking her over the side table. *I refuse to admit it, but my god, please spank me.*

"Okay, at your wish, fuck my rules, Mila. You can eat those words later, with my cock. *If you're so lucky.*"

"Ahhh," Mila screeched as cold liquid poured down her lower back. It slammed the retort back into her throat, right where Blake's erection should have been. The chilled Cabernet Sauvignon dripped down the sides of her hips, ass, and into her asshole and her already soaking wet papaya.

Like a dog his tongue lapped upwards from her slit, meandering slowly and then twining around her clit, to that soft perineum. His tongue played there for a moment, delicately placed, then her legs shook as he continued up into the opening of her buttocks.

"You're but a virgin," he gasped, sexy chuckle only making her want him more.

Grrrr, she bristled inwardly, as he mentioned her anal status. She decided to play by his rules.

Blake poked his tongue into her asshole for a moment, centimeter by centimeter, niftily moving his way inside. His whiskers the only roughness against the folds of her soft derrière. Now her breaths were still, almost nonexistent as he penetrated her other haven. She wanted him back in her cunt. Or if he stayed in her ass that was okay too, but his manhood was the only remedy.

Fuck me slow, fast, however, Blake, please!

Blake removed his tongue from her asshole. “We still aren’t in sync, Mila.”

Fucker, you perverted fucker, just fuck me! What do you want from me? Eyes pleading to do his bidding, Mila turned around again, making a loud, exaggerated exhale. His index finger swiveled. A small whimper rippled through Mila’s body as her glance trained on the headboard once more.

No more words passed between as Blake repeated the process. The chilled wine slid through her lady parts, taunting her.

Then he leaned forward, offering her the bottle. She gingerly took it. Gulped down some, and on second thought, took another sip, as something chilled and round dipped into her pussy.

Her eyes narrowed, but leveled out as the small circular item went deep. THE GRAPE. Mila realized as he began to chew.

“Wow, Mila. This grape was ripe, so very succulent before, shit, I do believe your wet pussy has this deliciousness to it.”

She arched her ass more as Blake dipped another grape into her, and turned back around. It was the only penetration, and by damn, she embraced it. He laughed as she tried to meet more of his finger, but he slid the grape from her velvety fold.

“Where the fuck are my manners, Mila? You want a taste I’m sure.” He leaned over the bed. “Turn around.”

He placed the grape on her lips, allowing her juices to slide over her mouth. “This also reminds me, later, my cum will adorn that sexy mouth of yours.”

"Talk to me, gorgeous." There Blake went, deciphering her again. Those eyes had swept over her body a thousand times during sex as if he knew where she wanted his hands or mouth or cock. He read her to his benefit.

But no, Blake couldn't be attempting to manipulate her as his eyes warmed.

"Well." Mila snuggled into the nook of his chest muscles. The fit was perfect. Just as his dick had been last night, all though stretching her to meet his girth. "I slept so damn hard, and so good. Feels like I've been out for years, or at least caught up on the sleep I've been missing."

"Good, sleeping beauty. It brings me great pleasure to satisfy you, Mila. This is a smart bed, destined to identify exactly what your body needs. Did it do your body well?"

This man made everything transform into sex.

Blake was sex personified.

Staving off embarrassment, Mila rubbed her hand on her face and chuckled. He put her in good spirits. "Well I do believe, Mr. Baldwin, you have done my body so very damn well it's a sin."

And shit, she meant it. A bubble of laughter erupted from her. She felt too old to be a giddy, whoring school girl. But she laughed until she cried with Blake holding her, claiming her...

Mila wiped tears from her eyes, and Blake took her hand before she could wipe the other cheek. He kissed the soft flesh of the inside of her palm. Then Blake licked those tears off his lips. The taste of her skin made him murmur. Last night he had toyed with her emotions, sexing her body in so many ways. It was as if there were two or three Blake Baldwin's that needed to be satiated.

Her breath became heavy as his tender kiss went from her palm to the inside of her wrist. That soft skin which had *never* received an act of intimacy made Mila smile. Then his lips went to the last bit of tears on her left cheek. He wanted to kiss away the pain she had endured. A married man, he sought in his own way to make her whole... Or so she perceived it.

They lay beside each other for a while, and the silent contentment almost scared her—it had the ingredients of a good marriage. Fresh air flooded Mila's lungs in a deep sigh. She found herself asking about Blake's abdominal scar as her index finger trailed up the deep welt.

"Uhhhhh…. I've got so many fucking scars. Let's see, where did I get that one…"

"You've done all kindsa crazy stunts, huh?" She grinned. There were more slight nicks over his body, but all the scars enhanced his beauty. He had this aura about him, as addicting as her first take with Hewitt Corporation.

"Yeah." He nodded. "Adrenaline is my drug of choice. This scar came from Annapurna II. I was climbing the West Ridge." With bulging biceps, Blake pulled Mila on top of him. From his position, Blake looked up at Mila. "The Mountain was so fucking gorgeous, and at my fingertips. In my mind's eye, I was no longer a rookie. But was I really ready for the glory of her. This breathtaking soul before me."

Those two divine hands glided across her dark flesh, curving across her hips, to *own* every inch of her ass. Her hair became a cascade shrouding out the daylight, enveloping them into privacy. Mila's pearly teeth sought and clamped down on Blake's bottom lip. The act made his hardness spear the center of her thigh as she straddled him. She kissed Blake until all inhibitions floated away, then sat up to take a breath. Still holding Blake siege with her thick thighs, Mila ran her fingertips up and down taut skin. Last night she knew his body. If they never leave this room again, she'd die with every piece of him engrained in her soul.

"I'm hungry..." His words were nothing short of a growl.

"Oh." She began to move a leg from around him.

"No." His large hands stopped her retreat. "God made woman out of man, Mila, to be his everything. It's only right that I taste the sweetness of sustenance and that, my dear, comes from you."

She licked her lips. "Daily dose of vitamins?"

CHAPTER 12

HE NODDED. *Daily* dose of vitamins; the phrase had him laughing now. He felt like a mindless teen. For half the night, his blood had gone straight to his cock, which attributed to the teenaged hormones.

This was the woman of his dreams. The good girl Diane pretended to be when they first met. A few days ago, Blake returned to receive an envelope from Tom. Pulling out the money order from the lovely Miss Ali blew his mind. Yeah, he planned on fucking her. Mila returning his money didn't offend him in the slightest. In that instant, Mila reminded him of the woman who helped raise him when his own mother was too busy.

Last night, it irked Blake to no end when she walked into his home, making demands. Her tenacity was fucking heavenly, but it alerted him that she planned to keep some of herself from him. That wouldn't do.

"Blake…" Mila strummed his name while licking the silky pink of her lips. Those gorgeous brown eyes shied away for a moment. "Why do you look at me so…"

"Nobody's ever looked at you like this before," he asked, voice thick with sex. "As beautiful as you are, I don't believe it."

"Nope, never. Well, I've been flirted with before, but the way you stare…"

He wanted her to say more, waited even, cocking his left eyebrow.

With a tilt of his head, Blake gestured for her to climb on up his face. As Mila crawled up into position, her knees above his shoulders he said, "Well, I like a woman who isn't easy, who's challenging. An innocent woman with morals and a head on her shoulders. A woman who has ambition is a fucking turn-on. And to get to her to fall to her knees is even better."

"Hmmm, but I'm not the one on my knees, Blake. It's you that is below me."

"Touché." Blake grinned as she lowered her lady parts. His tongue had already conjured up the taste of those sweet lips and the crème that lied within as he helped her adjust herself around his shoulders. Head back, Blake got to work as she gripped the headboard and gyrated. Those soft moans were slightly muffled by her muscular legs near his ear, but when his tongue delved deep and began to lick away her desire, a deep moan erupted from Mila's mouth and became his persuasion.

A dog. She'd turned the billionaire into a begging animal. His hands again clamped around her ass and hips, he plunged her pussy down harder. Damn, he'd almost gotten his chin in there. Blake's dick tapped against his thigh, thirsty for a taste, too.

The quivering in her legs prompted Blake to heft her up even more. She needed support to survive. Fuck it. He could do it. He needed her essence to survive. Shit. She gave her nectar like water. The most vital source.

Golden sunrays washed over their naked bodies. Though time was a non-factor, Blake supposed it had to be around noon as a bright glow beamed down upon his newest, most prized obsession.

"Time for a shower." Blake's command warmed Mila's entire body. She snuggled closer into the safe haven of his arms. He gave her slender, curvy body a quick squeeze promoting her reply.

"Mmm, maybe later." She took a deep breath; it tickled his forearms. "Blake, I just want to rest again."

"Rest?" His tummy rumbled with laughter, and Mila became putty in his embrace. "It's your sexual demands have—"

"Those demands are still conclusive."

"All right, Mila. You be the analytical one. On the other hand, I'd allow you to tie me any way you'd want. My only goal is for you to fully surrender. You'd be more relaxed if—"

"Fully *surrender*?" She turned around. "And allow?"

Though delving in a jovial mode, Blake's gaze countered her confused almond glare. "Yes, *allow*. Yes, let go, Mila." *You belong to me now.*

Insulted, Mila snapped, "Have you *not* explored my entire body."

He reached over, grabbed her high cheekbones and allowed his forehead to touch her own. "As I've said, get rid of those preconceived notions. I've seen your entire body, but fuck no, I haven't explored it in a way that we both can truly enjoy."

Mila moved away and got up from the bed, grabbing the linen around herself. "I've already told you that this—" she gestured at her chest, then him, "—this was a one night..." Then her eyes continued to glance around as if searching for a path to fly away.

The softness of her body had woven into Blake's memory. He wanted Mila to be real with him. He wanted to keep her and placate all the uncertainty swarming through that gorgeous mind. "Continue."

"Stop that!"

"Stop what?" *Shit, last night we were almost there.* He bit his lip, recalling how good the sex was once he'd gotten Mila into bed. That quick fuck downstairs should have taken the edge off. The way he kissed every inch of her body, in this very bed, now *that* should have had Mila more at ease.

"What was I thinking? I don't care that you and Diane can screw other people, even on the same fucking continent." Her hands flew to the heavens. "Blake, I think it's time for me to go home..."

CHAPTER 13

AFTER FOUR MONTHS of being stuck with just her own thoughts, the night had been jam-packed with more passion than Mila could take. As Lamb drove her home, she took into consideration the quick fuck upon arrival. Blake gave the release she needed. Why hadn't they smashed like rabbits all night long? Better yet, why hadn't she thanked Blake for his service and not gone through the dread of going upstairs?

Shame on me for staying. Mila's head sank against the headrest as all of the "what if's" crossed her mind. Heck, an even better question was: why hadn't he grown tired and offered a predetermined stack of cash in an envelope, or further insult her by pulling out a checkbook and scrawling the amount he assumed she was worth?

Blake had done neither. The blow-your-mind sex, infused itself into her essence as she'd slept. His scent, the way his five o' clock shadow prickled the inside of her thick thighs, all solidified in her memory. He'd become that tangible. Like graduating from college, or marriage, or thc birth of your first child, Blake would forever be that memorable. And the moment she awoke in his arms, Mila knew she never would be the same. Let the sex continue. And so it had, until Blake implied he wanted to know more of her mind.

There were dark corners of thought, such as the young Somali mother and son, things she'd rather not divulge. No, Blake couldn't have really wanted—to know *her*.

Blake was supposed to be her six-foot-two, thick, sexy dildo. A big piece of plastic to give her sexual liberation and stymy all other emotions. She'd heard before that anytime a woman lays with a man, she loses a piece of herself to him. And in return, he leaves a part of himself in her. That was the biggest weight. She expected Blake to leave her momentarily placated. Mila wasn't stupid. He didn't love her. A married man like him never could. But she needed to feel alive for just a nanosecond as sure as she needed air to breathe.

Blake gave her that.

Then he surpassed her expectations. He touched her body in ways no man ever had. Mila couldn't say she had no experience, having bedded three men. But she couldn't lie, either. Never had she felt so much like a woman.

Those frosted eyes glanced through the rearview window as Lamb drove.

Playing with fire would come one of two ways. Blake Baldwin had the ability to make her comfortable. Even when he casually implied that he wanted to know her mind. Mila had wanted to talk to him, tell him… everything. But she decided that it was his allure. The more Mila got caught in Blake's spell, the less the determination she had about taking his money. And that meant clinging to morals, emotions.

The Staples Center came into view as she decided emotions

wouldn't do. Leaning back on the headrest, Mila knew it was the safer bet.

~~~

Mila called Clarissa, and they decided to take a run along the beach. As they jogged down the steps in the back of Mila's house, the sky was a plethora of colors in the horizon as daybreak crept in.

"Oh Mila. I've been calling and calling. I came by late on Friday night with the girls to tempt you to a night of heavy muscles and cocks of every color."

"Yeah, I was… asleep." Mila let the lie roll off her tongue as she followed behind Clarissa. "You know I don't prefer strip clubs, either. Anyway, you have a realtor friend don't you?"

"Leanna, sure. If you hadn't been such a sleepy head, you and Leanna could have chatted. Wait a friggen minute." Clarissa stopped at the bottom step to turn around. Her hand went to narrowed hip as she conducted an inspection.

Mila lifted her leg and allowed her ankle to lean against the railing as she stretched. "Those bony ass legs of yours are going to feel heavy. Ten miles, Clarissa. Get to stretching."

"Not so fast. You weren't home the night before last. Girl, don't let me think you have been avoiding me for no reason. You've been slutting around. Why not have Blake help sell your home. You know those rich people—"

"Wait, what?"

Clarissa spoke quickly, as if a defense attorney clearing the guiltiest of thugs. "You and I were at The Yardhouse for lunch when
~~~

I grabbed that magazine about Blake paying your mortgage. You were in there for a long time, and I know for friggen sure that Blake has some goodies in his office."

Mila took a deep breath. Her friend was on point. The damn man had an oasis in his office. She almost smiled at having the bravery not to give into Blake even then.

"You didn't want to go to the spa last week; I'm betting Mr. Money Bags worked those kinks so good he damn near broke your back! So forget Leanna, have one of his realtors' take a look at your home. The property is *gorg*. Now where is he moving you to?"

"Clarissa, you're worse than Lido." Mila began in a slow jog while stretching one arm across her chest, pulling her elbow.

Clarissa kept stride. "Talk to me. What happened?"

"Okay, what happened…" Mila scoffed and stopped her run. She wasn't in the mood, anyway. She'd dreamt of Blake all night since running away from him yesterday afternoon. *I'm too damn old to be infatuated with a sex freak.*

She missed Warren, her equal. Her bank account qualified as the butt of many a standup comedian's joke. But she refused to disclose it for fear of being perceived as a failure. But she already knew the truth. She was indeed a big, fat failure...

As Clarissa hungered for just a morsel of Mila's 'fairytale', Mila sighed. "Girl the sex was so good I saw the Holy Ghost himself."

"*That* good?" Bright red strands slapped Clarissa's face, and she grinned.

"No! Not *that good* because I'm far from poetic. I need a friggen thesaurus to find the words! Clarissa, let me tell you, girl… it was even better."

"So you're his new slut?"

There it was. The part Mila didn't want to get into. The moment people assumed the worst. Not that Mila censored herself around Clarissa—heavens knew she didn't judge. Her good friend embrace whoredom. Mila just didn't want to compromise herself. Being Keith's friend in college had done this very thing. People thought they were more than platonic, even when he brought around a different chick for every encounter. But with Blake… Mila actually tried, and failed at keeping everything kosher with him.

"C'mon Mila! Spill it already. Where did you do it? How?" Her eyes brightened further. "What size is *it*?"

"None of that matters. I won't be laying eyes on Blake Baldwin ever again."

Clarissa paused. "But you sound sad... Did he... Was he one of those rich creeps that like it rough? You said *no*, he *refused* to stop! Do we need to tell my brother, Wyatt?"

Cool air glided across her skin, conjuring the feeling of Blake kissing all over her body. Mila shook her head no.

Clarissa held a hypothetical belief of cheating. The fox toyed with the opposite sex. But when the shoe was on the other foot, her big, beef head brother Wyatt made all the pain go away.

"Okay, so Blake isn't a creep. I don't mind telling Wyatt, you know he's head over heels for you. What should we do?" Clarissa followed as Mila kept a brisk pace. Mila shrugged, and they walked silently for a while.

~~~

Monday's were always particularly trying, but this one took the cake. She'd spoken with Leanna after her run with Clarissa, and they planned to meet tomorrow evening to view Mila's home. While she'd made the call, Mila remembered the day Warren first brought her to this house. He made her put on a blindfold while driving up Pacific Coast Highway, then his Porsche had lurched to a stop. The sound of the ocean below tempted Mila, but he wouldn't allow her to take off the scarf. The cool salty air feathered through her hair as he took her hand and led her out of the car. Even in her darkness, Warren's happiness wrapped around Mila, making her giddy. And the sight before her eyes was a dream come true.

A vision of herself jumping into Warren's arms popped before Mila's eyes as she pulled up the winding driveway. But just as quickly as her fiancé flashed before her, Mila felt the warmth of another man. The *wrong* man.

All her thoughts these days led back to Blake. How had he worshiped her body so well? *If he can sex my body any better*— Mila stopped herself from wishful thinking. She'd ruined any chance of happiness. If you could call sleeping with a billionaire without commitment *happiness*.

She turned the wheel and moved pass the wrought iron gates. Then Mila's breath caught when seeing an Aston Martin in the driveway.

Blake...
~~~

Every instance they crossed paths, Blake drove a new toy. Nonetheless, Mila had poked a hole in that ship before it could even set sail. Desire pooled in her mouth, and she had to gulp down the anticipation. *Stop it*; she warned the warm swelling of her labia.

Mila pulled alongside the baby blue coupe, but he wasn't in the car.

Her eyebrows knitted as she looked through the suns glare in the window to get a glimpse of Blake's sexy face as he paced back and forth near the clay fountain.

The height was all wrong.

Mila grabbed the banana leather purse from the passenger seat and stopped her huff of disappointment as she got out the car. *I ran away like a raging lunatic. Blake doesn't want to be bothered with me anymore.*

Like the coiling of her abdomen, Mila's luck continued its turn for the worst.

The man was 5 foot 11. Dreamy, dark brown skin, clean shaven head. All Keith had to do was turn around and the slight slant of his dark eyes would bring her back to memories pre Warren.

I thought we would end up together, was the 'nicest' thing he had said a few months after claiming to be content with their friendship. The four roommates were all packing, ready to close one chapter in their life and step into the field of their respective careers. Keith flipped out—

For the past few years, Warren saved her from Keith's presence. Keith had married, but everyone who knew Keith knew that a band on his finger and words said before God meant nothing. The announcement of Warren and Mila's engagement had been conducted in front of a large group of family, and she remembered Keith's speech when he heard the news.

"Well big bro, I've been so used to the hand-me-downs over the years. Thanks to mom that didn't occur with my very first car." Keith chuckled, eyes on the bubbling champagne instead of the friend he'd known for years, "But I see the situation has reversed. Congrats on your engagement."

The stinging came instantly to Mila's eye ducts as she clutched the purse like a barrier to her heart. An image of everyone clutching their wine glasses as their eyes flitted back and forth, determining if they should drink to the 'toast' or not, flashed in 3D before her. That had been two years ago. He'd apologized, but nothing would ever be the same.

It was too late to toggle the stick shift and high tail it back out of the wrought iron gates. He'd seen her.

No. This was *her* home. Well, for a little while. She sucked up those tears threatening to break through, and took a deep breath.

Keith's gaze stroked up and down her body, assessing her burgundy pantsuit. His mouth arched to the left in approval. To Mila's dismay, she too, drunk him in. No, not as the dreamy boy she'd crushed on at a tender age, but in calculation, in a desire to perceive his brother. Keith didn't wear khakis or polos or nerdy things like Warren. A custom suit adorned his athletic body. It didn't bring her any closer to the man who once held her heart.

“Hello, stranger.” He rubbed his sharp laid goatee.

“Hey, Keith.” She dug through her purse. The keys had slipped underneath a square-like contraption.

“You've been gone all weekend, Mila. The family is concerned,” he said in a tender tone. The very one he used to apologize to Mila after Warren had a long hard chat with him at the engagement party. What good that did; Keith tried his hand again when the Save-the-Date invitations came out. He’d cornered her while Warren was out of town, reminding her of that kiss they shared.

She put up a finger while gripping her keys. “The concern isn’t necessary, Keith. I am a grown ass woman so tell your *concerned* mother to keep her nose out of my finances.”

He chuckled at the mockery. The corporate attorney had become more stoic by the moment. Gone was the laughter he extended when she took difficult General Ed courses such as biology or psychology. These days, she stayed away from Keith, even after the apology. Warren had made it easy on her.

“No, Mila. I came by on my own accord—”

“You sure it isn’t at your mother’s insisting? You know what, maybe I’m wrong. That would be pitting her beloved, baby boy against the Somali village whore!”

“Oh grow up, Mila.” He’d grown stuffy since embracing his mother’s requests: Make partner at the law firm. Marry out of your race. All that was left was to have two children once he turned 35.

“My parents didn't force me to come see you. I wanted to check on one of my longest standing friends. You've also been gone a long time?"

She met his challenging glance, did an urban play on a do-se-do and continued past him to the wrought iron and frosted glass door. Eyeing the Coca Cola can and gourmet sandwich bag on the cement bench next to the wall fountain, Mila paused. Curiosity triumphed the irritation of wanting Keith to leave. "How freaking long have you been lurking around?"

"I came by on *Friday night,*" Keith spouted, as if the timeframe instantly made her guilty. "Saturday morning before playing golf. And today, long enough for lunch a few business calls and to tell Nancy I'll be home for dinner."

Mila tried not to smirk at the mention of the blonde with no official graduate education—who his mom had approved. *I should have met Warren first...*

"Then you should get home for dinner," Mila tossed over her shoulder, letting herself in. She went to punch the alarm code in as Keith picked up his trash and made a beeline for the kitchen.

In the foyer, Mila sunk onto the cushiony leather chair with silver studs. She took off her wedges, lamenting having not made any sales today. Though Lido paid the three months of mortgage, and offered to continue until the home sold, Mila still felt restless. Restlessness was uselessness. At the sound of pots and pans clanging down the hall, Mila hopped up.

What in the world? She thought he'd bumped into the pans hanging from the ceiling, but he had two burners aglow, with pots on top.

"What are you doing?"

"C'mon, I'm hungry. Just making us hot dogs with my special chili sauce."

"Special?" Her hand went to her hip as she reminisced about college days. "Boy, you would add a little pepper and more salt than necessary to the darn store-brand canned chili."

His head popped back out of the stainless steel refrigerator. "Damn, tell me how you really feel, Mi'."

"I'm not hungry, Keith. Go home. I'm sure Nancy cooked." *Or at least ordered take out....*

"Snippy are we? That's the kind of convo I could expect when beating your ass at the batting cages in our dorm days."

Her listless eyes landed on his playful ones. He'd reminded her of moments she'd never get back. Running with the crew, with *him.* Even when she worked for Hewitt Corp, Keith had been her motivator. He gave her the cutthroat pep talk she needed at times. She'd transformed into an asshole, just like him. Keith knew the game changed the second she left the Fortune 500 company and decided to start anew. They weren't friends, not anymore. "Keith, I'm really not hungry. You know how Nancy gets when you're away too long..."

"Nah, she only gets that way when I'm with you too long. Especially on those days when Warren had to go out of town for work and I came by to check on you."

Mila cocked an eyebrow. She had forgiven the engagement fiasco, but it would be a cold day in hell before she forgot. In the past, Keith tried to make it right—even after that last attempt while reality sunk in, when he had received the Save-the-Date. Now, Keith dropped by unannounced. She'd feign busy or sick or... any thought that popped in her head. In Mila's mind that saying "fool me once, shame on you, fool me twice…" Hell, she never got there with people. Though Mila never provoked or flirted with him. Even after the way he acted at the engagement, she refused to continue to provide him with ammunition. *I am not target practice.*

Mila sighed. "So this is what we're doing?"

"What exactly are we doing?" He added his "special" seasonings.

They were getting comfortable with each other like they once did in their grad apartment life. Or at least, Keith had inserted himself into that role, while she stood there, a stranger in her own body. Mila had once grown accustom to being Keith's wingman. She shrugged off any sort of lie to get Keith out.

Maybe we can talk about Warren. That thought sparked a warm feeling, and for the first time Mila mirrored Keith's idea of being friends.

She climbed onto the silk stool on the opposite side of the island. "Do you wanna talk about Warren?"

Keith simply stared, his smile almost faltering. Warren had been eight years older than them. It was as if the younger brother regarded him as a deceased associate. Not even a good one. But Mila knew Keith better than anyone. Despite his running after females or putting work first, it would take time to mourn his brother.

On her part, the tears came. If something happened to Lido, or even Yasmin, Mila's heart would be dead. .

He came and leaned between her legs, hugging her. If Keith could actually give a fuck about a person, perhaps she'd be on the top three—his parents came first.

"It's okay..." She told him in a shaky voice. Mila meant for Keith to back away and leave her be. Yet his thumb grazed her chin, tipping her face upward.

"Mila, you mean more to me than you know. At the funeral, my only intention was to respect your grief for my brother." Keith sighed. "I should have come sooner, but I won't let you go this alone."

His breath tingled against her earlobe. His lips had hovered so near she could taste it... Mila opened her mouth to cease his confused notions, but the alarm blared. Keith let her go and hurried toward the stove, Mila at his heels. The water the hot dogs boiled in had evaporated. A pungent odor had clouded the room.

Keith quickly grabbed the pot, and then it crashed to the floor. "Fuck!"

"Oh, hold on." Mila turned off the heat and removed the chili from the stove. "Keith, see what happens when you over think things?"

"No, I don't."

She knew he was irritated, and perhaps embarrassed for trying to rekindle things with her.

As she placed ice cubes in a sandwich bag, Keith leaned against the counter. His jaw tightened, and his teeth gritted. She placed the compression against his large palm.

"Where've you been, Mila?"

"Nowhere." She kneaded her temple.

"*Nowhere*?" His hand dropped the ice pack in the sink. "Nowhere? Well I've been by all weekend. I called your parents. Your sisters..."

She wanted to curse him. Mila's parents had actually liked Keith. After she declined the pre-arranged marriage, her father had gone the extra step against their culture to embrace his daughter's wishes, believing Mila loved the man. When she told him otherwise, her father had given in to their friendship, in hopes Keith Jameson was the one. When, really, Mila was just transforming into the split image of him. Out for self. Her ma was willing to work with Mila's love for Warren. But by the time she became engaged, the well wishes had overturned.

"Mila!" Keith forced her attention.

"Don't yell at me in my damn house. I will cuss you out and kick you out, Keith!"

"You went on vacation? Did the insurance finally come through?"

"Why, do you want a cut?" She snapped. *No, and the agent refuses to take my calls!*

He looked at her as if she'd slapped him.

Mila took a deep breath. "No, it hasn't. Those people have taken me through the ringer, Keith. Sorry."

"You already said sorry. I don't need apologies. I need to know where one of my *closest friends* spent the weekend. I need to know how you've been coping and whom has been helping you through!"

Flabbergasted, Mila's mouth opened, yet no sound came out.

His palm slammed down on the granite counter. The very one that had a red sneer from being burned.

"Keith, I swear." Mila tried to keep poise. Today, she wasn't in the mood. "You need to get out of my business. We aren't friends like that, not anymore, and we sure haven't been for a long time. Go home!"

CHAPTER 14

FROM DEEP WITHIN his loins, Blake had become bewitched by Mila. She was the first woman in longer than he could recall that hadn't become putty in the palm of his hands. The challenge was welcoming, but with the chase came another feeling. An emotion almost as strong, and counterproductive… guilt.

But she hasn't accused me of murdering Warren since that one time she fainted. He clicked at his ballpoint pen, deciding Mila was overcome with grief. *Yes, that's it. Mila was learning to deal with the fact that the man she wanted to spend the rest of her life with died. For Christ sakes, she was distraught–*

"Hey, hey nobody wants to listen to U2. C'mon dude!" One of the techies became the antidote to his newest obsession. Reality returned.

In the large room with millions of dollars' worth of electronics, his hired geeks sat around arguing about which music to play.

"Blake," Todd cocked his head toward Blake's office.

After a quick nod to Todd, Blake decided to address his team.

"All right guys, stop jacking off to internet porn. No matter how well your benefit package is, if you get arthritis, your asses are outta here," he said, inciting a round of laughter. "Fuck me." Blake shook his head. "I'm surrounded by horny-ass high schoolers. All right, listen up. I want us to work on more inventive things. We're number four right now in terms of gathering new customers, Zuckerberg and the rest of those douches are good friends, but I'd like to brag the next time either one of us has an event. So, turn off the fucking music, unless you're reaching for a good ol' gospel blessing."

A round of laughs ensued as he and Todd went into his office that had only three uses: working hands on with his team; fucking gorgeous secretaries; or times like now...

Ten minutes later, he allowed Todd's concerns to sink in.

Blake liked to keep his circle as tight knit as possible. He didn't have time for this bullshit. Taking a deep breath, he asked, "So you're fucking telling me, you're the best goddamn tech I have and someone is still trying to penetrate the system?"

Todd rubbed the back of his neck as he sat wide-legged on the chair across from the table.

"You can out-hack any of these dudes, straight out of college or even in your age range." Blake leaned forward. "Is it time for you to retire?"

"Man, Blake, I'm doing the best I can..."

"Fuck your best. If it doesn't exceed my expectations, I don't give a damn." He sat back again, fingers steepled. "How about this? The next time I'm in Asia climbing Karkoram, you should be worried that I'll return with your motherfucking replacement."

There was too much private information in the system to be infiltrated. Beads of sweat formed above the Todd's brow.

Blake turned in his leather chair. Todd took his leave.

"I'm on it, Blake," Todd said, before shutting the door.

Blake glared at the sun setting. People ran, walked, and roller-bladed the trail below. Two minutes later, Nina entered the room, her perfume greeting him before she rounded the large table.

"Blake, what should we do about that smile?"

He frowned harder.

She began to fall to her knees.

His cell phone rang on the inside of his suit pocket. Blake pulled it out. She huffed, backing away.

As soon as the call connected Blake made his case. "Jace, The Dolomites sound tempting ..."

"Do I hear a *but* coming on, when total liberation is a hop, skip and a parachute away?" Jace shouted over the sound of a hard gust of air. He had to be near a chopper, with his climbing gear.

"Yeah, well I got shit to attend to."

"What, man? You pay people to *pay people* to do shit. Or is it the girl that had us all taking the kiddie trail in The Matterhorn?"

~~~

At the office, the workers made their own schedules. Since the big boss was there, his employees had gotten stacks of pizza, and hardly even worked. Around nine pm, Blake donned a black vicuña wool suit. Tonight, he'd dine alone at the exclusive Xi restaurant in the Hollywood Hills. The reservation list was atrocious, but the owner wouldn't dream of turning away Blake.

"Alone, Mr. Baldwin, please let me know if you desire company." The maître d' grinned.
~~~

He extended a smile, not the least bit interested. Diane had called incessantly, knowing he was staying in California. Blake had been tempted to turn his phone off, when he received a text.

Mila: *Meet for (drink emoji) at 2378 5th Street, Los Angeles.*

Less than a second later, she'd sent another text. Mila: *If u want...*

He smiled, though wondering whether Mila had inserted him into the category of booty call. A title Blake had no issues with if she were any other woman.

Blake googled the address. A bar. Not in the best area of Los Angeles.

Around 10:45 Blake's Ferrari stood out between a rusted yellow Hyundai and box-shaped Volvo. Stale cigarettes and stiff perfume emitted into the smoky air.

This bar had transitioned. What at one point had been *the* spot went downhill fast. In the center of it, Mila was a breath of fresh air.

"Hey, hey, I won, sucker!" Mila slapped her open palm on the bar. Upon first glance, she appeared to be hanging out with a guy friend. Until the man tried to grab her ass, leering in her ear. He seemed to be whispering some obscenity.

Though she carried herself well, Blake stomped over. Glaring at the man, he greeted Mila.

She appeared more startled at his arrival than slapping the lewd gesture away. "You came..."

"Move, pretty boy," the guy shouted.

Blake's head snapped over. "Who the fuck you calling pretty?"

The man didn't get a chance to retort. The air parted as Blake tossed a punch, smashing the man's Adams apple. A mist of spit expelled from the guy's mouth. Unfazed, Blake finished him off with a hook.

Then with finesse, Blake gestured over to Mila. "Are you *honestly* enjoying yourself here?"

Mila watched, eyes wide. The guy doubled over and wheezed as the bartender came over.

"Hey, c'mon man!" The man pointed at them. "You two gotta go. She's taken just about all my clients money anyhow."

Blake began to pull out his wallet as the bartender mentioned her tab.

"I got it, Blake." She removed crumpled dollars from her jean pocket and counted out the exact amount. "These prices must be why this place has gone to shit."

CHAPTER 15

THE DAY HAD gone downhill the moment Mila arrived home. Keith had left her longing for Warren's arms. The pillow of curled hair at his chest had been her everything after a long day's work. But Warren was no longer here, and in his place stood a man she could never truly be with.

Sporting a good buzz, she followed Blake out of the bar.

"Let's go, Mila." There it was again, that controlling tone of his.

"Yeah, well, I'm not done drinking."

"Fine by me, but you're not driving."

"I'm not drunk, a little tipsy..."

Blake's dark look didn't yield.

Mila sighed under her breath, "Just comfortable in my own skin."

They ended up at a swanky lounge. Extremely elevated ceilings played up the vertical differences in the place. Chandeliers, at least twenty feet long, brought the focal point upwards. Low seated couches, thick with plush cushions sunk almost to the ground, were studded with beautiful, posh people. Everyone leaned into each other, pawing, touching, murmuring to the sound track of the live band. They connected in a manner which made Mila want to trace her hand along every one of Blake's adventurous body scars. She wanted to feel his freedom. *Yes, that must be how he draws me in...* Mila thought, since he wasn't the first wealthy man to cross her path. At Hewitt Corporation, the affluent came a dime a dozen.

In the outer perimeter of the lounge were alcoves for the ultra-elite. She sunk into one of the most sought-after couches in a recessed area that had a slight distinction from the main lounge area. This area had an atmosphere of its own. In a fluid motion, Blake sunk next to her, and *he* became the atmosphere.

His scent soothed her in the same manner as Warren's, and it jarred Mila. But, she rationalized, Blake was all physical. If he didn't want to know her, and her brain's only impression of him was that of a hard release, there'd be no problems. She had to force herself not to enhance cognitive schemas, such comparing Blake to… love.

I'd be stupid to fall for this man.

A blonde in a black dress which clung to each of her curves stood before them. She held an iPad, ready to serve.

"I'll take anything with a kick," Mila said, yet the servant's eyes never turned her way.

"Your best champagne," Blake ordered.

"Champagne?" Mila's eyebrow cocked. She waved a hand, but the server only had eyes for him. Mila tried not to grumble. She didn't want champagne unless it numbed her enough. "You know what, whatever. It's as if I'm invisible when you're around. As long as it has the much needed *kick*."

"Why?" His eyes trained on Mila as the blonde punched in the order, who seemed reluctant to walk away. And after one more longing glance, the blond strolled off.

"Well, you can judge—"

"I haven't made any judgmental conclusions, Mila." His breath felt erotic against Mila's ear, his sexy lips so close that it almost felt like a kiss.

But it didn't seem as if sex were on the menu, since Blake had that glint in his eye. The one which indicated he wanted to know her.

She scoffed, "Yeah right, you're at the top of the totem pole, born swaddled in gold, with a diamond encrusted pacifier."

Blake shook his head. "Far from the truth…"

She didn't catch his disagreement of her own judgmental assessment because in Mila's mind, schemas where building as to… friendship? No, that had to be far from the truth. Though it was hard for the notion to wrap around Mila's brain that any person could have sex without building a relationship. However, that contradicted her need to fuck him without so much as a care. *I use to be able to think like a man…*

"Look at me, Mila. We're more alike than you think." Due to the low lighting, a smile parted the sexy, dark contours of his chiseled face.

"How so?"

"You're the me that I've strived not to be—"

"Thanks."

"Just listen. You're so engulfed with what you believe are preconceived notions of you that you make the wrong moves."

"So Mr. Baldwin." She scanned him up and down. *I'm not*

supposed to judge, but I know you've had me investigated. A man like you doesn't just fraternize with any damn body. Mila had to believe that Blake was one of those power hungry rich men—everything was at their disposal. If he was calculating, she'd brush up on her old skills and become just as cunning. Besides, how else was Blake so spot on? Preconceived notions triumphed happiness in her world. But Blake and Mila? They were far from the same. Though she decided to humor him.

"How are *you*," she shook her head, "like me?"

"There was a time that I gave a fuck about other's opinions. Now I change people's perceptions. My first million dollars didn't even turn the heads of any potential benefactors in my field. Or how about more recently? Not an hour ago didn't I redirect that man's notion of me being a rich, pretty boy?"

She pointed at him. "Blake you are ridiculously rich; And that dummy lied to you, buddy. You're drop dead gorgeous, not really pretty, but more so rugged…" She gasped, palm to forehead. Perhaps those drinks at the bar hadn't been weak, but truth serum. With a raised index finger, Mila decided to read the billionaire. "Okay, you were a *sickly* rich kid, may…be. But those eyes, that hair, you were born with. Wait, scratch that. You perhaps were sickly as a rich kid. Then you grew up and conquered mountains in all aspects of the word; am I right? Wikipedia was vague on your upbringing. So you grew up and climbed mountains, parachuted, sky dived. Due to being born with that affluent mindset you have no breaks when it comes to redirecting people. Whether its business related or with those fists." *Gloriously scarred fists...*

"I wasn't born rich. Yeah, as a kid, other people's perspective got under my skin. These days, I train people to see things my way."

Though Mila wanted to counter that his money trained people, a heaviness at the pit of her stomach told her otherwise. She wanted to know more about Blake. A man who stayed in the limelight. His internet bio began when he struck gold while inventing an application when cellphone apps were expensive.

"Now, Mila, why'd you call me?"

She contemplated that for a moment. The 'fuck me' line was the easy way out. He was a crack shot when it came to her g-spot.

"The finest champagne we have to offer, a 1995..." The waitress eye-fucked Blake. With a graceful wave of her slender hand, she displayed the Dom Perignon White Gold bubbly and its laser engraved insignia.

Blake nodded, his attention instantly back on Mila as the server poured.

"So what are we drinking to, Blake? My tipsy feel-good is coming down, give me a reason to celebrate."

"Not so fast, Mila. The last time we spoke, I wanted to know everything about you." He seemed to glance straight into her soul.

Blake just told her that others perceptions didn't matter. Now he still wanted to mind-fuck her. Mila just couldn't dash the feeling that anyone and everyone could see into her soul.

The confession was too easy. "I feel like I've been mourning a good friend, not a lover or a fiancé."

She wanted Blake to fuck her into submission. To extract the guilt of not being *in* love with Warren a man that treated her too damn well. Instead of a stolen caress from Blake, or even allowing their tongues to dance in the middle of the lounge she told Blake about Warren...

Mila skimmed over Hewitt Corp; the big name often scared people. Not that it would send a self-made billionaire into a tailspin, but it would surely let Blake know exactly the kind of person she'd become.

"I worked 80 hours per week, fresh out of grad school, Blake. That was before Warren, but technically he knew me all the while. We were the type of … I guess you'd say friends… yeah, friends who got together for chats when there was a large group."

"What changed?"

"With Warren?"

"No, with your job. The 80 hours."

Mila's eyes glided away. "One day, I decided that just wasn't life for me." Mila tried not to allow her mind to wander to the young mother and child when her family fled Somalia. Then there was that one reason she chose not to take partnership, that very day she'd taken a Taxi from Downtown Los Angeles, got out and proceeded to walk for hours…

"Talk to me, Mila."

"There was a time I was in love with Warren's younger brother, Keith." Mila ran a hand through her freshly pressed hair. This was a safer topic. "What do you think of that?"

"Tell me about it," Blake said, though his eyes didn't reflect the same disgust as Mrs. Jameson or anyone else who thought she and Keith would one day get together.

So instead of telling Blake how she'd almost compromised her soul for Hewitt Corp, Mila mentioned how cute Keith once was to her. He'd been her first kiss. "I went back home after that summer. Out of sight, out of mind, I guess. Well, more so…" she paused to consider, "I bonded with the boy I should have married."

"You were a teenager, and you already knew who you'd want to marry?" Still inquisitive… still *not* judgmental.

She gave a thoughtful nod. "Yeah, arranged marriage, Blake." *But there are reasons I couldn't go through with that, like the mother and child in the wilderness. Where was the father while this young woman had to go through life wondering if she and her baby would make it–God, I just want to know if they survived!*

That emerald gaze stayed connected on Mila's. He had more questions, his demeanor made it evident. He wanted to know more about said arranged marriage and why she didn't go through with it.

"I chose education. Out of a gazillion Angelinos, Keith and I went to the same school. I didn't even know Keith got into UCLA. This might not make a lick of sense, but Keith became my crutch. I've always taken the easy way around things. Education was my first, and having him as a friend kept my eye on the prize. But I can't say he didn't get under my skin this evening. I wanted to slap the black off his face. So there, the reason why we're here. Because Warren was a good guy, a wonderful man that I loved, but I've never been so…shit, I don't even know the word."

"You've never been in love with him."

"Yeah," Mila shook the confusion from her head. Then a smile perched on her lips. "Blake, you of all people—"

"Deflecting."

She took a deep breath.

"You're deflecting; not to mention I sense another round of judgement, Mila."

"No, I'm not judging. It's just that my sister Lido is the only one to know the full story. Okay, this is how people see me: a slut who went after both brothers. I shared a dorm room with one throughout college. Then it seems like I traded the young one in for the already successful Warren." Mila paused. Blake didn't seem to agree with her assessment of herself. "Okay, so I've only shared an awkward peck with a boy who had dimples! The other, who nurtured my mind, chased me for the longest time. But I was in love with Keith as a kid. I never got around to falling for Warren."

"Hmmm. Mila, you're all over the place. Look, Keith was the first cute boy you stared at. I remember the first girl I liked in elementary school too." He paused to chuckle at the absurdity. "You can't compare kiddy love to the grown folk stuff. Now, back to us. Mila, your debating is fucking praiseworthy. Arguing with you makes my cock so hard I want to bend you over and slap you with it. But when it comes to the two brothers, your debating sucks. You're still assuming I look at you the same way as other people."

"Let's drink. We've been sitting here for fifteen minutes with perfectly good bubbly." She squirmed. Blake was right. Even if the love she once felt for Keith was puppy love, it held more weight than her feelings for Warren. "Have you dug into my mind enough, Blake?"

"Sure, but there's always later..."

Though she smiled at the thought of some sort of future with a *married* man, Mila glanced at the Dom Perignon White Gold with its luxurious casing. If Blake wasn't going to fuck her brains loose, this would do. "So what can we celebrate?"

That forest green gaze swept over her skin, so palpable and rich, then landed on her eyes. "We breathe, therefore we celebrate."

Their glasses clicked.

After a few drinks, an imaginary magnet made them scoot closer to each other. Mila leaned into him and began to nibble on Blake's ear. She wanted him badly. The man could have been unattractive, ugly even, but his ambitions and egotism made her horny as hell. And let's face it, his cologne only enhanced Blake's charisma.

"I've missed it..." His package felt like titanium as Mila's palm fondled the rich material of his pants.

Blake turned toward her. He nipped at her bottom lip, sending a pulsating jolt to her lady lips. "You drunk, Mila?"

"Not even."

"Good, I wasn't going to fuck you if you couldn't remember shit." The dark look on Blake's face told her she couldn't even fathom what he had in store for her...

CHAPTER 16

PAIN REFLECTED IN those chocolate brown eyes. A sadness that Blake Baldwin knew so very well. She'd said he was privileged. Mila came up with a good enough back-story than the one Blake had always provided the media. But just like Mila, the happiness, the stability of living was torn from him. So instead of growing up privileged, Blake knew something of the sadness that Mila clung to.

He wanted to give her a release. Blake realized climbing Mount Everest or skydiving in New Zealand might be goals he had to steer Mila toward. For now, there was this one spot he just had to take Mila. A place so beautiful that her tensed shoulders would relax and that brain of hers got a rest. She'd already asked him three times on the way to the airstrip if his wife would be okay with them going on vacation. He'd told her the terms of his open relationship until her hesitance had ceased.

"Where are we going?" Mila asked, glancing at the seatbelt light on the upper counsel of the Learjet.

"Somewhere ugly," he teased.

"Oh, I'll pass." She played along with a coy, shaky smile, starting to unbuckle the seatbelt. He placed a hand over hers.

"We aren't even in the sky yet, Mila." His tone blanketed her with comfort. "St. Bart's."

A gasp rushed past Mila's sensually parted lips, and Blake realized the fear had begun to break away. "St. Bart's is ugly?"

"There's nowhere on this universe to rival your beauty, Mila. Trust me, I've been all around." Blake slipped his hand into her dress and let his palm slide over her breast. Mila's rock hard nipple pierced his skin, and followed the rolling of his hand. His lips went to her ear.

"Hmmmm." Mila's breath shortened in a moan. "Am I to assume you've had much practice telling many pretty girls this while … whisking them away?" She raised her eyebrow at the bullshit he fed her, though it tasted as scrumptious as his cum sliding down her throat.

"I'd never do that, recycle lines."

Something told her that he spoke fact, not fiction. Or rather her mind was blown by his thumb and forefingers squeeze of her rock hard nipple.

Then Blake undid his seatbelt. Greedy as she was, Mila's mouth moistened.

He got on his knees, parting her thighs with strong hands that stung her silky skin with desire.

"Miss Ali, may I eat your pussy?"

Jaw dropped, eyebrow raised, Mila hadn't expected him to be so gentlemanly. Blake rarely asked, and usually it was to make a point, or delve into her thought process.

She nodded.

"I must hear the words, Miss. Ali..." Those golden flecks in

Blake's eyes were so profound, she had to assume he was toying with her.

"Blake, go down—"

"No, no, I'm asking to taste your pussy, beautiful."

She scoffed.

"Oh, I did forget." He licked his thumb, then pushed his hand beneath her skirt. Blake made circular motions with the sweet rounded bulb. "You were so ridged when we met. No tying up or down. So many stipulations."

"Am I ever going to live that down?" Her legs opened wide, but fingers, Blake did not provide. Just that intense caress of her clit.

"Blake, please." Mila's tensed breath hissed through gritted teeth when he removed his thumb. But Blake again licked his thumb and went back below, adding a tormenting amount of lubricant.

"Blake! St... Stop fucking with me."

"But I'm not fucking with you, gorgeous." Blake gripped her hips and slid her even more down the luxurious leather chair. Emerald gaze locked onto her shaded brown marbles, he said, "You won't release for me. So I have yet to begin fucking you."

She glanced at his mouth, licking her lips. Knowing her thoughts Blake turned his head before she could kiss him. An irate, feminine grumble on her part made the left side of his mouth rise.

"Well I won't play these games anymore, Blake." Mila tried to close her thighs. The muscles shaking as she found out the hard way that her shapely legs were no match for the strength of his biceps.

He maneuvered his slender hips between her legs and staked

claim to Mila in a tight embrace. Hands pawing at her ass and hips, Blake tongued her down with a vengeance. Their tongues collided, twirled, and danced. Lungs ready to explode they parted ways. She'd learn to submit once she learned her worth. Blake threw Mila's thighs over his shoulder so quickly that she yelped. His hands glided up beneath her dress, his head disappearing. Mila gulped an air-full into her lungs as he nipped at her panties, bringing them down with his straight, white teeth. Her mouth went slack in amazement, and she tried to wipe the drool from the corner of her lips but he reached up to kiss her.

A whimper radiated from deep in Mila's delicate frame as Blake went back down. His tongue twirling erotically slow around her clit.

"Fuck me, Blake." She moaned. "C'mon please... Please eat my pussy!"

Those were the exact words that Blake needed to hear…

CHAPTER 17

IT STARTED OFF with a French kiss to her two *other* lips. Slow, seductive, and juicy, he growled his delight. Her entire body ached, since she'd waited so long for this penetration.

And... then..., Blake's tongue dove in, almost reminding Mila of a tiger dipping its long, thick tongue into a pool of water. His sustenance. His vitamins. Or so he said. Yet Mila chose to believe she was Blake's life source.

Pussy power, wow, she held in a giddy chuckle as her body went through the ringer. Though Warren wasn't her first, she'd had one other boyfriend, a fellow business major during undergrad school, and a few other guys during college, her lady parts had never had so much attention. Mila gripped the leather, realizing that she was scratching the buttery soft material, she began to claw at Blake's shoulder and grab his hair. He growled as Mila's hips twerked.

Then bliss blinded her. Stars blossomed before her eyes. Mila's left hand went limp in Blake's tresses as did her entire body.

Blake leaned back up, lips glossed over. "The games are adjourned, Miss Ali." He undid his belt, and his cock plopped from premium designer boxers. Blake began to rub on his dick. A wet, pink tongue came out and slid over her lips. The taste of his dick had been impressed upon her memory, like a Christmas feast. She wanted to deep throat Blake and gobble down his seed. Mila lurched forward, and slammed back as she realized her belt was still on. They laughed like teenagers as he helped her from her seat.

~~~

"... I'm supposed to be working today," Mila said eyes wide as they lay in a hammock over ultra-white sand, turquoise waters glittering before them.

"A few weeks away will do your body good." Blake rubbed her wonderfully fleshy ass.

"Weeks?" Her eyebrow arched. "That's a no-go, Blake. You squeeze in a business call here, a board meeting there, and even had a few men in suits meet us for dinner a couple nights this week. But I don't have enough power to do business overseas. Besides I have an ... er … engagement this evening that I must return for."

"Hmmm... Engagement. With whom?"

"Nobody you know."

"Why do I feel as if your mind is on the other side of the world at this moment? We've already talked about this, Mila. You're stressed and at a turning point in life. I'm doing everything that I can to be there for you."

"Blake." Mila rubbed a hand over her face. So he and *the wife* had an open relationship. *My god, I'm hating on a woman. I don't even have that right! And why does Blake want to be there for me?* "I'm meeting with a realtor to sell the house."

"Not necessary."

"*Not* gonna happen."
~~~

From her home in Ethiopia to here, Mila had seen this a hundred times over. Men dangling their assets in a female's face. It was one of the reasons she hadn't followed Yasmin's footsteps and acquiesced to her father's request. Even though Mila knew his only intention was for the betterment of her life. *If I had listened to father, I'd be married with at least two children right now... To trade in sex on the beach for pulling out my hair while preparing for my first child's fifth birthday... hell, I already know that answer.*

Instead of thinking about something so dear to her heart as bearing children, Mila's buttocks bumped back against Blake's cock, spurting a full blown erection.

~~~

The next morning, Blake woke Mila, saying that they were going on a hiking trip. She'd laughed it off while the gourmet chef prepared brunch on the veranda. They'd already been on endless shopping sprees, buying more clothing than she'd ever wear. None of which would do for a hike. After their stomachs settled, someone knocked at the door.

Mila stood just behind the opening with a cocky smile, and nothing but her birthday suit on.

Blake smiled, admiring her as he answered the door.

"… All of your gear, Mr. Baldwin…"

Mila watched as a backpack like she'd seen on the show *Running Wild with Bear Grylls* was passed to Blake.

"And your items for your lady friend…" The slutty voice seemed to end on a sigh.
~~~

"Oh shit…" Mila sighed as he handed over her own gear. "You weren't kidding."

"Nope."

They ended up in Saint Vincent. As the helicopter made its descent on the lush land, Mila's forehead was glued to the window in awe. "What a beautiful mountain…"

"La Soufriére is actually a volcano."

"Say what?" She side-eyed him.

"The volcano's last recorded eruption was… uh… 1979, we'll do fine."

She moved away from his touch. "Doesn't matter how diversified I become, volcanoes will never be on my bucket list. You have fun hiking, I sure will enjoy myself swimming."

Not two hours later, were they on a trail. Her legs burned. Mila thought running along the beach was an intense workout. This was torture. "Well what kind of vitamins are *you* taking?"

The hike had begun easy enough, with a series of bamboo steps. Then they meandered through passageways, over slippery rocks and streams. The sound of rushing water came from all around.

"We're getting close to it," he said as they traveled over a rocky terrain of lava rocks. Then they came upon another duo. The man seemed overzealous, just as fit as Blake, and Mila could tell this wasn't his first rodeo. The woman, who obviously hadn't been on a hike like this before, sat on a large lava rock, holding her ankle.

The man's large hands were in his blond hair. "Brittany, weren't you looking–"

"What seems to be the problem?" Blake cut in.

The man puffed out his chest and held out a hand. "I'm Derek, this is… Holy shit, you're Blake–"

"Yup," Blake nodded. He shook Derek's hand, then turned to the woman, only to find Mila tending to her. "Mila, you shouldn't…"

"I got this." Mila noted the swelling in Brittany's ankle. She extended the same smile she did while helping at her father's practice in Ethiopia.

Blake gave her a peculiar look.

"Let's bandage up your ankle." Mila knew this was more than just a twist. The swelling was extreme, and she knew a fracture when she saw one. She just didn't want to scare Brittany, who gritted her teeth against the pain.

It took twenty minutes to bandage up Brittany's ankle. Mila and Blake worked as a team, using his first-aid kit. Either he was capable of reading her mind, or he'd been in a similar situation before. He handed her the gauze

"Are you a doctor?" Brittany arched a painted on eyebrow.

"Nope." Mila shook her head, handing the rest of the gauze to Blake. She started to rise, eyes on Derek. He had to have burned a thousand calories pacing back and forth in the time it took her to care for his girlfriend.

As if Blake knew she wanted to tell the man off, he spoke up. "Derek, buddy." He patted the man's shoulder a little harder than necessary, making the blockhead wince. "Take Brittany back down the hill. There's a little resort on the west side of the island. Let them know you and I are good. They have a doctor who can take a look at Brittany's ankle, redress it. Get a couple's massage, dinner, the whole nine."

"Wow, thanks!"

Mila helped Brittany up, glaring at the man. Brittany thanked her profusely. She watched them head down the hill, and saw Derek actually taking his time down the mountain, holding Brittany. Then Mila felt Blake's fingers glide through her own. He pulled her close, kissing her hard on the lips.

"You're fucking gorgeous, Mila."

"Why, because I helped that lady?" She let him go. Blake's touch was welcoming and the taste of his lips divine, but the act of helping Brittany made Mila think of her father. She could almost feel her father patting her back, telling the ten-year-old how well she'd done.

"Blake if you don't stop staring at me as if I'm some sort of new species…" She didn't want him to ask how she knew how to bandage so well.

"Damn, I'm just surprised. You're fucking amazing, Mila. I've broken a few bones, and pushed another man's femur back into … adequate position in my day. But –"

"Blake, I am halfway out of shape as it is, climbing this friggen volcano. A *volcano*? *Really*? We can chat later." Mila joked.

Blake had stamina. He had the same aggression which caused poor Brittany to try to keep up with the fitness psycho Derek. But he was kind, and in tune with her needs. She just didn't want him to be attune with the old Mila. The one who helped her father bandage Somali refugees all throughout her teen years. The *good* one that once held her father's love.

Mila sucked in a deep breath when Blake didn't try to pry. Instead, they were content with each other's presence for a little while longer. He took her hand once they stepped onto the lush foliage. Sea views sprang forth from every direction, making Mila's pupils dilate with astonishment. Then she looked into the circular rim of La Soufriére's crater. With Blake at her side, Mila felt each stitch of her broken heart slowly twine back together. Even though he didn't offer a future, the present would be enough to sustain her.

Later, as Blake cooked dinner, Mila moaned with delight as he held the ladle for her approval.

"Wow, you're totally remarkable, I just want to fuck your mouth, Mila." His mouth devoured hers, and he scooped her into his arms, placing her on the black onyx countertop. "Wait a minute…"

Left breathless and a tad confused, Mila looked up at him.

"I know for a fact that you've had my food before, Mila."

Her gaze wavered, then Mila sighed and confessed, "I'd made such a fool of myself that one day you came to my home and I accused you of killing Warren. Although it was a simple case of transference, Blake. I've seen too many *Lifetime* movies to trust you way back when."

Her smile returned, sweetened with guilt and self-embarrassment.

Blake's hands blazed under her shirt, fingers tickling her ribcage.

“Oh, you suspected I was a bad boy?”

Large hands grasping at Mila’s fleshy thighs, Blake dragged her closer. His lips teasing her earlobe, “I like that.”

“Obviously, you’re a bad boy,” she countered, nibbling at his ears as her legs captured Blake’s strong waistline. Mila’s hands wrapped around his body, firmly gliding along taut muscle surrounding his spine. He pressed his erection into her thigh.

CHAPTER 18

Two weeks later

A SMILE NEVER made its way across Lamb's thin lips. As Blake sat on the back veranda with his wife, he gestured for Lamb to step forward as soon as the man posted himself right outside the back door.

"Any *illegal* activity that I should stay away from?" Diane asked, her eyes trailing over more food than they'd eat in a week. The gauzy light pink dress that made her milk white skin creamier blew in the wind. She snatched up the China dish of marmalade to apply to her piece of toast.

"You can step away if you'd like, Diane." Since returning from St. Bart's a week ago, he'd spent a few nights at Mila's. Today he had business to attend to. When Diane scoffed, he countered, "I promise that these activities may be illegal in a different sense of the word."

Again, the platinum blonde grunted, standing in a long silk robe. The sheer act caused a slight uprising to the left side of Blake's lips as a plethora of memories rushed through him. Mere moments later, the effect vanished along with the place in his heart he'd vowed belonged to Diane Baldwin. They'd been in each other's presence long enough. Sex last night was pretty good. Breakfast this morning was sufferable.

Lamb took post right next to Blake's table. Blake wanted to jokingly say *at ease soldier,* but just gave a head nod, adding a dash of salt to his sliced tomatoes.

Lamb sat and took out a Manila envelope, tossing it onto the table as he leaned back.

Blake forced himself to smile. He didn't want to open the contents. Shit, to be honest, this wasn't even really *why* Lamb made millions of dollars a year.

He took a sip of his espresso before grabbing the envelope opener that a man servant held on a tray.

He took out a single photo. The woman in it had striking good looks. There was a subtleness about her grace that resided in tiny titties that could fit into his hands. A thin, alluring body that he could pick up, toss around and fuck every way till Sunday. But she presented a problem.

Blake paused, rubbed his hands together and then asked, "Is this woman related to my first issue, or the second?"

"The first."

The world ceased spinning as Lamb elaborated. Nothing in the entire universe meant a fucking thing if this supermodel type was linked to a primary set of problems as opposed to a secondary set. Money was always primary. *Secondary* meant his current fix. His current desire standing at five-five, dark eyes, luscious hazelnut skin, raven hair. Ass too damn fat. Should he continue? Certainly not, because this secondary problem could be easily rectified. He was working his damnedest to keep Mila, and that's where she'd stay.

Blake's mouth tensed as he listened to how the woman in the photo was sticking her hands into his conglomerate.

Face set in cement, Lamb concluded, "I'll probably be gone a while after I handle this young woman, Blake."

With a quick swipe, the modelesque female's photo went back in the envelope, hopefully, to never be seen again.

He sighed, and the axiom 'more money, more problems' sunk in. "How the fuck did I get involved with Warren's fiancé?"

Sitting back, Blake glanced over his wife, who'd taken her meal to the gazebo across from the lap-pool. Unlike the trust-fund baby Diane, Blake hadn't always been the richest man on the block. He had been one of the poorest white boys to make it out of the hood. With blood, sweat, tears, and true grit, he'd climbed the fuck out of the gutter, no matter who fell in his wake.

As a teen, Blake took on virtually any hacking request to make a buck. He once hacked the Feds for an Italian mobster. Blake went on to obtain a full ride to Yale. He had so much money in scholarships that he thought himself rich, even then.

"Mila doesn't know a thing about Warren's death, she still believes it was just a faulty plane malfunction. You've got the background. I've only got experience." He wanted to believe that his experience of cultivating beautiful women indicated that he understood Mila. She didn't fear him. She didn't see him as a murderer. Well, except for when he'd first come by her home. The woman had been suffering from exhaustion.

Lamb thumbed the side of his prickly jaw. "Miss Ali is in the clear."

Good, Blake's instincts were grounded in Lamb's scientific proof. Mila was none-the-wiser. The tightening of his abdomen subsiding, Blake took a bite of his turkey sausage. Regardless of how long, or how often he'd been surrounded by talk of death, he'd never get use to that shit. "What's the update on our connect at the insurance company?

"For the moment, it's still a no-go. They're not pointing any fingers per se, however Miss Ali, as beneficiary, won't be collecting anytime soon."

"Those motherfuckers." *I will not claim guilt I won't fucking do it!* Though he gave the usual motto, Blake figured that screwing around with the lovely Miss Ali would not fare well for the investigation.

He grabbed the flask of alcohol and poured the amber liquid into his coffee. The action made Mila's warm brown gaze flash across his mind. Tears would be streaming down those soft cheekbones if she knew the real Blake, and what he was capable of.

Fuck that. He had to extract the guilt from his gut. Blake had taught Mila not to apologize, which was in the same spectrum. He put the model from the photo out of his mind, deciding to figure out how to help Mila Ali. The life insurance policy was for a cool $8 mill. A drop in the fucking bucket, but Mila was much too ornery to take his money. Maybe helping Mila keep her home would cancel out his guilt of Warren's death.

First things first—Blake decided Lamb would handle the model. Then they'd return to the primary issue—someone trying to fuck with his money. Blake would cut someone limb from limb for taking just one of his crumbs. After all, he had grown up with just crumbs....

CHAPTER 19

LAST WEEK, Mila settled. If she didn't fully stop to ponder the dynamics of what she'd become, then there'd be no issue of how she'd begun to compromise her heart. Her most prized possession, her heart and soul, were up for grabs. The most unworthy man—a married man—held the key.

Blake's nearness did something to her. He had the ability to transform her into his mistress, his whore. That only occurred when he was near. Or when her mind was consumed with thoughts of him, the domineering man was the sweet taste of sin in her mouth.

Cool, wet mist scoured Mila's skin as she ambled toward her car. For work, she donned a pair of GAP khaki's that firm-fitted her ass. The linen shirt and cropped leather jacket accentuated her waistline and hourglass shape. As fog evaporated, Mila glanced up at her house, which proved she was worth much more than simply being Blake's current obsession. *I'm not that far gone from grace.*

She turned the key into the ignition, considering Leanna's competitive listing price of $2.99 mill. She cranked up the music, backing out of the palm tree studded lot. Her radio screen flashed as Keith attempted to call her for the umpteenth time, but the ignore button was but a press away.

An old Alicia Keyes song had Mila joining in, trying to

harmonize. The bridge began, the song faded, and another song from back in the day came on. It was a love song. Mila quickly changed the station.

Steve Harvey's Morning Show blared through her speakers. Unlike other stations that got the boot once a song went off, or the DJ played a tune she didn't feel, Mila relished Steve's flair.

Except, Steve wasn't administering a morning dose of funniness. Catching the conversation mid-way, Mila figured he was talking about thousands of postings on Facebook… Not at all social media savvy, Mila said, "Au revoir," to one of her favorite radio personalities.

Toni Braxton's sultry voice reached out from the surround sound stereo and enveloped her in sadness to the tune of 'Unbreak My Heart'.

Blap! She reached over and slapped the power knob. Warren had been a good man. Though work was always at the forefront, and Mila never complained, he'd had this uncanny ability to regress at the nick-of-time. And when he put her first… that to Mila, made her love him dearly. Tears flowed from Mila's eyes. One minute, Warren would be chatting statistics, the next he'd explain the stats on how much he loved her. A bubbly laugh broke through Mila's tears as she turned onto Pacific Coast Highway, with only five more miles to Versa Home Improvements.

He'd start off mentioning the distance from Pluto, while allowing a trail of kisses to descend her body. Then the distance for Neptune, Uranus, Saturn… more constellation orbits that Mila had ever even known while loving her body. Warren Jameson's intellect had spurted her attraction for him. *I loved him, but why didn't I fall into that maddening type of love? Why wasn't I 'in' love with him?*

~~~

A few days later, tingling sensations consumed Mila as she sat on the phone late that night with Blake. Her lover often frequented her home, or she'd frequent one of his. Tonight, she hungered for Blake as she often did on days when he was away, but tonight, things were different. This wasn't just an overwhelming desire to fuck him. Every tendon placid, a giddy aura surrounded Mila as they chatted for hours.

"You're smiling from ear to ear," Blake stated.

"Oh, so you get off on mentioning just how well you move me." Mila bit her lips.

"Yeah, what's in store for me?"

Mila's mouth twitched, but she couldn't shake off the grin. "Um-hmmm, I assumed you were operating off pure altruism. You know what, a few days ago I think Steve Harvey was talking about you on the radio. I was looking for jokes from Steve, instead he's hyping up this mystery man."

"Mystery man?"

"Yes, mysterious and rich and well, maybe Steve added in a quick joke about believing this mystery man to have a good heart. Good enough to buy housing upgrades for people in the community." She sighed, recalling the shock she felt this afternoon as Versa Home Improvement reverberated with applause. There
~~~

were a few sneers from sales representatives who were always on the field, wondering how a Sales Supervisor had gotten the highest level of sales this quarter, especially when Mila had come back, glowy and happy from an extended vacation. She'd put two-and-two together, as Mr. Versa congratulated her, and jokingly asked her to take him to lunch.

Mila realized that while they were on vacation, he'd had a mass social media competition set into effect. Needy families from around the country posted reasons why they needed new home upgrades. The "secret benefactor" chose from those thousands of requests. Mila's eyes were stinging. If she ever got around to it, Mila wanted her nonprofit organization to be someone's testimony.

Blake's team had made arrangements with these families through Versa Home Improvements, with Mila as the sales representative, and she hadn't a clue about it. Her check would be large. She shook her head, astounded by some of the poignant YouTube videos participants from around the nation had uploaded as a "thank you" to the mysterious benefactor. One of the families had been squatting in their condemned home due to a fire. They made it on Good Day LA this morning.

Each story, even more poignant than the last.

"Damn you, Blake Baldwin, you had a certain payment on your mind when conducting that anonymous contest for families in need."

"You know me, Mila. I've spent hours envisioning your appreciation."

Mila's sex swelled. She wanted Blake in her bed tonight. But how could she have the audacity to even ask these things when he had to be at home with his wife?

They chatted for a while longer, longer than she'd ever dreamt.

"All right, Blake, I need sleep. I'll do my best to exceed your expectation's tomorrow, scout's honor. Will you release me for rest?"

"Release you?" His seductive voice twined through the receiver.

"I'll come back."

"In that case, I'll grant it. As long as you always come back." The way he spoke made every word seem of importance, as if her presence mattered, though he was somewhere in a mansion with his *wife* near.

"I'll see you tomorrow, Mila."

"Mmmm." Mila nodded off, her head dipping on the goose pillow. "When? No wait," she smiled, waking up a tad bit more. "Don't pull that move that you did when coming to my job again."

"So I can't eat your pussy?"

"Ye... Yes anytime anywhere -but my job."

"I'd love to tell you otherwise. But I won't be seeing you at your job tomorrow, Mila –"

"No," she damn near whimpered. He'd just fucked her through the phone. "Later then? You'll spend the night? I mean if you can..."

"Do not question me, Mila. And do not question my capabilities. *If I can*," he almost mocked. "I'll see you bright and early. We're leaving for Japan."

"Japan?" Suddenly fully awoke, Mila sat up.

“But I have work, Blake.”

“You’re going to be sick.”

“Sick?”

“So call in sick, Mila,” his voice was a tad testy. “You have over 300 hours of sick time at work.”

“How do you...”

“I'll be there bright and early.”

As they got off the phone, Mila wondered how long she'd have to be sick to go to another continent with Blake. A few minutes ago, Mila needed sleep. She’d been consumed by raw happiness all day today, in spite of the haters at work.

Her home would be paid off in a few days, with the commission that Mila received due to Blake’s silent good gesture. He’d saved her home.

CHAPTER 20

Tokyo, Japan

UP UNTIL THIS moment, Blake had never been to Asia without his climbing gear. If Jace and the gang knew he were within a hundred-mile radius of one of the largest mountains in the world, then there'd be no way to live it down.

Hundreds of floors up, they lay entwined in a cashmere blanket in Blake's penthouse apartment. The sun began to rise. Mt. Fuji beckoned him off in the distance, but the soft, feminine creature in his arms gave him the same heart-thumping in his ears.

"If you try to get me to climb *that,* I'll start a riot." Mila's smooth voicc warmed his cheek as she bestowed kisses to his ear.

"We've got all the time in the world to work our way up to Mount Fuji, Mila." He palmed her hip, pulling her closer.

"Oh yeah, all the time in the world."

He realized that talk of a future was taboo, even more so, her status as his mistress meant her time may come on a whim.

The phone in his pocket vibrated before Blake could reassure her.

"Blake, you've been screening your calls all week…"

Unable to declare his affection to Mila, Blake took the chance to answer his cell phone.

FUCK.

"So you've taken your slut on vacation again…" Diane's words were slurred with a heap of venom, pills, and alcohol.

"Don't allow the latest magazine headline to move your emotions so much that you forget who the fuck I am," Blake responded, censoring his words. Not in the least out of concern for Diane's feelings, but because Mila was in close proximity.

"Oh, I apologize, Blake. I fucking apologize for acknowledging your whoring around after the vows we've made!"

"Fuck that, Di…" Taking a deep breath, Blake gave a monotonous, "Guess I'll see you when I see you. On the other hand, feel free to enjoy the show."

Diane began to go off as Blake hung up. With the blanket swathed around her, Mila started to stand. She meant to leave him cold, and alone. His tanned body dominated the lounger. A warm hearth nearby would suffice, but a warm body meant everything. His hand went to her wrist.

"Blake, I heard the entire conversation," Mila stared him up and down. "Let's not pretend that you and your wife are over… 'Oh, don't worry Mila. Diane's in Bora Bora, Maui'…" she paused, shoulders rising as crisp air filled her lungs. "Yeah, I'm sure that was a lie. Don't worry, I still like to fuck you as much as I *think* you enjoy fucking me. But for the moment, I've enjoyed the sunrise. I'll take a nap. You can go out, do one of your *business meetings*. Let me know when you require my services." She bowed curtly. Resistance was met at her attempt to remove his hold of her wrist.

Strands of hair caressed across her bare shoulders and Blake knew Mila's knuckles were taut as she held herself away from him. In shame?

"You're done?"

Sparkling wet eyes, obsidian in hue, turned his way. "Yup. I'm not stupid, Blake. This is how the story goes. You want me. You get me. *Then you fucking treat me like your wife.*"

The way those full lips puckered as Mila cussed made his dick hard. He wanted her mouth on his cock, yet there were tears in her eyes. He nodded, still holding her captive. "Oh yeah, that's fucking cute, Mila. So you think I'm cheating on her? You think I'm cheating on you?"

"*Cute*? Glad I could fully entertain you, *Blake*." Again she attempted to wrestle her wrist away, but the asshole had a good grip. Though not hurting her, his callused hand held firm.

Though Mila had more grit than any woman he ever knew, Blake realize she was pretending to play the game. A fucking game he had no hand in as she mockingly made her request, "May I be released, *Blake*?"

He yanked her back onto his lap. The cashmere blanket slide to the ground. Now, she was just as bare as Blake. Except his tanned, taut body didn't display one goosebump while her silky skin shivered. Fire burned like magma in his veins. *She,* his current obsession, had that effect. It was like the very first time Blake had climbed Mount Everest.

"Diane and I are separated, Mila."

“Whatever.”

“You and I have gotten serious. The day we came back from St. Vincent, from climbing that fucking volcano, I told her–”

“Yeah, okay, Blake.”

He gripped both of her biceps, and pulled Mila in for a kiss. Her face dashed to the left, Blake’s teeth sunk into the flesh of her jawbone.

“Soon as we set foot on USA soil, I’m so fucking done with you Blake.”

If she wanted to play hard to get, he’d go vampire on her ass. His large hands staked claim to her buttocks. A moan streamed past her just parted lips. Blake grabbed the hair at the nape of Mila’s neck, turned her head quickly and devoured her mouth.

Reading her mind, Blake pulled back, leaving Mila breathless. Those Hershey’s nipples fully erect, rising and falling at the panting of her lungs. He clasped her throat with his hand, and again tasted her lips so damn good that all thoughts vanished from Mila’s mind. And it vanquished all his guilt about Warren’s death.

“Those fucking lips love to curse me. Taunt me. Threaten me.” Blake’s forest orbs took siege on Mila’s glance as his hand held her cheeks.

“Blake, when I say something, I mean it. Since we’ve gotten here, it’s been you reading your iPhone. Stepping out of the room, or declining calls. It’s been fun. True to form, you’ve helped mend my broken heart. So you’ve kept your end of the bargain. When we get back home, let’s call it a day.”

"My end of the bargain?" Blake scoffed. "This is all business to you, Mila. We're back to square one with you wanting to leave, too fucking bad."

"Too bad." She struggled to pull away. He refused to let her go, and he readjusted the blanket around her bare shoulder.

"Yeah, too fucking bad, Mila." Blake's arms gripped around her waist, he pulled her closer. Blake bit her bottom lip. Mila's pussy jolted against his thigh. Sugary wetness began to trickle over his leg. Blake refused to address her attempts to leave as her hot naked body warmed against his. "You're wet for *me*, Mila. You can talk shit, but still be ironically so motherfucking wet for me!"

She gulped, mouth wide, yet didn't say not one word.

"So what else is that mouth good for, huh?"

Not a half a second later, Mila scooted down beneath the blanket. Her lips flew to his cock. Those pillowy lips reminded Blake of her swollen labia. All the anger rolled over Blake's shoulders as her jaws got to work. His eyes went to the clouds hovering around Mt. Fuji off in the distance. Since Mila's mouth could work a multitude of miracles, he grabbed a fist full of hair and began to massage her scalp as she moaned. The head of his tool slamming down the back of her throat. Then Blake's fucking toes curled under as she drunk of him.

~~~

Strawberries had never been Blake's favorite, even in his past life. While others enjoyed what was considered a sweet taste or exhaling just the essence of a ruby red delight, Blake chose not to.
~~~

Just his luck, he stood before a strawberry blonde with pleasing pink lips that were curved in interest. How fastidious, those lips had been plumped by one of the woman's many suitors, yet she'd chose to forgo the standard Double D-breast job most mistresses received. Now back to those lips, they were perfect. Blake wouldn't mind the feel of those plush pillows on his cock. Yet given the circumstances he mirrored her poker face. False satisfaction.

Her alabaster skin-tone clashed with the slate-gray cement walls of her vast estate. The home was taciturn, her *façade* charming. The model from the 8 by 10 photo Lamb delivered almost two months ago, in the flesh.

"Hello, Mr. Baldwin, I'd say it's a pleasure, nevertheless I've delighted in many a billionaire before and have acquired a taste for ones who've seasoned in their assets."

His mouth twitched as she dissed him, then those muscles settled on a smile. "Blake. Call me Blake," he continued with the fakery as Lola invited him inside.

The servant in silk kimono who'd greeted him a few minutes ago kept her slanted eyes downcast as they walked by.

They walked past rice-paper walls in which allowed Lola and her many suitors the luxury of privacy in such a wide-spaced home. The place appeared even larger due to its minimalistic furniture.

"Well Blake, what would you like to drink?"

"Whiskey."

"Hmmmm…"

"Elaborate."

"Oh nothing," she nodded to her man servant who most likely doubled as a fuck partner. "Martini dry,"

"You're here about Warren Jameson?"

He nodded with a closed mouth smile.

"Suppose I should give you what you want, without any extra *lip*," Lola arched an eyebrow to clue Blake in on the fact that she had an inkling of his dirty thoughts.

Lola wanted to submerge him into a past where Blake had been watched like a hawk in the corner liquor store, or underestimated as 'not going to make it out of the hood' by inner-city school teachers.

"Thank you." Lola nodded to her man servant while Blake just took his drink. He downed it and complemented the whore on her good taste. The only words he spoke to the staff were, "another."

"Now back to this persuasion, Blake. You're one of the hottest billionaires ever. I've heard delicious stories about you." Lola licked those faux lips.

"You'll have to thank the gossipers for me."

"Ha ha." She laughed tensely. "Funny, though, the gossip is always ever in your favor. My friends, the *agreeable* ones can't get enough of bragging about you." She paused for effect. "Then my gorgeous friends who have a negative opinion of you… well, they disappear, Blake."

Instead of genuinely laughing at Lola's accusations, Blake shrugged. "This is a vacation area."

"Yes, it is. But I make many friends who vacation. You know," Lila tapped her lip with her index finger, "some vacationers transform into lifelong friends. As a frequent voyager, Blake, surely you've cultivated a few friendships on various continents."

He nodded. There was Jace and the other adrenaline junkies. And like Lola had just said, there were women. Some of which he'd see again, others… they were stolen moments out of a lifetime.

"Lola." He leaned forward, second drink in hand. "You have to be rather paranoid to conclude that some whores you once chatted with, stopped chatting with you because of me."

Her delicate shoulders rose. "I guess those are the makings of a coincidence, Blake." Lola smiled. Instead of accusing Blake of murdering these women, she changed the subject, "A few minutes ago, I was preparing to congratulate you on being an anomaly. Sexy. Billionaire. Although *new* money. You have this swagger about you as does all the other self-made billionaires. You keep your mistresses on gilded shrines, yet offering only morsels of yourself. Now, like I said. You and your kind, this new breed. Well you all have *nothing* on inherited money. Those types, though harder to snatch," she said with a curled upper lip, "are the crème de la crème for mistresses. Old. Money. Is. Everything. So I fuck them, or mere millionaires who aren't frugal." She held up her hands as if a weighing scale, "old time billionaires or measly millionaires who like to wine and dine a girl. I've heard your eyes are set on one of my old lovers."

Blake's eyebrow rose. Lola was curving toward his goal, without him even having to ask. Lola liked to talk and judge.

She shook her head. "If I could get anywhere near Mila Jame—oops, she didn't quite succeed in obtaining the name. So guess I really wasn't a mistress when it came to Warren, huh? He just liked to have chats, with back rubs and stuff like that." Lola shrugged. "Funny, I was there before he even got Mila. He liked her ever since meeting when the girl was in college. While I rubbed his feet, he told me all about sweet Mila. I knew when she popped his fucking cherry. Anywho, I'd like to think that Mila and I are friends. She wants to own a resource center. I like her friggen idea, really I do. Coming from a working class background in the small town, I remember my dad complaining about the *blacks* getting welfare and the rich, oh we all know how that story goes. Back to Mila, I wish I had a way to talk to her. I'd tell her to run. Whadaya think of that?"

"To be honest," he began, "nothing at all. You're hot shit Lola, which is why I've entertained your stupidity for over a second."

"Oh, so is this the part where you threaten my life?" She snapped. "I know all about your fleet of jets. Warren was on one of them, he took a business trip. One of his stops was right between these thighs," Lola said, opening her legs titillating and slow. "Warren had been tense. I thought it was because his bitch was forcing him into marriage."

Blake's eyes locked onto Lola's. She'd called Mila out. She was tight-roping on a thin line, and her demise already played out in his head.

"But nope, it wasn't *his bitch* that made Warren worried. It was you, your company… So are we at the part where you threaten me?"

His smile was pure, utter evil. Sociopathic tendencies allowed Blake to stay so fucking reserved while smiling in Lola's face. Voice smooth as usual he inquired, "Why threaten you, Lola? You don't know how *far* I've come to get to where I am. You sure as hell don't deserve a fucking piece of me either. The moment I leave you can voice all those half-cocked ideas."

She had endeavored to make him feel ashamed of his poor roots. Blake had done even more illegal things to make it in this world than what was about to transpire. The soft, tiny, gorgeous thing before him wanted to blackmail him? Fuck that.

Now Lamb stood before them, Lola's sapphire gaze almost popped at the sight of the silent, sly Lamb.

"Like I just said, there's no *use* in threatening you." Blake guzzled down the whiskey. He slammed the snifter glass into the empty fireplace. The sound of shattering clung to his ears as did Lola's shouting at him for this current move.

CHAPTER 21

THE WAVE-LIKE vibrations rolling over Mila's larynx signified ultimate bliss. Her almond eyes had slowly closed as her breathing became a melody. A melody that added to the tranquil vibes playing through the PDA on the veranda of Blake's apartment high in the clouds. The masseuse's strong muscular hands caressed her body to new heights.

The change in pressure awoke her. Mila's eyebrow arched, she turned slightly. A sardonic smile brightened her face. "Hmmm, Blake. You've been rubbing my back this entire time?"

"Yup."

"Yeah, right." She almost wondered where he'd run off to. They were all the way in Tokyo so it couldn't be… No, it wasn't another woman. At first, Mila didn't care about Blake, albeit the sex made her momentarily weak. Earlier, she'd tried to give him the 'out.' Starting the argument had been comparable to handing Blake the gun and bullets. All he had to do was admit to cheating. *What the hell am I thinking? Cheating on his wife, cheating on me… I don't even have the right.*

Still, Mila had glanced at the digital clock on the wall just inside of the apartment before he'd began the world's best back rub. As usual, he'd slip out the room and a trained masseuse completed the deed. Blake must've been gone at least two hours.

She hopped into a seated position and hugged him. "Blake, baby, we really gotta…" The words lodged into her throat. She wanted to tell him that even though she was angry earlier, these sexcapades had to end one day. Yet, Mila realized he didn't hug her with the same zeal. "Blake..."

His arms seemed heavy as they slowly draped around her.

Though he now held her tightly, her lover seemed lightyears away. The other day when his wife had called, Mila had been livid. Even after they'd sexed like rabbits she'd began to torment herself over the affection that she felt for Blake. *Why am I doing this to myself? Do not cross the line, Mila, Blake is just a momentary reprieve.*

After forcing herself not to be so gullible or emotional, Mila went right back to wondering about *the wife.* Was she in Diane's shoes every chance Blake stepped away? Blake was never satiated. Their fuck fests were heavenly. But did Mila satisfy him enough. She'd been talking shit when telling him to turn to any whore while they were here in Tokyo. But… "Blake, baby what's the matter?"

"Hard day." The last time Blake had to leave her presence, he'd expressed his distaste of having to leave her in an unfamiliar country to complete a few meetings or PR conversations. As if he knew all, his hand went to her throat and thumb grazed softly over her lips before Mila could offer to be his ear if need be.

"These fucking lips." His eyes bore through the raspberry pink flesh of hers as his thumb print continued to love her mouth. "I love these lips."

His tongue went into her mouth. Mila's eyes swept across the open patio. The masseuse had disappeared. There were no servants moving about the living area inside the open sliding glass doors, but the lust in Blake's eyes read that he was going to fuck her here regardless. Mila sucked at the soft ridges in his thumb and imagined that she were conjuring his seed, sucking his cock. Like she'd done out here, but underneath the covers. Now the railing didn't shield them from the tall post where she'd just gotten a massage.

"I could take you down right here Mila." Blake's voice was breathy as they leaned against the post. "Or out in the open." He delved into the warm wetness. His eyes scoured the buildings across the way as if he sought an audience. "To have you begging me to take you under, to make you cum how sexy would that be with envious onlookers."

She stopped delighting in the taste of his thumb, "No Blake. That wouldn't be sexy at all."

The left side of his mouth curved upwards. The emotion, the life, the perceived heartbeat seemed to slowly seep back into the man she'd fallen so damn quickly for.

"You're art to me Mila. The most gorgeous piece I have acquired."

The words were a lofty complement, yet she had no desire to be owned.

"It took a while for me to enjoy art." Mila assumed it was because his rich parents had probably shoved it down his throat.

“When I first took interest, it was because of an elegant museum curator. She taught me the art of standing back, to just observe art for its uniqueness,” Blake said pushing a strand of hair from her face. “it changed my concept. I thought they were fucking assholes. Selfish. Disgusting pricks for not allowing the world to observe such beauties. Then my eyes landed on you Mila.”

Her pupils dilated; he'd gotten her exactly where he wanted. She'd fuck him in front of an audience of a million if he wanted. A tender gulp slithered down her throat. She wanted him to slam his dick straight into her pussy right here. Even if there were people walking by.

CHAPTER 22

Los Angeles, CA

SUNDAY BRUNCH WAS worse than Sunday service. Mila had already felt the judgement of being in the large cathedral structure with a melancholic Jesus, palms open wide, yet gauged out. Ouch. The pastor, though, didn't further condemn her by biblical verses of adultery. No, the man upstairs had left that for her older sister, Yasmin.

The once a month Sunday brunches and token church attendance on Mila and Lido's behalf had begun to even out, now that Warren wasn't around. Veronica stayed at home on those days because Yasmin had chewed her the fuck out one time.

At the table of shiny silverware and crystal which caught the sun and sent rainbows across the room, Mila and Lido sat across from Yasmin and her husband, Faaid. The family got together at the same upscale Beverly Hills buffet for years. Faaid had once enjoyed Warren's company. Warren had been nice enough to keep up with soccer—actually more statistically interested—in order for the two to chat while the sisters caught up. They hadn't had been here in almost six months, meaning Faaid hadn't gotten used to it just being him with the ladies.

"Where have you been, Mila?" Yasmin forked up baby arugula.

Those enchanting black marble eyes never wavered. Yasmin kept her hair in silky short tousled curls. Her buttery brown skin always seemed pampered, though she never invited her younger sisters to the spa.

"Mila just got back from Tokyo," Lido interjected with a devious smile. The look in those eyes didn't speak volumes to her *walaashay weyn*. Mila gave a quick elbow to the bony broad's ribcage. Lido wanted to start an argument.

"Tokyo, is that true?"

"Why? You sound like father! Are you going to tell him?" Lido's eyebrow arched.

Faaid mumbled something about not being full. Nobody acknowledged his presence; Yasmin didn't even care.

"Can't I make small talk with my *Walaashay yar*?" Yasmin snapped.

"Most definitely." Lido nodded. "You started the chit-chat, but keep in mind I always got the back of my *Walaashay yar.*"

Mila sighed. It was hard being the youngest. "Yes, Yasmin, I stayed a few weeks in Tokyo. I even sent in a few–"

"*Few*?" Yasmin's eyebrow arched.

Mila's shoulders deflated. Of all people, she wanted to tell her siblings first about sending in the proposal for a few government grants. With the commission Mila made for Blake's altruism, Mila had paid off the house. She also had enough for a down payment on a building in West Los Angeles. Today, she planned to see if her sisters wanted to tag along to view a few locations her realtor had found. But,

"Twenty-eight days, let's just call that a month," Lido gestured, wanting more of a rise out of Yasmin.

Yasmin had already texted Mila that church and brunch would be a cordial affair. So it was clear to them all that Yasmin was curving her judgmental attitude. Though they weren't close, Yasmin seemed to be trying for Mila's sake. She'd even called during the months since Warren's death. She didn't attend the funeral, but calling without forcing the family card for them to have get-togethers was a good thing.

"Well, a month in Japan." Yasmin sighed. "Sounds like a tranquil vacation. So, Mila, you had good news to tell us. I'm happy about that. I've been a bit worried about you, Mila…"

"Yes, the good news." Mila turned in her seat so she could glance back and forth at the both of them.

"*Worried*?" Lido said. "Yasmin, you've been worried. I didn't see you at Warren's funeral. We haven't had brunch since he died—"

"Mila's trying to tell us something," Yasmin stressed. "Look, I texted Mila about brunch the week after the plane went down, Lido. Why must everything be a show for you, huh? We have to measure our love."

"*Texted*?" Lido screeched as if the rest of Yasmin's statement went straight over her head.

"I've called her a few times too. Lido, does that meet your standards." Yasmin turned toward her baby sister.

Lido put her hands together in a round of applause. "Now, me, myself, and I, *oh,* and my drop, dead ..."

Mila mumbled, "Now introducing Veronica." *Every time we get together Lido has to slap her sexual relationship in everyone's face.*

Lido continued, "... Gorgeous, 104 pounds of sexy—"

"Veronica, just say it damn," Mila cut in, her resource center plans fading to black. "I love Veronica like a sister, Lido, but damn, its physically impossible to shove a person down other people's throats. So stop trying. Yasmin is just—"

"Just what?" Lido folded her arms.

Mila shook her head. "Who the hell are you representing today, Lido. Huh? I had to tell you all something, but now it doesn't even matter. You're so busy wanting to cause problems. You're so ready for war that you forgot who you're representing."

They both took a moment to regress. Mila gave a quick smile to Yasmin for not engaging in combat with Lido, as was the norm. How quickly had the conversation hopped to different subjects? When it came to Mila being in Tokyo, her oldest sister had really tried not to judge. Mila never cut in when the two argued. She found it just as exhausting trying to speak when Lido dominated the entire conversation.

Finally, she took a breath as her sisters began to eat. "Listen, I know you've been worried. Everything is fine now; I've paid off my home." And so as not to allow Lido the ammunition to strike, Mila further elaborated, "I've been doing well at Versa."

She decided to save the nonprofit organization talk for another time. Especially since she was scouting locations and awaiting a response from the government, which could take months. An hour later, as the ladies handed their tokens to the valet, they gave each other the customary goodbye. Yasmin seemed reluctant to leave while Faaid stepped forward to tip the valet.

The willowy Lido got into her Bentley convertible first. Her older and younger sister smiled in pride as every eye, from valets to old folks getting out of luxury cars, were on the model. Some knew her by name, others were just as awestruck. Relishing the attention, Lido waved while pulling away from the curb.

Instantly, the attraction faded. Each sister returned to her own thoughts. Faaid waited in the driver's side of their BMW as Yasmin embraced Mila once more. "May I make a suggestion, Mila?"

Mila teetered on the heels of her ballerina flats. She'd driven her trusty Honda Accord, even though Blake had surprised her with a Maserati Alfieri. The sleek, carbon fiber luxury sports car was at her home when they'd returned from Tokyo. She hadn't complained, since Blake wasn't dropping funds into her bank account.

Now here she stood, certain that Yasmin was about to read her like a cheap, raunchy eBook. "Sure."

"I don't just agree with any magazine I read in the grocery store check-out line, but there are pictures of you and … and a *man*." Yasmin paused, as if bottling the anger brewing in her gut. "A married man, Mila. It doesn't matter if a man is to marry another, or another, or another," she said with a shake of her head, "You are much more than a second or a *third*, Mila."

Now they were at the pivotal point in this discussion. Gaze cast on the asphalt, Mila asked, “Are you going to tell father…?”

CHAPTER 23

BLAKE AND DIANE use to fuck so hard, so loud, so boisterously. Diane lay on the bed next to him, but it wasn't that cosmetically plumped pussy that got his dick hard. His tool had stood at attention with all those dirty words flying out of her mouth.

"Can you still put it down, Blake." Her fleshy lips sneered. "Can you still fuck me like a real man?"

He rubbed his face. Though he cared so much about Mila, his wife had just challenged him.

"Oh yeah, like a real man." The *ching* of his leather belt being unbuckled proved this was real; that he indeed was consenting to fucking his wife. His tailored pants dropped. Diane's metallic gaze fell onto his boxer briefs. She licked her lips while his hand disappeared beneath the cotton fabric.

"You want this cock, Diane?"

Her shiny crimson fingertips toyed with her clit. "I'm so fucking wet right now, Blake. I'm fucking myself… you use to hate when I pleased myself, greedy bastard."

He licked his lips. "Yeah, I'm fucking greedy, Diane."

Diane's mouth went slack as she plunged a few fingers into her swollen center. An orgasm rose, making that fuck face of hers even more gorgeous. *She's not real.* Blake told himself. *I'm fucking around on Mila, the woman who belongs to me.*

Diane's slender, glossy fingers came up to her lips. A pink tongue dipped out and licked the liquid sugar. "You want to taste it? I'm so fucking wet for you, Blake…"

He bit his lip. "No, I don't wanna fucking taste it, Diane."

She simpered, that frosted face of hers percolated with jealousy. "Guess I better find solace in the fact that you'll soon treat your mistress in the same manner that you've treated me. But tell me, Blake, do you eat your mistress's pussy like you once ate mine?"

"Now do I have to answer that?" Blake pulled out his throbbing cock. "C'mon Di', ass up."

A hard glare sent daggers his way before Diane complied. Her backside wasn't too fat, but then again Blake hadn't been an ass man before he met Mila. And furthermore, Diane hadn't had an ass at all when they first met, no matter the fact that she actually worked out to stay fit.

He palmed the soft flesh. Before she could brace herself, his erection pushed into her asshole. Damn, he couldn't even retreat into the areas of cognition that were solely for Mila. So he pumped in and out, to Diane's moans. Giving it to her harder and harder. Raw, no emotion. Blake gripped her ass cheeks, watching the small of Diane's back as she came all over his balls. But he refused to spill his seed…

~~~

Later that evening, for Diane's sake, they lay in bed, watching *Eyes Wide Shut*. The movie held a certain level of nostalgia, being
~~~

that it was the first movie the two had seen in a theater together.

Diane's ivory tone glowed as she held the bowl of organic popcorn within her thighs. Blake took a deep breath, reached over and grabbed a handful for himself.

His cell phone buzzed in the side table. A quick glance showed Mila's gorgeous face popping up on the screen.

Mila: *U busy?*

A deep grumble radiated from Diane's fragile body as he reached over to grab it.

"Blake, please don't ruin our evening together," Diane implored, placing a hand on his shoulder.

Blake*: I can be there in less than an hour*. The ride from Bel-Air to Laguna Niguel took 70 minutes without traffic.

"Blake," Diane's grainy voice wove into his moment as he waited for Mila's response. "After that guy's funeral, you said we'd start working on us. How can you do so while running after—"

PING.

Mila: *That's okay. I just wanted to talk to you... Call if you can.*

His senses piqued. The demure Mila continually requested less than her worth. He arose from the bed as Diane's subtle petitions became more demanding.

"Fuck you, Blake! I know for a fact that you ignore *my* calls! You never want to talk to *me*!" Diane got to her knees, and tried to grasp his arm as he walked past toward the master suite exit. She sailing forward when Blake didn't stop.

"Calm down, Diane or I might *not* return." Blake closed the door to her silent guilt-laden sobs. She'd brought this on herself, no amount of marriage counseling was going to make him put her first again. Either Diane would consent to a divorce or this is where they stood, stuck in limbo.

He retreated toward one of the guest bedrooms and grabbed a pair of Nike's and a leather jacket. As he ambled down the marble steps, he called Mila. "I'll be there soon, babe."

"Blake, please don't come."

He grabbed the keys to the Range Rover, saying, "Fuck that, you sound—"

"Regardless of what you say, Blake, I don't know the dynamics of your marriage. I respect the fact that I probably shouldn't, Blake." Mila's raw emotional tone stopped Blake in his tracks.

Had she found out what happened to Warren, or worse yet, Lola?

He stood at the entrance of the show room, lights brightly displaying his favorite goodies, fast cars, SUVs, Humvees. He considered the Ducati, and riding dangerously. He craved Mila's soft rounded ass and settling some of her nerves.

No, Mila was moved by other emotions. Blake stayed quiet to allow her to rid herself of his presence. "Clarissa and Todd stopped by this evening, I gave them your Maserati."

He chose not to correct her. The pink slip to the new car had her name on it.

"Todd will bring it to work tomorrow morning. Blake... Are you listening?"

"Yes, gorgeous. I didn't want to cut in, you seemed… determined."

"Determined," she sighed the words. He could only imagine that pearly white row of top teeth was doing *his* job delighting in the succulence of her glorious mouth, via grating her bottom lip. Then Mila's stern, business voice returned, and he almost smiled, remembering her first attempt to boss him around: *No tying me up or down. No spankings. No gags, no debasing...*

"Yes. You're right, Blake. You could say I'm determined. Mr. Baldwin, you made me fall..."

There it was again. That expectancy. She knew that he *knew* she wanted him to fight. He had yet to begin. Of course, Mila was worth the wrangle, but Blake always operated in a manner that allowed women to "go with what they know" or at the very least what they *thought* they knew. Once Mila saw the error of her ways, she'd be back in his corner.

Blake allowed her to hang up the phone on that note. *Shit.* He jangled the keyring in his hand.

With a hand over his face, Blake considered. This very woman may have been the only one to deny him once, twice, but he wasn't going to let Mila away three times. She'd called him a dirty asshole to start. Maybe that was the addiction? Mila was the only person on the universe who hadn't given into his current status.

He'd courted her slowly. Now, regardless of the danger of formulating a relationship with Mila Ali, he'd take her the way she was meant to be taken. As his. He just needed to wait for the perfect time.

~~~

It had been seven days since Blake received the Maserati car full of everything he'd bought Mila while they vacationed in the Bahamas and Japan. Todd had handed over the keys, mumbling that the hacker hadn't tried his/her luck lately.

In a slate gray suit, Blake readjusted his BB diamond encrusted cuff links while his Lamborghini crept through the towering wrought iron gates of the Hyper House, a grungy old factory sitting on the top of the hill in West Covina. There were lines and lines of luxury sports cars pulling up to the red carpet. The factory had views of downtown Los Angeles sparkling in the dark of night.

Cameras flashed as the world's most gorgeous people stalked toward the entrance. He sighed. Flashing lights and limelight in general weren't Blake Baldwin's idea of a good time.

Inside the airy building, white thick drapes surrounded the cement walls, flowing down at least a hundred feet or more. Servants held silver trays of endless champagne or French creations. Along the center of the entire factory supermodels strutted down a suspended platform.

Blake noticed Lido Ali first, as her velvety, dark brown giraffe legs took the runway by storm. With each strut, the material about her thighs moved around, allowing a perfect peek-a-boo of her nether regions covered by some sort of barely there shimmery material. This was the sort of crap Blake would buy for Mila to tempt other men and then later on tear to shreds.
~~~

He licked his lips.

Then through the crowd, Blake found Mila. Her eyes were on his, tossing burning chocolate daggers—*shit*, he thought, *she thinks I'm staring at her sister*. She sat in the front row, with a metrosexual male and a female in suits as anchor. A thick thigh crossed over her other leg, and the shoes, the ones he'd purchased at Elle's boutique in Paris to complement the lingerie for their first encounter. Cock sucking crimson full lips were barely parted, displaying ultra-white teeth.

"Fuck me." Blake readjusted a blatantly large erection while he made his way over. His eyes locked onto Mila, compelling her not to look away, even as he passed crowds of people or said a quick *hello* to a few people attempting to block his path.

About fifteen yards away, the connection broke. Mila's glare swept across the other side of the large space. She rose, provocative ass teasing him while she moved in the opposite direction. Fuck that. At average female height and even in those heels, she could try him. But the panther was going to pounce very soon.

He almost collided with a server. "My apologies Mr. Baldwin." The servant's eyes widened in shock and before the girl could continue to apologize, Blake moved past her too. What on earth made Miss Ali believe she was capable of getting away from him?

Blake gripped her tensed bicep from behind.

"Enjoying the view?" Mila asked over her shoulder, scurrying away. He hooked arms with her.

"Yes, I am relishing the view." Blake's intense gaze slithered up and down her body, noting the rapid breathing at the pulse of her neck. With his arm still looped in her own, Blake whispered, "Are we being childish this evening, Mila?"

"Oh, funny. Stop wasting your time with me, go drool on *my* sister, asshole."

His bicep flexed, the effect tightening around her arm. "*Asshole?* Yeah, Mila, so we're back to our old tricks. I already had it in my mind to take you over my knee, and beat that heavenly ass before fucking you until you passed out."

"That sounds… psychotic."

Blake stopped in front of Mila, and let her go. "Then continue to tempt me, Mila. Either way, we're in for a helluva night."

The sex in his eyes had her all but shuffling over two left feet to get away. Cat and mouse became lion and gazelle, as Blake's fingers glided through Mila's before she could get away.

"Oh, Mr…" he decided to fuck with her and include an audience.

"Mr. McDougell," the man dressed in a tuxedo, with a blond, thinning comb over smiled at them.

"Yes, Mr. McDougell." Blake snapped a finger, keeping his hostage secure. "We met at the—"

"The Winestein Gala!" Mr. McDougell seemed to be eating every word in excitement. "Well, it's an honor to be remembered by someone of your stature."

"Nonsense, yours as well, Mr. McDougell, I'm afraid I've been sort of slow as of late."

"Humph *afraid?* Admitting incompetence? Let's just call that an apology," Mila said under her breath.

Well, she'd just set herself up then. "It has to do with these vitamins, Mr. McDougell you see I get these vitamins imported from Africa."

Mila's mouth dropped.

"Very good stash." Blake winked at the man.

"I'm sure they most certainly are." The old man's busy eyebrows rose, he placed his hands in his pants. It was evident what he also assumed these vitamins could do. "Say, where can I get these vitamins?"

Blake gave a half smile. "Unfortunately the darn things are very *exclusive.*"

"Yeah, I can just about tell. Exclusivity in the world of affluence," Mr. McDougell gives a pursed lip smile. "Every time I encounter the top two-percent there's always a pep in y'alls step as if you have the stream of life at your feet."

"I'm a one-percenter," Blake corrected. "The stream of life, it's the sweetest, intoxicating taste."

After they finished chatting, Mila scoffed. "Well that was very assholish."

"As I've just explained to Mr… uh…"

"You've already forgotten his name." Mila shook her head.

"Fuck his name." Blake stepped in her path. "I've missed my daily source of vitamins, Mila."

She took a deep breath. "Oh, wow, you should actually write a self-love book—not even have it ghost written. You can teach some self-bashing folks a thing or two. Blake, I'm mad at you, you know that don't you?" Mila tried again to be stern but only succeeded at enforcing the type of control that made horny middle school boys fall for their female teacher.

The subsequent chuckle was as smooth as black maple bourbon. However, Blake held in the lust. He nodded, seeing just how much she drunk in his looks. He imagined her mouthwatering as Mila took a subconscious gulp. He wanted to tell her that there was no reason to be embarrassed. Ever.

She looked up at him as people walked by. He knew her plight. A conversation with Lido Ali had told him that Mila was scared. Scared of disappointing a father that had long ago stopped caring anyway. Not having a father-figure himself, Blake only had one way of mending a broken heart.

The back of his knuckles drifted across the silk of her jawline. Mila's lips brushed the side of Blake's hand, then her mouth kissed his palm before she shunned such affections.

"We've had a… nice ride," Mila's tone indicated a 'but' was soon to follow, "Goodbye, Blake."

"That's a no can do, Mila." He grinned. Though Blake's appearance was jovial, he dominated every corner of the place. "I'm unable to allow it, Miss. Ali."

Her gaze narrowed. "You can't or you won't?"

Blake's broad shoulders shrugged, and he placed his hands in his pockets. The laidback demeanor implied that there was only one way for this to end: *his way.*

Her riveting almond gaze panned around the room. There was no foreseeable end to the runway with its eclectic designs and models. He speculated that Mila was analyzing the best course of action, a sure exit. He waited.

"Mr. Baldwin, find someone else to play with."

"Mila, we can go tit-for-tat, you insult me, call me asshole, or any other variation. But I've conquered Mount Everest, K2, amongst other beautiful deadly sights. The next sight I'm gonna enjoy seeing is your mouth filled with my cock."

"You haven't conquered me?" Mila's head cocked to the side. "But I could have sworn I could be placed on your trophy shelf… or is it an entire room?"

Blake's smile twitched. She didn't yet know him; they had time for that. "So we've resorted to the judgment again, Mila."

"Oh, forget about it."

"That downcast glance, the slumped arms, everything about you reads that you expect me to judge you to, Mila. Why can't I delight in the best parts of you?"

"You can't go around saying shit like this. *'I could offer you so many things to adorn your beauty, on the premise that you'd become exactly what you were designed to become.'* Blake, I've memorized the bullshit that you've dished out to me. Eaten every word. Do you know where Wetherby Lane is?"

Blake's eyes rose as he considered the location. "It's the street around the corner from my Beverly Hills home."

"Exactly. I've been day dreaming of us owning a home right

around the fucking corner from your wife. I've been pondering the cars *your wife* drives. The perfume *your wife* wears. What *she* does to have you, Blake!"

He wanted her to pause for a second; he needed to reiterate that he and Diane were separated. Anything to help Mila, but she seemed to be purging, deep, dark thoughts. Then her whispering concluded on a crescendo, "I have *feelings* for you, Blake!"

A few heads nearby snapped in their direction.

CHAPTER 24

MILA'S MOUTH OPENED and closed while she claimed her feelings for Blake felt so real. *It was real.* How could she be so stupid?

As a wildfire struck and ran embarrassing red heat from her neck to her cheeks, Blake pulled her into a kiss. The action held two goals: conceal her embarrassment as people seemed more enthralled by simple touches or kisses or anything sexual at the event. The other defense was his ability to muddle her mind–at least Mila considered in her paranoia. But a second later, the doubt clinging to her skin faded away. She transformed back into the dumb girl who'd noshed on her inner lip and fidgeted while waiting for him to fuck her for the very first time. Affection from Blake had *become* her addiction.

Her honey walls felt swollen with desire as she introduced Blake to Veronica and a few of the other people Mila knew at the event. Somewhere deep in her mind, wisdom ordered her to leave Blake Baldwin the hell alone. *The way you get a man is the same way you lose him,* she told herself.

The thought of ending up *broken* over Blake receded to the hindmost parts of her heart as she breathed in the fragrant cedar, patchouli, white musk, and testosterone of *him.* There was confidence in just Blake's presence.

"Look at the two of you," Veronica gushed. "Your yin and yang is on point."

They made small talk about the show. Then Mila's breath hitched as her gorgeous sister stepped over. Five inches taller than Mila, the beauty stood eye level to Blake. Lido donned what Mila could only explain as an expensive silk black handkerchief. The soft material looped around Lido's neck, crisscrossed in the front and grazed across her breast, then further crisscrossed to loop back over Lido's nether regions. Noticing Veronica gawking at Lido, Mila wriggled her eyebrows.

Usually Veronica would clutch her chest and feign amazement by stumbling back at just the sight of her lady. Then she and Lido would share a private laugh.

Tonight neither occurred.

Lido seemed to be ignoring her girlfriend. "So Mr. Baldwin, you caught up with my *Walaashay yar,*" she strummed along the Somali words in an erotic tone.

"Wala…" Blake tried to enunciate the word with a raised eyebrow.

"*Walaashay yar,*" Lido did it again, flirting.

"Oh, there's Gustavo." Veronica pointed as Lido explained the term meant *little sister.*

What the heck is going on with these two, Mila wondered, as Veronica flitted away. Mila turned to call after her, but Veronica blended into a sea of ultra-rich, attractive people before Mila could speak. The warm laughter from Lido brought her back to attention, making Mila's eyelid twitch. Lido reached out to paw Blake's lapel, unaware he slipped his arm around Mila. The way he held her close, claiming her made all the confusion disappear.

~~~

Later that evening, the butterfly doors of Blake's sports car ascended. He turned to give Mila a look, one she was unable to read.

"C'mon, Blake, you have to be hungry even after eating a hundred of those little finger food thingies." She grinned. "This is Mama Estelle's. You're always taking me places to try new things, tonight I'm catering to you. Well, technically it's too late to cook, so here once we pass that threshold we will be transported to New Orleans for a smidgen of the price."

"All right, Mila. The last time I went somewhere shady with you, I was called out of my name."

"A pretty boy?"

He nodded.

"And you handled that like a *gangster*." Her laughter liquefied into a tangible sigh that magnetized his lips to hers.

She rose on her tippy toes, and Blake placed a dominating hand on the small of her back. The very hand that had become accustom to spanking her ass so fucking good.

"Mmmmm, Mila. I suppose this kiss will make Mama Estelle's worth it. Though you should know, I've been to New Orleans more times than I can count. I already have a favorite spot."

"Stop being skeptical." Mila's fingers wove through his stronger ones as he guided her toward the door.
~~~

Inside of Mama Estelle's was the normal diner seating, with red faux leather booths along the perimeter. The furniture had seen better days. Being past ten p.m., Mila had no problem scoring her favorite booth. African American faces from ebony to butterscotch turned their way, eyes roaming from Blake's shiny Armani shoes to his suit, and then back down again. The process repeated for Mila.

"*My-laaaaa,*" one of the servers, Trina walked over with a wide grin. "You must be trying to get snatched up tonight, gorgeous. And you too, handsome."

"Well thank you, Ms. Trina. But we will be needing to try everything on your menu this evening. Mila has told me that this place is comparable to being in New O'leans," Blake said.

She nodded. "Just the same. This is a family owned business, Mr… Mr… Baldwin, so trust and believe we're all from that *deep* Louisiana. You want to try everything?"

"Yes, ma'am. Just one of everything though," Blake replied, to which Trina nodded and started away.

"Boy, we aren't going Dutch," Mila chuckled under her breath. "I've invited you out." She signed and leaned into him. "I probably should have sat on the opposite side of this booth. I wanted to show you something, but we gotta keep it on the low."

Blake's eyes zeroed in on her lips. "Mmmm, I like that."

She bumped shoulders with him. "This is not that kinda party, Blake. Later tonight I'll pay for breaking your heart.".

"Yes, you will. If this food sucks, then I'll know that you're stalling. You should know, it won't be pretty for that sexy ass of yours if you really are trying to stall. So, what are you showing me?"

She gave a come hither gesture, her body sliding down the booth.

"Is it the champagne that has you feeling good? Then I'm going to take you home now."

"Uh yeah right, bossy pants. Get down here."

Blake wriggled his bowtie in and then scooted down in his seat. She tapped her hand against the side of the table.

"The first time I came here was with my sisters and parents. We didn't know a thing about Creole food. I was 15." Mila paused. Blake never pushed, but he'd subtly mentioned her family on a few occasions after she'd bandaged Brittany, the young woman they'd meet while hiking La Soufriére. Telling Blake that her father was a doctor, and skimming the surface was as far as she'd ever gone. "I didn't come back in here till over 10 years later. The day I was offered associate position with Hewitt."

"Those are the big boys." Blake nodded. "Those fuckers approached me while my social media company hadn't even begun to hit the ground running."

"Yeah…" she grimaced as Trina silently dropped off two iced teas. "Hewitt is the type of company that always knows when to strike, right before the getting is good or when an owner is going through a few shitty quarters."

"You still have your soul, it seems."

"Humph, can't say that it wasn't compromised during the climb," Mila suddenly felt uncomfortable. She'd grown to care for Blake, just as she'd said during the event tonight. The words had

CHAPTER 25

AT BLAKE'S GLASS house in the woods, they had the sort of tap-out, kama sutra sex that porn stars enjoyed. All. Night. Long. Only to fall back onto a feathery duvet, glossed with sex, and the sweetest tears streaming down Mila's eyes. As twilight gave way for day, the two lay in the glow of lust, maybe even love. Giggles permeated from Mila, while a raw, baritone laughter came deep from within Blake's abs before they fell asleep.

The next afternoon, Blake awoke first. He pulled Mila's naked body closer to him. "Awaken, my sleeping beauty."

"*My*?" She murmured, still half asleep, "you think you own me..."

"But I do." Blake climbed onto his knees and nipped at her ass. The sound of his large, sharp teeth made her yelp even more than him biting her butt cheeks.

Mila hopped out of bed. "Damn you, Blake!"

He decided that they needed a shower, though this was to be an extension of last night's laziness, she conceded. Not ten minutes later, Blake delighted in Mila's spiel.

"Hmmm, dirty man, I see you have a fetish with showers." Mila took a gander around the outdoor shower, with its large boulders and tropical oasis style.

"*Dirty* man? I thought we settled that little squabble." Blake hooked his arm, capturing the small of her tiny waistline. Mila pressed back to his body, his erection spearing her thigh.

"But I like it dirty, Blake." A moan erupted past Mila's swollen, needy lips when his mouth scoured the soft silk of her jawline. It hurt so fucking good.

They stepped beneath the cascades of hot water from the waterfall faucet that was concealed by boulders.

Blake picked up the shea butter soap, opened it and poured the creamy liquid in his hand. It had a mild fragrance, yet not powerful to mask his woman's sex. He reached out, hand planting against the center of Mila's chest. The beating of her heart reverberated through him. His woman was the epitome of arousal. She wanted to ask to be fucked, but at this very moment, fucking her was the last thing on Blake's mind.

A warm sunny breeze beamed down on them, the glow masked the pleading in Mila's eyes. Blake reached over. His mouth locked onto hers, lips extracted the sweet desire to beg from her mouth. She need not beg, she was going to get exactly what *Blake* desired anyhow. The kiss left her breathless, too dazed to speak or even build schematic ideas within that gorgeous mind. She went back to being palpable in his hands as Blake rubbed the opulent cleanser against her body.

He picked up the soap; still one hand continued its domination of Mila Ali. It glided across her shoulder as he moved to step behind her back. The lather of his hands now caressed down her back. His cleansing hands glided back toward her front. Blake swiftly pushed her body back, that plump rear almost being seared by his rock hard cock.

A hitch of breath made Mila's breast rise, from his viewpoint over her shoulder. Then she mellowed once more, as she silently begged for a dirty fuck—the very thing he currently denied. Though the entire process was ferociously slow, yet erotically detailed, Blake slapped his hand onto Mila's hip and dug his fingers into her flesh just harsh enough to keep her still… when she had not one desire to run.

His other "cleansing" hand reached around lathering her nether regions.

"Blake…"

"Shhhh!" His harshness made Mila almost teeter, yet he held her closely. There had to be an echoing in Mila's mind even now, begging him, cursing him, willing him to fuck her.

Not a single finger breached the beautifully tumescent folds of her labia. Mila's head turned slightly, Blake reached around to bestow her plump lips with a kiss. As their tongues collided he continued to purify her body.

They got out of the shower. Her shoulders were taut, with agitation. A slight cock of the left side of Blake's mouth made her ask, "So what's so funny?"

Blake reached around, grabbing both ends of her terry cloth towel and held her gaze. "Now you've been Christened."

"Christened?" She snapped. "Well, I could think of many ways you could have done that Blake. All over my fucking mouth, in my face—"

"Is that not debasing?"

"Oh you're fucking with me, Blake, as usual."

"That's a half-ass assessment, Mila. If I were indeed fucking you, or your mouth rather, since you want my jizz all over your face, then I'd tell you to fall to your fucking knees, open that mouth wide. I'd grab you behind the fucking neck, perhaps even gripping your hair with my other hand and determine your gag reflex while letting the head of my dick beat the shit out of your tonsils. Is that what you want?" He teased already knowing the answer.

Blake could see her subconsciously gulp while nodding.

"Then get to your fucking knees, Mila."

She sunk to the floor, not a second before her knees hit the ground did her lips taste his dick. As warned, Blake's large hand gripped Mila's ponytail. He didn't hold back as he forced his dick to punch down her throat. She moaned and gulped, twirling her tongue around his dick. When Mila tried to put her hand around the base of his tool, he slapped away her attempt.

"Just that fucking mouth, Mila," he threatened. Shit, she was sucking him so good, taking him so deep, the head of his cock beat at her brains.

~~~

Every time they fucked, his woman seemed to grow into her own skin. They lay, clothed in the last bits of the sun's glow, that
~~~

evening. Mila found solace in his chest. His hands pet her mahogany tresses.

A deep groan erupted from Mila's throat. "I have to work tomorrow."

"You *choose* to work." He took hold of Mila's chin, guiding her line of vision to his own. There was no more uncertainty. It seemed the slither of doubt still clinging to Mila was beginning to wan. Reading her mind was easy, Blake determined that if their relations ended and she was out of work, that would be a setback. He got ready to convince Mila otherwise, yet her stomach growled.

"Sounds like a brown bear," he joked, his tone as fine as black maple bourbon.

"Oh, that was me." Mila grinned. Her eyes narrowed. "When did we last eat?"

His head cocked slightly. "*You* haven't eaten since Mama Estelle's."

She swatted at him. "As if you really *ate* this morning. Don't forget I drunk the sweetest taste I've ever known."

They started to get up and dress. "Out? Or should I see about someone hooking us up dinner?"

She grinned, shaking her head. "Nah, no outings. There's an endless wave of paparazzi. How about *you* cook dinner," Mila tested, eyebrow arched. "After all, you've put me through torture this afternoon in the shower."

He nodded. "Any recs?"

"Nope. Uhhhh…., I suppose I recommend anything we eat must

be able to be washed down with the taste of you."

Blake opened the door with a chuckle.

"I'll be down in a sec; I'm going to do something about this bird's nest." She gestured toward her hair.

"All right, Mila, but you're most beautiful after we fuck."

She mumbled about him being Mr. Candid while shaking her head as Blake stepped out of the bedroom. He sauntered down the stairs.

Blake pulled out fresh vegetables from the subzero refrigerator and two lean steaks. He considered making fingerling potatoes, and recalling the last time he'd lovingly cooked for his wife, Blake chose not to.

Fingerling potatoes, Diane, and old memories were a distraction. Once the steaks began to marinate and the rest of the food was all prepped, Blake glanced at the clock. Even if he was designated chef this evening, they had yet to have sex on the marble island.

He walked out of the room, started up the stairs. Whispered voices made Blake's ears perk. The angst in Mila's tone was disconcerting.

"Keith, are you even listening to me? Please *stop* calling me." Mila's voice rose the closer he got to the ajar door. "What the hell do you mean, 'we need to support each other at a time like this?' You haven't mourned your brother's death. Not one bit!"

Her voice drowned out. Less than sixty seconds later, guilt clung to her tone. "*Yes, I miss Warren.* ... I just haven't been home. Keith, how about this: go lean on your wife's shoulder. That's what being married is about." Mila's inflection increased. "Nancy loves you, Keith. You're drunk; you haven't dealt with Warren's death. You're in a bad headspace right now….""

Her voice drowned out. Again, Blake was unable to perceive the muffled response. Mila handled herself well, unfortunately it seemed to land on deaf ears.

"… Well, I dare you to be at my house tomorrow. When I get off work, I'm calling the cops!"

Every tendon in Blake's being churned. He started back down the stairs. Keith Jameson. Tomorrow evening, the least of that motherfucker's problems would be the cops.

CHAPTER 26

IT WAS MONDAY again. Though Mila's body had gone to heaven, her shoulders were rigid with worry. After the drunken Keith episode, Mila casually offered to take off work while eating Blake's wonderfully prepared dinner. Mr. Verse treated her like royalty these days. But Blake said he needed to step into his business and make sure there was more work than play going on. Then he proceeded to request that Mila return the favor of a good meal.

Blake promised to be at her place in Laguna Niguel around 4 p.m. His mannerisms weren't to be persuaded as candlelight flickered off his viridian gem gaze, last night. He'd pulled out all the stops for dinner so she had to comply. Damn, Keith's crazy ass declared that he'd be at her house that evening too. She'd given Blake the keys, and even now as she noshed on the tip of her pen, Mila considered not going home. Let Blake handle that...

Yeah, right. With the way Keith is acting, Blake won't believe that we never had anything more than an inexperienced peck as kids. He'll look at me in the same manner as Mrs. Jameson. Mila wondered what the heck was going through Keith's mind. They'd made better sporting buddies, cheering the UCLA Bruins, than anything. Though Keith once claimed, he thought they'd be together,

Mila believed it was just due to the shock of her and Warren beginning to date.

She walked across the bathroom section, patting an employee's back or telling a new worker how well he'd done on the last order, all the while considering last night after dinner, she wanted to bring up Keith. He was beginning to get out of hand. Come to think of it, there were piles of cigarette butts near the fountain. Had he really *frequented* Mila's residence on numerous occasions while she and Blake were in Tokyo? Tingles of confusion coursed down her spine. This wasn't a *Lifetime* movie where some chick was being stalked. Perhaps the grounds maintenance had grown lazy and the heap of cigarettes were thrown over a matter of time.

On the way home, Mila jammed to Adele, singing off-key.

"Incoming call from Veronica," a computerized voice advised.

Mila searched and searched, but the Maserati had too many facets. Blake had it returned while they spent the weekend hibernating.

The darn thing was connected to her cell phone but by the time Mila answered, Veronica had hung up.

"Okay.... So how do I redial, Veron—"

She swerved, ascending the steep hill toward a Spanish-stucco mansion. A loud cry from the tires gave warning as Mila headed into oncoming traffic. Mila yanked the wheel back over to the right and the side of the car skidded against the railing.

She looked back, the H2 window was down and the finger waved in her direction.

The Maserati crept to a stop at the wrought iron gate entrance of her home. Shoving the stick shift into park, Mila leaned her forehead against the steering wheel. Her heart beat mellowed back to normal.

At a sudden tap against her window, she almost jumped out of her skin.

Green eyes blazed through the driver window. A nanosecond after pressing the unlock button, Blake reached in her car. He pulled the belt button and grabbed her out, cradling her in his arms.

"What the fuck were you thinking?" He frowned, as if weighing the pros and cons of reprimanding versus caring for her.

"I... I'm okay," she stammered. The calming scent of his cologne and the rise and fall of his chest felt good to her soul.

Blake gingerly placed her on the hood of the car.

"Mila, what were you doing?" Blake growled, yet his gander assessed her for any signs of pain.

In that single moment, the tiny glimmer of horror emanating from Blake meant more to her than the world.

She reached up to grab his cheeks, but Blake pushed her away. "Mila Ali, if something were to happen to you..."

"Oh, Blake," she sighed his name. "I'm sor—"

"No apologies, Miss Ali," he spoke in a more formal tone, as if perceiving that he'd just bared his soul. A slight taste of vulnerability that Mila had no idea he obtained. Blake Baldwin the Billionaire, was falling for his mistress.

Mila's tiny hands finally clasped at the stubble of his jawline. "Blake, I made a dumb mistake, trying to answer a call, that's all."

"A call? Nothing is more important than your safety."

"Okay, baby." She kissed his lips. The intense alpha was acting like a cuddly bear; the sort of man who could only be tamed by his woman. "I'd say you're falling in love with me, Blake. So concerned about my wellbeing and all..."

"Mila Ali, I've loved you to the point of madness," his lips bruised her soft ones in a rough kiss. A fog crept forward from Mila's hindbrain. *I just said you're falling for me. Blake confirmed it!* She rewound this moment in her mind as he devoured her mouth.

Blake planted himself between her legs. She melted in his embrace. After the lung scorching kiss, he let her go. "Just one inhale of the scent of your body and I was gone."

"You fell for me at Versa Home Improvements?" She grinned almost woozy, those kisses were laced with opium.

He nodded it was true. Blake kissed her roughly down her neck. Then his hand entwined with her ponytail. "What do you have to say, Mila?"

"Uhhhh... You want to buy me a hair piece?" She giggled, aware of exactly what he desired.

His grip tightened bringing Mila's susceptible pulse to attention. His mouth scoured the silky ribbon at her neck sending tendrils down her spine.

Her sex tingled as she said, "I love you—"

VROOM! Keith's Aston lurched to a stop right next to Blake's Bugatti.

Mila hadn't even got the chance to slide off the hood before

Keith got out with a frown of jealousy, and Blake was his target. Blake's forearm tentatively swiped at Mila's waist, pushing her back behind him.

With the Maserati to her left side, Blake to her front, and his wide hand anchored just to the right, there was no way of getting around. No calming the brewing storm. Over the left side of Blake's shoulder, she was eye to eye with Keith, but her angle didn't allow him to see the anger of her gritted teeth. She cautioned, "Keith, I already *warned* you—"

"Who the fuck is *this*…" Keith ceased his rant as he distinguished *the* Blake. "*You*... You're Blake Baldwin." Keith's dead eyes turned to Mila. "So this is the reason you have been so hard to get in touch with. ... Blake, I'm going to call you Blake since it looks like you're *at home* here. Mila, you fucking this man in *my* brother's house? What does your rich ass have to say about that?"

"It seems you've already came to a conclusion."

"Oh," Keith gestured. "You don't want to clear the air? So you're a pussy, a punk ass bitch?"

She expected tension, or something. But then again when Blake fought that drunk at the bar, he'd given no sign that the disrespect had pissed him off. Even now the stacks of muscle in his back were taut as usual, but not nearly as tensed as when another man disrespects in front of a lover.

"Keith you're being…" Mila had difficulty conjuring words. This was frat boy Keith from back in the day; there'd be no swaying him.

"So you allow the female to speak for you? But then again B is for Bitch right?"

"Not at all, Mr. Jameson. But I don't talk shit, run after women, harassing them." Blake shrugged. "I make *waaaaay* too much for that bullshit. So I'll *allow* you to end this conversation."

Keith laughed. "Allow me? End this conversation? You're acting like you're from the hood. Shit, I'm not even from the motherfucking hood. But I bet my life, you aren't going to..."

Disinterested, Blake turned to Mila. "Let's get you in the house, beautiful—"

Two seconds later, Keith tossed a sneaky punch at the side of Blake's head. Mila watched in horror as Blake sidestepped the hit that would have had his right ear rendered deaf. Blake caught the side of Keith's jaw with a right hook. Off guard, Keith stumbled. Then there was a flurry once Keith righted himself. He attempted to punch Blake in the eye, his balled hand hardly meeting its target. This time Mila saw Blake's arms move in overtime, his fist pummeling Keith to the ground.

Blake took to one knee, his polo collar mussed and dirt on his slacks, he grabbed at Keith's suit collar, saying something into his ears.

In an instant, Mila shouted, "Bl… Blake, that's enough!"

Though blood dribbled from his mouth, Keith smiled. An imaginary gust of wind left goosebumps and raised fine hairs on Mila's forearms as she walked over.

"… do you fucking got that?" Blake's hands pushed Keith back into the ground.

She offered a hard glare which read: *we need to talk.* Then she turned to Keith.

"I swear to you, Keith Anthony Jameson, don't you ever bring your black ass around my house again. Don't fucking think you can catch me slipping without Blake. I swore to call the cops, nah, I got *some heat* for your ass if you step one foot on my lot. Keith, try me." She caught herself giving that confidently cocky ass grin Blake was known for.

The idiot stood up. He wrestled with his tie. Though Blake had to be behind her, Mila knew those devil-darkened eyes of Keith were on him. She backed away slowly, not that she believed Keith would hit her, but her father raised her better than … better than her current situation.

Mila turned to Blake. He licked the small crimson trail off his busted lip. As she stalked around the clay fountain, toward him, he sighed. "C'mon, Mila why the look? And I want to see this piece you have."

"Humph. Blake, you already know you're in trouble. Don't postpone the inevitable," she snapped.

Blake's glare was unyielding. Mila wasn't going to allow him to silently dominate the moment. She waged a finger at him. "Blake, don't stare at me like that! No. I don't have a gun, but that won't stop me from defending myself. And no, Blake you won't take me to get a gun, either. Now, tell me why you seemed ready to fight. You wanted him to blow up!"

CHAPTER 27

A SOFT CHUCKLE took over Blake as Mila added that he knew Keith by name. He followed her up the stairs. Her ass swayed, but Blake made sure to catch Mila's eye contact each time her narrowed gaze turned around. She knew that *he knew* exactly who the motherfucker was prior to Keith's arrival. It had been years since Blake got into a fight—the bar scene didn't count. That dude didn't fight back, and he was begging for it. Back in the day, he wouldn't stop until managing to tear a guy's head off. He'd had reason to fight. Always. Back then, guys didn't just talk shit. There were never words, just the tumultuous sound of fist to flesh, or the cheer of onlookers. Keith, the fucking lawyer, how farcical, he desired a tête-à-tête.

Mila wasn't like the girls he knew as a teen. They'd hoot, they'd holler, they'd cheer. It was all rudimentary, environmental. Mila wasn't a kid anymore; neither was Blake. But that didn't stop him from waiting for Keith to cross the line.

"Mila, we can rehash the dynamics of our relationship and how a man doesn't tolerate any motherfucker's harassment of his woman. Let's just get you comfortable first. You were just shaken up." Vulnerability swept over him. An unfamiliar emotion he hadn't been accustomed to in years.

"No." She kicked off one Manolo, which clattered across the wood floor and almost hit the fireplace. The other stiletto ping-ponged against the canopy bedframe.

"As you wish." Blake flexed and unflexed fingers that had grown accustom to hacking in his late teens—for funds of course. Then typing away code at his early twenties. Though his fingers got some action-time during comradery with Jace and the guys, he hadn't pounded a face in so long. He turned toward the sliding glass door to stop Mila's gander. He needed to hide the satisfaction he felt.

"Wow, that smug look on your face tells it all." Mila leaned against the wood post.

A tranquil sea breeze blew a few of Mila's amber tresses from her slick ponytail.

He turned around as she began to slide down her skirt, over one sexy left hip to the right and back again. So fucking erotic. Blake looked back up. Those chocolate orbs didn't reflect his desire.

"Mila," he said gesturing with both hands. "We just had a fucking epiphany! I'm in love you. You're in love me. You think I'm gonna allow any shithead to bogart his way in between what we've created?"

She staked claim to the accent chair. "Nope. I figure this is more than a dick measuring contest, Blake. There isn't even a question as to you having to wonder about me desiring another man. You know for sure that *you* have me wide open."

Then Mila's eye clouded. "I don't know what has gotten into that asshole. I already had settled how this craziness would end with myself and Keith. We haven't fully communicated as two friends over the death of Warren. You didn't allow that."

"Hmmm." His baritone murmur roamed across the room. As Mila grappled with her reality, just his presence made her lose her mind. He wanted it to stay that way. Keep Mila on her toes, yet at arm's length. Instead, he'd just professed the highest level of adoration to Miss Ali.

He was fucking go-postal in love with her. He'd just threatened that asshole's life. So off his game, Blake didn't even know what Mila heard.

"All right, Mila. Once Keith has settled down, you have that discussion with him." Blake came before her, dropping to his knees. His hands rubbed at her creamy thigh and he kissed her breath away. Then he continued to flip the script. "This weekend, I'm taking you home, Mila. I feel there's uncertainty that you're clinging to."

"Home?" Mila leaned forward. Worry clung to her shoulders, so palpable, if it were a color it would be more gorgeous, even darker than her creamy brown complexion. Blake could see Mila's chocolate gaze cloud as numerous catastrophes flooded her mindset all at once.

He didn't miss a beat when adding, "Yes. My family will love you."

"How do you say such things? Me, a *mistress*. I'm not even a *good one.* Our relationship should revolve around catering to you," a sardonic chuckle shacked its way past plush lips.

That was where Mila was wrong. Blake would fight Keith for her a thousand times over, or any other prick trying to ruin the happiness he'd found in the luscious Mila Ali.

On a daily Blake lived by the credo: live life to the fullest. He was a man with a keen taste, and had no qualms about whetting his appetite. He'd almost lost his life climbing mountains, jumping out of helicopters, and dirt biking canyons. No amount of money in the world was capable of thwarting his contentment, not even the guilt laden notion of the departed Warren Jameson's murder.

But going back *home*... He'd do that for her.

~~~

Mid-Wednesday was the halfway mark until Blake had plans of taking Mila home. She'd gone through the motions: happy, excited, worried, hopeful. At each step, he guided her, and reminded her that his family would love her.

They'd just gotten off FaceTime, since meeting Mila at lunch wasn't going to cut it.

Then his iPad popped up with Lamb's face.

"Blake, I'm on my way to Cambodia. Little bit of pleasure, little bit of business." Lamb's pale eyes sparkled.

"All right. Not too much pleasure," Blake recommended, though already aware that Lamb lived for the business aspect of his job.

"Just enough to get my point across..." Lamb's monotony curbed. "I'll be out of reach for a while. When I return, we got a lotta shit to talk about."

"Fucking awesome."

They disconnected the call. He rubbed his hands together,
~~~

looking out the glass wall at his closest employees. Though his social media site had many locations, this one had allowed a hacker to worm his way into the fold. Lamb was getting ready to fix this little issue. *Yes,* Blake sighed, *Now I can go home and fuck my beautiful Mila. At least that will get the dead strawberry blond chick out of my head...*

He physically shook his head, yearning for a momentary reprieve from thoughts of meeting Lola in Tokyo.

~~~

Later that evening, Blake let himself into Mila's home. The entire downstairs was dark, save for the entry light. He stepped into the kitchen, and opened the fridge. Blake poured his woman a hefty glass of Pinot Noir into a goblet, swirling the blood-colored liquid. He set the glass onto the marble island, leaned against the countertop, and took a deep breath. Lamb was cleaning up the biggest, deadliest mistake of his life. Blake looked down at his hands, and through the moonlight's glow, he could see his knuckles become an ashen white from the intense clutch.

These scarred hands that had fought hoodlums by the time he reached the double digits, to hacking, to creating million-dollar computer code, to making his first billion. It wasn't money that made Blake strive for the best, it was status. The status of being able to say he'd made it out.

How the fuck have I made it out of the hood? There are as many dead bodies surrounding me as there were while I was being raised! This wasn't the type of man Blake molded himself into. The family
~~~

who'd raised him taught him better than to let others orchestrate his future. He rubbed the back of his neck, and then grabbed the goblet in one hand and a bottle of bourbon in the other.

The sound of rain drummed in Blake's ears as he ascended the staircase. His woman was in the shower, washing off the day while he marinated in the horror of his future if the government came after him.

Blake set Mila's wine on the counter right outside the shower. "Hey, gorgeous."

Mila turned, the frosted glass shielding Blake from her heavenly curves. But her excited greeting carried through the sound of rain.

He sunk into the accent chair in the bedroom, the master bath door wide open. A fog moved slowly toward him, but Blake controlled his own destiny. Nobody was going to fuck with him and live through it…

He opened the bourbon. The texture was superb, caramelized sugar, thick warm honey, candied pecans. The closest comparison to his current addiction. The lovely Mila Ali's pussy.

Mila came out of the shower, her brown body dripping wet. Steam lifted from the silk of her skin as she stepped toward the wineglass. "I thought you'd join me."

He needed her to break through his resolve. Even with a sordid past, Blake never got accustomed to the thought of death, or murder. Mila's eyes sparkled questioningly as he held up the towel she'd had draped over the shower. Conceding to his desire for quietness, Mila sauntered toward him. She grabbed the towel, while waiting for him to have his say. Blake took another taste of the closest comparison to *her.* He could feel her breathing, thinking, desire rising. She started to wrap the towel around her body, but Blake stood, almost a head taller, and did it for her. Blake gripped both edges of the towel using its leverage to keep her stuck with only him as an exit. The sheer act spoke volumes, shouted ownership.

If every fucking thing fell apart around him, this woman would still belong to him.

"Blake, talk to me..." Mila implored, that angelic face cocked slightly with worry.

"Shhh."

"You're so near, I scent that rich, sweet, strength of your mouth, yet you're so very far away."

Instead of commanding her to be quiet once more, Blake held her jaw so hard that her lips pucker into a magenta heart. He kissed her bottom lip then bit it, sending thrills down to her love box.

Blake patted her dry. Then the look of confusion returned to Mila's face as Blake dropped the towel from around her. He grabbed her wrists behind her back, stepping her toward the edge of the lounge chair.

"Stop thinking about anything and everything, Mila. All I wanna know is, how do you want it?" his command enthralling in her ear while he pulled down his tailor-made navy blue pants.

"Blake, are you mad at me?"

In her mind, Mila strived to catch his heart. She wanted all of *him,* not realizing she was already the recipient of such a notorious love. He had no desire to give in at the moment to delve into his feelings because there was no way on this green earth that he was going to tell her about Warren. Instead of replying, Blake gripped her hips and forced her back so that her ass cheeks melted against his stiff erection.

"Mila, how the fuck do you want it?" Blake slapped his dick against the side of her buttocks. Though a deep craving was warming its way across her body, Mila looked back at him torn between a primitive need for his cock and a love, a love that worried for *him*. The very man who'd put her in the situation of *not* being married soon…

Blake's lips teased the back of her neck, alternating from stolen kisses to heated bites. He smacked her left booty cheek. "Guess I'm going to tear that ass up, Mila?"

Instead of turning around with the same apprehensive gaze, Mila reached for his lips. His hand claimed the back of her neck, as he kissed her hard on the mouth. Her eyes sparkled with enjoyment.

Then Blake twirled around his index finger. Mila again planted her hands on the back of the armchair.

"Toot that ass up," he ordered, gripping a fleshy hip once again. The small of her back dipped. Those gloriously rounded buttocks were two chocolate arches as his ivory hammer began to inch its way inside. Not in the mood to take it easy, after about seven inches, Blake slammed the rest of his erection into her hollowness. Hard and slow was what she was in for as Blake worked out his frustration. He loved this woman. He didn't mean to hurt her so bad. These large white hands that encased such celestial dark skin gripped harshly as he took her to the pleasures of pain.

Each time his lips touched the small of her back, Mila's legs weakened. She'd lose a little more of her mind. She started to slam her ass back on his cock. Blake slapped her hip so hard, he realized it might leave a mark.

"Fuck me!" She pleaded for genuine agony. For all of him…

His big hand glided across the soft skin of her tiny stomach, over her belly button. Mila steadied herself once more, hands still anchored on the chair. Her breathy pleading for more and more cock spurred Blake on. He pinched her nipple while his balls repeatedly smacked against her ass. The fuck was long and hard, almost reminiscent of the first time his dick tasted her pussy. She'd been defiant, business like, desiring control. Blake worked her body until his sweat shackled her almond roasted skin once more.

They took another hot shower, just lazily holding and loving each other. She no longer asked what was eating at Blake as she'd done when seeing him sitting in her bedroom. Bodies colliding across clean sheets, they fell asleep.

The sex should have been such a drug to keep them on the other side until way past morning, but Blake awoke as Mila began to stir.

"Damn, beautiful, are you taking shots to my ego? I thought I put you to sleep," Blake chuckled softly while shaking her ass with his large hand as Mila leaned over.

"I know, baby," Mila spoke groggily. "I'm sorry. I… hold on a sec," she answered the phone. "*Maalin wanaagsan, Hooyo. Sideed tahay?"*

Unable to perceive the Somali dialect, Blake determined from Mila's bittersweet facial expression this was a call she'd take any single moment in any given day.

"It's my mom," she whispered. The glossiness of Mila's eyes wasn't indicative of a young woman engaging in a heart-to-heart with her own mother after midnight—however, Blake didn't have a control variable in which to make an accurate assessment. Blake didn't have parents at all to compare to.

"*Sababtu waa maxay*?" She sounded heartbroken, questioning even.

The call finished quickly. A sliver of a tear trickled from Mila's glossy chocolate eyes to her ear and soaked into the pillow.

"What happened," Blake forced himself not to growl, not to be upset with people he didn't even know. A doctor and a mother who raised three daughters while taking care of home. That was all he knew. Oh, and that her family left Somalia for Ethiopia, but Lamb had told him as much.

"She told me not to call on Wednesdays, that's all."

They were at this stage. Learning of each other, and slowly entwining the bests and worst parts of themselves into the storyline. Mila hadn't been shying away of talks of her parents, but she hadn't mentioned them either. While Blake had kept any sort of familial cohorts from the topic of discussion, because Mila simply hadn't asked before. Although, she had come to her own conclusion about Blake being born with a silver spoon. Offering to take her home had been on a whim, another puzzle piece at displaying his love of the beautiful, strong woman before him.

His long arm scooped Mila closer.

After a few moments, she elaborated, "There are certain times I can't call. Now, Wednesdays are off the table, too. My dad has been coming home early from work on Wednesdays. My mother didn't answer me earlier today. I should have known."

"Known *not* to call your own parents?"

She sighed. "It's not like that. Last Wednesday, she didn't answer. Usually if she doesn't answer, I remember to call at a different time during the weekday. Blake, my family has their preferences."

"You mean your father?" He corrected. "Your father has his preferences."

"Yes, he does."

"Talk to me, baby."

"My father prefers not to see my face ever again, Blake!"

Fuck. Blake held her closely. Mila was too shaken to even talk. He wanted to know more, but this wasn't the time. Blake rubbed Mila's back until sleep claimed her, the woman he'd fallen for all too fast. They'd known each other almost a year, but there'd be no going back.

CHAPTER 28

JEANS, TEE, KICKS. Simple. Too damn simple even for the woman that would rather wear khakis on the weekend—unless it were an outing with Blake.

But this is an outing with Blake.

The lavender shirt slid gracefully off her shoulder. Mila's hair had been swept into a messy bun. He wanted simple. Dark washed jeans for a soupçon of class. A beige blazer, cut at the waist to accentuate her ass, draped across her Birkin bag. She was happy to toss the nude heels back into the closet for her old, beloved pair of Nike Cortez shoes. Realizing the kicks didn't look well with the rest of the outfit, Mila opted on shades of purple-and-earth-stone sandals. Not half as comfy but from the follicles of her hair, to her flawless nude face, to the soles of her feet, Mila was a natural beauty.

All the while they boarded the jet, Mila considered his parents. Maybe these rich people were down to earth? They had so much money that... Damn, she couldn't even continue to meditate over bullshit. *Blake says they'll love me. Nothing else matters.*

All the while, Mila extended Pinterest-style quotes of self-love, a flurry of emotions consumed Mila by the hour. He was her rock. Her everything. The way such peace consumed her after her mother forbade her to call on Wednesday afternoons. This was a brand new feeling, having a man to love despite not being loved by her very own father. And having Blake to hold her closely while crying last night, well, nothing in this world topped that. Mila endeavored to train her mind from hoping to steal his family from his wife. But as a flurry of white clouds passed by, she took that into consideration, too. The woman, Diane Baldwin, couldn't love Blake like she loved him. So the discussion went sort of like this… "So where are we going, Martha's Vineyard?"

"Not exactly."

"San Francisco?"

"It's a surprise, Mila."

She'd asked about various quaint places to match their casual attire. Each time Blake smiled and ended the conversation with a kiss to her lips, cheek, forehead or nose. And that ever calming reassurance of his love, and that of his parents…

A metallic glimmer caught Mila's eye as the plane curved to make its descent three hours later. The Gateway Arch.

Her almond eyes tapered just slightly in thought. "St. Louis? All right now, before we meet your parents you're taking a chick to Sweetie Pies?" Mila patted her belly. "I could eat."

"No Sweetie Pies. I'm taking you to an even better place."

~~~

An Escalade was curbside at the private airport. Blake had obtained the keys from one of his personal attendants as they'd gotten off his Learjet. The scenery had Mila wondering if Blake was strapped. The billionaire handled Keith in a way that still left her
~~~

astounded even now. But this was a city full of diversified folks. In the greater Los Angeles area, she knew where to go, and where not to go. Even as a fifteen-year-old, visiting her father's family.

The place had the same character as Mila's old drinking spot near UCLA, but with a rawer feel. The barebones of the inside were red brick, yet the ambiance didn't waft of stale cigarette smoke and cologne but the aromatics of genuinely good food. The spices of ribs having been marinated to fall-off-the-bone and melt-in-your-mouth consistency wafted into the air.

Hands strummed together, Blake led her across the scuffed natural wood floor.

"B!" A black woman shaped like a figure eight stepped around the hostess podium. Mila's pupils dilated at the sight of her ass. Jeans had a hold of the heavy curves she was rocking left to right. Besides having the type of ass that men flocked to, those damn dimples had to melt a man's heart. Any ol' *married* man…

"Zenobia, how are you, girl." Blake took her into one of those tight embraces.

Mila noticed that his tone had a dialect to it. When he was bossing her around in the past or unappreciative of her not showing him any play, his tone had mellowed into the one he currently used.

"My bad, Zennie, allow me to introduce the love of my *life*, Mila Ali. Mila, this is Zenobia Washington, I haven't seen this little girl in a few years."

"Little girl?" The walking-wet dream retorted. "Whatever, nerd." Zenobia turned to Mila. "Mila, you have yourself... Hmmm... Let me just say an *ambitious* man. Though after all the stuff he's been through, I see him as a brother, in other terms—B, close your ears for a sec— ambition is equivalent to sexy sexy."

Mila nodded, still at a loss for words. Blake shook his head, wearing a genuine smile. The sort of smile that could never be the norm for a billionaire, a person used to having more and more…

"Yeah, so he leaves you speechless too?" Zenobia chatted as if the women were friends from high school. "One minute Brendan is hacking into the FEDs and the next week he's at a prestigious university."

"Zennie, the Feds, really? You're supposed to keep that on the low." Blake chuckled deeply. Yes, it was the same expensive black maple bourbon chuckle that melted the thong right off her ass. But who was this man? Who was *Brendan*?

"Brendan?"

Then another person shouted 'B.' For a rather sleek establishment, nobody seemed to take offense to all the banter.

The black man had a butterscotch complexion, and low-cut fade. A button-down, with vest, added a certain level of snazziness to his jeans. He resembled Zenobia, but had to be at least 5 years older. Around Blake's age.

"Damn, Brendan fucking Walker, how're you going to come through my spot without a call? Now I gotta go kick out good paying customers for my closest."

"Man, don't put anyone out for me." They gave each other a brotherly hug. "Isaac, allow me to introduce you to..."

"The woman of *my* dreams?" Isaac looked Mila up and down like candy on a stick.

"Not even big bro," Zenobia shot over her shoulder, as her voluptuous body strutted back to the podium.

CHAPTER 29

HE WAITED FOR her to react. To make an inquiry. Though the restaurant was packed, Isaac squeezed them at a quaint little table, on the deck outside.

She'd ordered a mojito. Downed it. He took a double shot of whiskey, since the bourbon wasn't recommended. The waiter treated them like royalty, not because of Blake Baldwin's current status, but due to his association with Isaac. Salads arrived.

"Can I get the beautiful lady another strawberry mojito?" The waiter placed the salad atop the black cloth napkin.

"Sure, I'll take 'em back to back. Oh, and stronger than the last…"

When he stepped away, those almond orbs glided to Blake. "So when were you going to tell me who you are? Google. Wikipedia. Your very own company bio is this big," Mila held out her index and thumb in measurement. "It sure as hell didn't say anything about you being an alias."

Noting the irritation in Mila's tone, Blake gave a soft chuckle. "For months you've been very wrong in your judgement of me. And in your judgement, you never stopped to ask me one question about my past. Now that you belong to me—"

"*Belong*?"

"You belong to me; I belong to you, Mila. Is there anything brand new about that?"

"No. I love... To be honest, how do I finish that sentence? The 'I love you,' simplest fucking phrase ever doesn't seem to strum together just right if I don't know you. *Brendan Walker*."

He nodded, mouth somewhere between a grin and an irritated snarl. "Yeah, so you think I'm a fucking name? You think knowing me is all in a name. When I know every fucking thing about you, Mila. You bite that sweet, softness of the inside of your lip when nervous. So much so that I want to grab you by your fucking neck and bite it for you. You think, think, think, and goddam it, you think some more. Last week, you worried that I'd consider less of you. That's why you refused to enlighten me of the Keith-stalker bullshit."

She rolled her eyes.

He snatched the wooden chair closer. The pulse at her neck invited him, but Blake chose not to kiss her. "But I've tasted every inch of your body." He licked his lips, murmuring in Mila's ear, "Your gorgeous, sweet pussy has this slight salt to it in the morning as if you've marinated in the love making we've had during your dreams. Oh, I also know when you're dreaming too. Not that you don't snore. You do, just a tad. You pull closer to me after falling asleep and delving in an erotic dream. If the dream is bad, like the one you had after speaking to your mother, your pillow is your comforter because you're so use to going it alone. Or let's bring Keith back into the discussion. You're used to being his wingman from undergrad and grad school. You regret Warren falling for you, you never loved him."

"I told you I was never in love with him, Bl—*Brendan* or whatever the fuck you wanna be called."

"Yup, never in love with him. You were in love with his brother."

Smack.

The sound drew eyes. All eyes on them. Mila picked up her fork to toy with her garden salad. Blake tossed back a double shot. Then the entertainment began to shift back to each individual table. So maybe he hadn't meant to take a low blow, but all she did was take digs at him, even from the start.

"I was. But that was a long time ago."

"Yes, Mila I know that. From the day you opened up about it, I've always known it was only puppy love. The thing is, there's absolutely nothing wrong with you having fallen for Keith as a teenager. But you don't see it that way. Ironically you've spent more time trying to convince others of the truth and it has left you in a predicament."

"Hmmm, I guess you're going to continue to tell me about myself then. Huh?" She shrugged. "What kinda predicament?"

"The kind where life passed you by. Good, I'm glad life passed you by. You settled for Warren because you saw love as a fucking ancient pyramid, unyielding, with the man always and forever on top. Mila you're capable of so much more than you've always given yourself credit for."

She glanced away. There was this one relationship before Warren that had the potential to be so much more than she allowed. And even with Warren Jameson, the love had blossomed on his end. Only to begin to bloom on her own. Yet, she was so afraid of giving away her heart… The truth was real.

“Then I arrived,” Blake tugged his collar, more for smugness than for show. “so I'm glad you didn't know love until me.”

She took a deep breath.

“See, I know you, Mila.” He kissed her ear. “Now, are you done thinking I'm an asshole, or a number to my bank account.”

“Blake, I've never...”

“You've never used me, Mila.” He stopped to chuckle, genuinely baffled. “Do you know how long it took me to consider a way to get money into your hands after you chewed my ass out about the mortgage? Soon I'll tell you how I fell. When we meet my family. But you've never placed yourself on the pedestal, exactly where you’re meant to be. Let’s eat, then make love all over this fucking town. Tomorrow we meet the folks.”

CHAPTER 30

MILA HAD NOT thought of her dad too much since meeting Blake. Not that extracting her father from her over-worked mind wasn't a good thing. Last night, Blake made love to her. He was becoming even more of a stronghold into her life.

There'd be no getting over Blake. And these days, he rarely went home to his wife. Nor did he remove himself or ignore a call. The calls seemed business like so Diane must've really been enjoying her pool boy or whatever the case may be.

Again, Mila donned a casual pair of jeans. Blake wore tan khaki shorts that showed off strong limbs, so she was certain his family would take her as is. But doubt began to pool in her stomach when the Escalade didn't take the freeway exit for the airport. They weren't leaving St. Louis for somewhere exotic or luxurious to meet his parents.

As Blake made the turn for Florissant Avenue, he slipped his hand into her fidgeting fingers. Bellefontaine Cemetery gates came into view. Mila looked from Blake and back again. Then she softly squeezed his hand as the SUV climbed over the entrance. The car took a one lane road across vast green lands with plots and burial monuments. A clear green stream came into view when Blake stopped. He parked, got out, coming around the other side of the car.

"Are you ready to meet one of the two most important women in my life, Mila?"

"Your mom…" her throat was constricted. Was it too late for her condolences? She knew nothing about Blake's family at all.

"My Aunt Serenity. Isaac and Zenobia's mother. Serenity Graham, she was pretty good friends with my mother." He shrugged. "Serenity knew my mom a heck of a lot more than I did."

They linked hands and as they began to walk. "I wanted my mom to be here, too. She's buried in not such a lavish place."

"Oh?" Her steps faltered. From the beginning Blake had been there for her. Albeit with sexual intentions, he listened intently given her desire to talk about Warren.

"C'mon, Mila. You have questions, I've got answers."

"I know, Blake. You're always so real with me."

He stopped before her. Mila hesitated, as those forest green eyes held nothing back. She asked, "Why isn't your mom buried here?"

"We didn't have a pot to piss in when she died. Or rather, Auntie Serenity was trying to take care of us all, my mother included. When I made my first million, I appealed to every political facet to move my mother's body from the mass grave with all the other convicts; they refused all but one hypocritical politician who offered to help. But I didn't want to financially back such an…" his tone drowned out as they stopped before a plot that had an angel molded into the side of a cross. Serenity Graham died less than three years ago.

"Here's my mama, Aunt Serenity. Mama, meet the second important lady in my life."

The love Blake had for his Aunt Serenity was tangible. Serenity and Blake's mother grew up neighbors in the same housing authority. They both had teen pregnancies. Except the seventeen-year-old Serenity saw peace in Isaac's eyes while Blake's mother continued along the same path.

The young mothers were supposed to take turns attending night school and watching each other's children. But Serenity often did it all, even taking the toddlers, along with crayons, to evening classes at the junior college. Blake and his mother lived off and on with Serenity, and each time his mother went to jail, he had a safe home.

Mila's heart broke as he told her about living in the street with his mom. His mother would become so stubborn when Serenity tried to break through to her best friend. His own mom was in and out of jail for petty theft, though she'd tried to take care of Brendan.

"I remember one time, I had to be about six years old, sitting in the backseat of an Oldsmobile when my mom went into the grocery store. My stomach hurt so fucking bad for hunger," Blake said, there was no shame as he looked Mila in the eye. "The cops came a few hours later, they took me straight to Serenity, not telling me a thing. I knew. Shit, I always knew when my mom was stealing." He rubbed the back of his neck. "I would fucking hate myself for being happy to go right on back to Aunt Serenity's house. Then one day, mom stopped picking me up. The in-and-out of jail crap was done for good. Mom had to do real time."

Blake briefly mentioned his father. The sort of man Mila couldn't even keep from wincing from as Blake talked about him.

She knew the man was mixed into human trafficking. Blake stopped to grin at Mila while he told her this horrible story. "You're thinking about your center?"

She nodded, eyes wet with tears.

"You remind me of Serenity, Mila." Blake shoved his hands into his jean pocket. "Not just the fact that I was blown away when Todd handed me an envelope from you. By the time you told me about sharing the meal with the transient, I was batshit in love with you. But back to me falling for the lovely Ali girl…" Blake looked far off in the distance, a smile creased his chiseled, usually unreadable face, "Serenity cussed me *out* about ten years back. I had deposited money into her bank account. She said I was family; I was her son. That no way in hell was she going to take my money."

The corners of Mila's mouth tugged upward into a smile as she felt the love in his voice while he talked about her helping at Warren's funeral. Blake took her hand, "Serenity use to work as a pregnancy advocate. She never took a vacation or a break. One day you're going to have your resource center, Mila."

Mila's eyelashes brushed across her cheeks as her eyes closed to his kiss. She loved him with every part of her. It was as if Blake held the same vision for her. He didn't try to shovel money into her hands, Warren had offered countless of times when Mila stressed over funding proposals. This was something Mila had to do for herself, and knowing how hard his Aunt Serenity worked, made it all the more important.

"I… I can't believe how wrong I was about you, Blake…"

"That's all right. You've got all the time in the world to make it up to me," he said, his tone didn't hold the usual undertones of sex but of hope. Hope for a future.

"I apologize."

"C'mon, Mila, no apologies necessary." Blake kissed her lips again. "I'm a firm believer it takes time to get to know someone. Like I just said, all the time in the world."

Mila nodded. She wanted to believe in this image of a future with Blake even though the knowledge she learned at Hewitt Corp taught her otherwise. This sweet love that they delved in was the highest level of risk.

~~~

"Meat, meat, meat," Clarissa attempted to whisper at the Asian Moon in Laguna Niguel. The casual restaurant was tucked into a strip mall, and by no means were they here for the ambiance. Unless it was the type of restaurant where the lights went out. Asian Moon was a gem, and one of their favorite spots. Also the only reason Mila got her bestie to meet in her neck of the woods.

"*Meat*? Girl, why can I just imagine that there's dick of every shape and size roaming around before those catty little eyes of yours." Mila shook her head. Her face still glowed from meeting Blake's family in St. Louis two weeks ago.

Clarissa placed down the jade tea cup after a delicious sip. "You got the green light from the government, to help with your resource center. So we both have things to be happy about. If you must know,
~~~

Todd has been under stress at work these past few weeks. Meaning—"

"Code for you've been just about breaking your neck to get cock elsewhere?" Mila chuckled. After leaving Serenity's grave site, Mila turned in the application Warren had harped was more than perfect. She had just gotten the news this afternoon while preparing for dinner with Clarissa. She'd told Blake first. They were going to celebrate later this evening. "Girl, you keep on. I swear, Clarissa, you're going to be in one of the health classes about STDs."

"Are you as smart as you are gorgeous." Clarissa laughed. She twirled around rice noodles since all the a la cart items of Peking duck, dim sum, bok choi, the girls would buy more than they could eat and always take doggie bags.

Mila's cell phone began to vibrate. Veronica's unblemished face popped up on the screen. "Oh, shit I never called Veronica back. I'm going to tell her and Lido the news. Excuse me, Clarissa."

With an upbeat voice, Mila answered her cell phone, "Hey, Veronica…"

"COME GET THIS BITCH NOW!" Veronica's tone made Mila certain that this was her sister instead of the more amicable of the two. But nope, it was *Lido* in the background, caught in a loud rage.

"So you want me out, trick, is that what the fuck you want, huh?" Lido shouted.

"I'll be there shortly." Mila hung up just as Clarissa gestured for the check. Her friend pulled out her purse and tossed more than enough cash on the table.

"I can drop you off at my place on the way?" Mila asked as they made their way through the mall, since Clarissa had driven to her house and they rode together.

"No friggen way. I'll stick with you. Two cats going at it can get dangerous. Should I call my cousin?"

Mila didn't even answer that. It took them over an hour to get from Orange County to the Hollywood Hills home. Her Maserati zoomed up the stone fragment to the towering cement walls of the mini-mansion. At the sound of glass crashing the two friends gawked at each other than hurried to the door. Mila began to bang on the right side of door, but the continuous crashing and abrasive large noises didn't cease. The left handle gave slack as Clarissa jiggled it.

The door crept open. Every chromed chandelier from the two story ceiling swayed. "Watch your step," Mila said in horror as her stiletto boots crunched over broken glass. Canvas paintings on the wall were torn. A photo of Lido from her younger years had been ripped to shreds, the top portion twisted, falling to the floor.

"I have given you all of me, *all of me!*" Veronica's voice echoed off the cement walls.

They followed the sound to the gourmet kitchen, where Veronica stood, back facing them, a butcher knife in her hand. Lido's penetrating gaze followed her lover's every move. She was dressed in a red lace teddy. Blood blotched the floor, with foot printed red smudges. A quick evaluation of Lido's half-naked body proved she'd only cut her foot on glass as she'd tried to run away.

"Veronica, what are you doing, beautiful?" Mila said softly.

The model's frail shoulders jumped. The knife dropped from her hands as she turned around. The buoyant beauty willowed into her arms. Mila's heart broke as she crashed into her. On her heels, Lido stumbled back, but held Veronica as tightly as she would any of her *walaashays weyn*.

Mila's shaky hand went to Veronica's golden mane, and her other hand rubbed Veronica's back. "It's okay, it's okay…"

Sniffling and crying resonated off the frail woman's body as she continued to rub her hair and back. Mila's eyes went to Lido. The nimble black beauty hobbled with Clarissa's help to one of the stools.

"Let me get you some ice." Clarissa's gaze flitted toward Mila, then she shrugged. "I think Lido just stepped in a bit of glass, is all."

"That's *not* all." Veronica let Mila go. Her hands were tightened into fists. "Do you know how much I love you? I could kill you, I could take you out, then my heart," she tapped her hand at her thin chest, "I could just die right now."

Never had Mila seen the look of remorse on Lido. Even as children, reprimands brought anger, not anguish.

"I… love … you, Veronica," she cried. "You're my world, V, I'm sssssorrry."

"If it's any consolation, Lido has never been so genuine in her life," Mila offered.

"I take no solace in that. Because this bitch has been my all ever since I laid eyes her. Your dumbass sister just lost a great one."

The willowy woman turned and stalked out of the room. After a wave of her hand and a deep breath, Mila turned to follow her. "Veronica, let's all sit down. We can talk. Look, I know you called me a few weeks ago. Have you two been at odds this long," she asked as they made it to the vast entryway.

Veronica stopped at the staircase, head lowered.

"I almost killed myself trying to answer the phone. So I never called back, I'm sorry."

"Mila, your only fault is your ability to apologize. You're the backbone of the Ali girls. The one always trying to keep the peace. But one day you'll really get to know Lido Ali. For now, I'm the sorry one," Veronica scarcely looked her way. "Sorry that I ever set eyes on someone so … so ugly."

Heart pounding in her throat, Mila had no words. Lido was a bad child, there was no way to get around it. But for the first time in Mila's life, justification of Lido's actions stayed dormant within her mind.

Veronica was the antithesis of a supermodel. A divalicious mask grazed her face when the lights came on, yet only while the camera shutters clicked. Once over, she became just Veronica. Nice-nasty wasn't even in her repertoire. *What did my sister do!*

Mila ambled back into the kitchen, where a few shards of red-tinted glass were on the sleek white counter. Clarissa looked up at Mila, then back down at the task at hand. "They're not too deep, so Lido will be just fine."

"What did you do, Lido?" Mila asked, hands on hips.

Lido waved a hand. That stark dark glare she was known for

blazed through her little sister. "The fuck is wrong with you, Mila? I'm in pain—grrrrr," she paused as Clarissa began to bind her right heel with gauze. Retreating to the same ol' Lido, she squared her shoulders. "Get my shit! I'm not staying here one more night. That whore is going to murder me as I sleep. I'm too fucking sexy for *Snapped* to find someone to play me."

"I'm not a damn valet, Lido! You can hobble your little black ass upstairs but I'm not getting anything or doing anything until I know what you've done."

PLAP! *PLAP*! They all turned to the entryway as black trash bags sailed from the sky. Veronica had to be throwing Lido's things from over the railing upstairs. One bag took out the chandelier entirely, and glass scattered to the ground.

"Get yo' shit, don't *ever* come back!" Veronica shouted from the top railing.

"This is my house too, goddamn it. As far as I'm concerned we're in a fucking common law marriage. You just continuously refused to say 'yes.'"

There was loud stomping upstairs then another bag flew over to the ground. "Bitch, why would I say yes? You're no good!"

Mila held up a hand before Lido had the chance to say another word. "Veronica, if I walk to the door am I going to get hit by any bags?"

"I wouldn't try to hit you, Mila. No matter what, I still consider you as a sister. I love you, but I hate that cunt! Just a few more things…. Okay?"

Clarissa drove. On the silent ride home, Mila asked what had occurred. Lido was smack dab in the middle of the back seat of the Maserati with bags all around.

"I'm a bitch when drunk," Lido said after a while.

Mila chose not to address the obvious. No amount of alcohol had the ability to alter Lido's mindset, not in a sense of making her worse. Lido was a bitch, period. "Veronica is your better half, Lido… She just woke up, deciding that she's over you?"

"Mmmm, well, I've been cheating too."

"With whom?" Mila interrogated through stressed teeth, looking back at Lido.

"Naomi Campbell."

"*Try* again."

The sisters glowered at each other.

Finally, Lido smirked. "Okay, I have standards. Vanessa Fucking Williams."

"Clarissa, feel free to stop the car. Where are we, Santa Ana?" Mila peered at the N Grand Ave exit. "Lido can stay at the first hotel we pass by."

"Like hell! I'm your *walaashay weyn,* Mila. I don't care if I have a gazillion bucks. This sexy ass, right here," Lido said, provocatively gesturing to herself, "is staying with you. That's what the fuck families do!"

"As it should be. Yes, we are *family*, Lido. Who did you cheat with? More importantly, why? You shunned a marriage with a very affluent family back home because you were so in love with

Veronica. You fucked over family then, but I will not be hypocritical, because I've stood by your side. I tried to vouch for you. The two of you have been together for over ten years. You were talking adoption a few months back."

"Veronica was yakking about adoption. But the little angel wouldn't marry me though. It was a man. Every once in a while I like penetration with a heartbeat."

"Every once in a while? You've been cheating on Veronica all along?"

"Yeah," Lido shrugged. "I didn't tell you because you care about her."

"You damn right I care about Veronica." Mila turned even more in her seat. "Listen, we both have done things that have turned our father's head. Turned him away from *us*. It didn't work out for me. You disgraced our family for no reason!"

"Yeah, so maybe I did. It's not my fault dick is as good as pussy. Can't a chick have it all?"

Clarissa chuckled. "Here, here, the power of an erection."

"You," Mila pointed at her best friend, "You don't egg her on. Lido will never need a mascot with all the demons swarming through that head. Now Lido, no you can't have it all. When you're in love, truly in love, nobody in this world can come between that. The two of you walk around so blinded by love that Antonio Banderas's accent in Chris Hemsworth's body doesn't do the trick. No, you both gotta have it all! Every damn lustful gaze that turns your way."

"I'll take both," Clarissa countered.

"Thank you for these words of wisdom, Mila. You are all knowing." Lido chuckled. "Says the woman whose madly in love with another *woman's* man. So I hope Baldwin walks around with his eyes closed in front of that perfect, perky titted wife of his. Furthermore, do ya know what they say about sluts who set the foundation of their relationship on another's?" Lido barely paused. The slight slur to her intonation had evaporated. "Oh and mistakes? You're telling me that you made a mistake by not marrying some Somalian stiff? Bitch please. You wanted to play Keith's shadow just so you had a means of not marrying some boring, baby faced idiot back home. Shall we call that weak, pathetic? We all knew Keith was never the one. If you opened your eyes, you'd have known that *his* pussy is bigger than all the whores I've fucked—male or female—while with the goody-goody Veronica."

Mila turned in her seat, almost ready to double over in disgust. "I can't even talk to this woman right now…"

~~~

SPLASH. The slushed ice water that Mila had poured from the refrigerator drenched her sister's face and the silk pillow Lido brought with her from home. Warm sunlight streamed into the room as Lido began to choke, rousing from her peaceful slumber, dressed in a peach silk camisole and short set. Her bare arms and legs prickled instantly, her backhand held high.

"Don't!" Mila pointed a finger. Unlike her older sister, who'd just been so very serene, she hadn't had a wink of sleep. They both
~~~

vehemently glared at each other. She said, "I've been up all night. Drinking? Fucking every Tom-Dick-and-Halle that you can get your hands on? You are an Ali! You are better than this."

"Yes, yes I am," Lido's chin jutted out as she climbed from the soft pillow-top mattress. There were clothes shrouded around the bed. Mila had told her to get her own sheets out of the hallway cabinet after Mila and Clarissa lugged most of her items upstairs. But the diva was just too lazy. She'd rather wrinkle embellished runway pieces.

"I know my worth, Mi-la. You're the one running after a married –"

"Don't you dare speak ill of me or my man," Mila cut in. "He is separated from his wife, but that isn't none of your business. *And you know your worth?* I could sit here, taking bashes at your character. Lord knows you have flaws, but I'm not with the female-against-female thing. There will be no stepping on each other's back to feel better about ourselves. Do you hear…" Mila paused, and was met by utter derision. "Hear me loud and clear. I have never failed you, Lido. Despite your ability to be cruel, you've always had my back. Like I just said, I've been up all night. Our substance abuse program begins this evening."

"Our," Lido snarled. "Substance, what? Bitch I'm not on drugs."

"Alcohol, Lido. You won't go this alone." A deep breath discharged all the anger she felt.

Those deep dark marble eyes of her sister's lulled for a trice. Mila turned on the heels of her bare foot and left. After completing grad school and commencing the most difficult course of attempting to find a job, Lido and Veronica supported her. Since she hadn't returned home, Mila's father had washed his hands of her. There was no way Mila was turning her back on Lido. Not for a man. Not for, hell, even the diva herself…

CHAPTER 31

Four Months Later

BLAKE AND MILA had been dating for a year next week, and for the last few months Blake would either spend the night at Mila's or she'd frequent the glass house. During the week, he'd stay with her so her commute to Versa Home Improvements would be easier. But with her sister being there, Blake found himself coming over late and leaving early.

Though Blake kept himself out of the sister's business, he appreciated seeing support like that. It was the same love that lingered behind the tired eyes of Aunt Serenity when his mother strolled in and out of the apartment at all hours.

He stood at the window of his business, waiting for the phone call to connect.

"Hey, handsome, it's lunchtime," Mila's delicious voice wove in his ear. "I'm sitting in the employee room."

"Someone there?" Blake smiled wickedly detecting that she was halfheartedly whispering.

"Yeah," she murmured. "But I'm still hungry."

"I know, beautiful. You went to the meet last night, then there was this thing at work this morning."

"Yeah, tell me about it. Lido finally found an AA meeting she likes. There were those few weeks she forced me to drive her all the way to Lancaster or Palm Springs or all the way to Bakersfield saying she'd heard the meetings would be the best."

He shook his head, knowing just as well as Mila that her sister had been playing her. Mila was much too good to her, even putting the resource center on the backburner. Her plans were up in the air for such a selfish person. Lido would say that going to those far off places for rehab kept her incognito. He'd offered them use of one of his jets to go anywhere on God's green earth, as far as Tibet for meditation and detoxing.

They got off the phone, with promises of good love tonight, and Blake went back to ruminating over their one-year anniversary. He planned on taking her across the Mediterranean by yacht. They'd begin at the volcanic island of Santorini, Greece. Its curved caldera and steep cliffs had been created when part of the island fell into the sea due to a volcanic eruption. After wine and relaxing walk trails, the second stop, he wasn't entirely sure about. Somewhere with a mountain would be good, but he smiled considering how he had to butter Mila up to climbing. He knew where they would end up. There last destination was to be the utmost important one.

~~~

He'd whisked her away to a shopping spree at Oscar De La Renta in New York City just to prepare for their one-year anniversary. She didn't know where they were going and with items from bathing suits to ballroom gowns to lingerie that he had to tear off her body at tens of thousands a shred, Mila was growing
~~~

accustom to extravagant surprises.

As they strolled down Madison Avenue after putting mounds of glamorous paper bags into the car, Blake's cell phone buzzed in his blazer. He slipped his hand from around Mila and took a glance. His jaw muscles tensed as a text message popped up, the messenger even clingier than his wife.

Blake slid the phone back into his inside pocket.

"Baby, you need to answer that..." Mila said, sexy mouth slightly tensed.

"Nah."

"Well, you answer *all* of your calls when I'm around."

His emerald gaze hazed over as Blake planted himself in front of Mila. There were people walking by, but he placed his hands on her arms, and rubbed softly. "Mila, you mean the world to me. Yes, there are calls I must answer. Some can wait."

"Other business calls or *other* calls in general?" She folded her arms.

Blake cocked her chin up with his thumb. "All I've ever been was faithful to you, Mila. I've offered to show you the legal documents for my separation with–"

"Forget a piece of paper; introduce me to *Diane and her* family, since those blue bloods are so against divorce... or so you claim."

"Mila, don't fucking take it there, beautiful," Blake shook his head as her shoulders tensed, guard up. "Baby, I've shared things about my family that Diane doesn't even know. Do you think she's even been to my Aunt Serenity's grave? Fuck no. Mila, you mean so much to me. You gotta stop accusing me when all I ever do is show how much I love you."

Her eyes closed for a nanosecond, pain and fatigue showing on her face. Blake leaned in to kiss her. "I'm sorry, beautiful."

Her gander was wet with tears, "No, Blake. I'm sorry. It's this whole thing with Lido."

He fucking couldn't stand her sister, but just the way she stood, her entire demeanor reminded Blake of Serenity each time his mother had gotten out of jail in the past. The guilt coiled in his abdomen as Blake thought about the text message on his phone. But it was too late to stop the madness, he loved Mila too much to let her go.

They stopped in front of Cartier's. He held open the door. Mila's eyebrow cocked. "What do you need, new cufflinks?"

"Nope."

"Uhn-uhn, Blake, we're not here for me. You're always giving me beautiful trinkets," she tried but his grin was unyielding. "Baby, I just made an ass of myself accusing you of not answering your phone."

Blake took off his black leather gloves and grasped her hand. "But I need your assistance."

An attendant hurried to do his bidding. "Mr. Baldwin, Miss Ali."

Blake smiled. "I came to put you to the test."

The redhead gave a triumphant grin. "Please do."

"Find me any piece of jewelry, forget cost, that could adorn such an exquisite being." Blake's hand grazed Mila's arm.

"Hmmm.... Let's see, what's beautiful enough to rival Ms. Ali's eyes? I know a pair of couture earrings that may very well come close."

They were ushered toward low seating leather chairs. Strawberries floating in Champagne were readily offered, along with imported chocolates.

"What diamond shape do you prefer?" Blake asked casually.

Mila's eyes narrowed in mock suspicion as she took a sip of the sparkling champagne. "Boy, I like every diamond you gave me this past year. Furthermore, you know what I like more."

He mirrored her teasing smile. When the attendant brought over the chandelier antique diamond earrings, the style popped against her sparkling dark brown eyes.

"A timeless beauty," the attendant assured. Her words about the earrings being paved with brilliant cut diamonds went in one ear and out the other.

"These *are* pretty." Mila smiled looking at herself in the mirror. She turned and mumbled about the price, but Blake insisted she had to have them. While the receipt was being rung, Mila went to the restroom.

Blake followed Mila toward the front as her ass swayed mockingly. She'd just propositioned her desire. Gifts, diamonds, not even Cartier would do. His love had but only one fancy.

HIM.

Blake spun her around with a tug of her wrist. His lips locked onto hers, tongue seeking the sweet elixir of her mouth that had made Blake lose it.

There it was...

That tiny moan only his ears could hear. Her body melted for, and into him. Blake's hand took to the small of her back then down to the pear of an ass that belonged to him. Hand wide, he clutched as much plumpness as possible, guiding Mila backwards toward the only unisex restroom.

His eyes never left Mila's as he held her against the door and jiggled the handle. He breathed against her lips as the door held firm. The sparks in his lady's eyes made Blake beat on the door.

"Sir..." A suited security guard began from the gallery but Blake's every attention remained on having Mila soon.

The door freed from its hinges as a young girl with floppy ponytails exited. An older couple took the happy girl's hand, none the wiser about their urgency. Blake backed Mila into the room and slammed the door on the security guard.

Deep chocolate eyes bore straight through him. They'd had a long day. He'd scented the sex on her dewy chestnut skin for hours.

"I'm fucking you right now." Blake's stormy green eyes glued onto Mila's. As the statement boomed against the marble bathroom his lips automatically sought hers.

"Bl...Blake, everyone outside knows…" Mila stammered as the buttons of her blouse popped. His calloused hand roamed beneath her black silk custom bra. In that very moment, Blake's quest ceased.

"I've been trying to get us back to the jet for hours," she held up a hand. Blake had toyed with her desire all day.

Blake stepped closer, allowing his thumb to flick against a swollen, hard nipple. Mila's grumble died as a moan roamed over her tumescent lips. He did the pleasure of unclasping her bra from behind. The haste, the urgency had been doused. Blake leaned down and kissed the chocolate morsel. His sexy mouth opening, warm, wet breath becoming the satin of her soft skin. Mila sighed. He growled, with a mouth full of her breast. His teeth softly clamped onto the melon. The pressure tantalizing enough to make Mila lean into him with her body and as extra support, leverage a hand on the slick counter. His teeth grazed over the curve of a breast he'd been waiting to love on and slowly dragged to her nipple. Pressure releasing softly as he continued.

Blake again kissed the tip of her nipple then looked up at her.

Blake's hand went to the silk of Mila's almond-roasted skin, his hand drug up her shapely thigh and beneath her skirt. He guided her leg upward and over his shoulder. The only sign that through her he'd reached ultimate pleasure was the slight uprising of the left side of his pleasing mouth. Blake reveled at how ambidextrous Mila was. Soon as her stiletto was perfectly positioned over his left shoulder, Blake pushed her thong to the side and dug in. Her complaints about him needing to be quick evaporated into thin air as he sought the honey within her body.

"Bla… Blake," Mila clasped one hand over her mouth and the other grasping the countertop for dear life! After leaving her spent, Blake stood up and licked the glaze from his full lips. He kissed her mouth, the fragrance of her cum tasting so fucking good. Then his hand skimmed down her inner thigh, as he silently positioned her leg all the way up over his shoulder. With them standing there, eye to eye, he confessed, "Do you know how fucking magnificent you just made those earrings, Mila."

Her graceful neck lengthened as Blake's glance was only for her.

Blake dipped his pelvic bone back then his dick slowly pressed into her body. She clutched his biceps as his cock explored her nether regions. His mouth clamped onto her own, he offered the sweet notes of her own sex, and he offered his undying love…

CHAPTER 32

THE DAY TRIP to New York had been a much needed reprieve. At work Mila had secured an even better position in management. She placed the new social proposals on the desk before leaving the job for a two-week vacation with Blake.

One whole year? Wow!

Since she would be leaving Lido in her sister's care, Mila wanted to have an outing with them before leaving. As Mila's Maserati pulled into the valet line at the outdoor theater, she told Lido of her plans to be out of town. "… And Yasmin is going to attend the meetings with you every Tuesday and Thursday."

"Okay," Lido said, tone almost dripping with covetousness, but Mila blamed it on the chilly evening as they walked up the stairs toward the cinema entrance. Her cell phone vibrated, Mila slipped her hand into her jean pocket to grab it.

Clarissa: I think Todd is breaking up with me ☹

Damn. she paused to consider what to type. All of Clarissa's relationships ended in the same manner. Her good friend didn't have anything in common with the computer tech, so she quickly replied about them having a "man bashing" evening soon to which would placate her friend.

Mila tuned back into Lido.

"Okay, Mila. I'll see Yasmin this Tuesday and Thursday. Have fun, be safe *walaashay yar*. You can go, as long as you come back."

Mila smiled as her sister rubbed her shoulder. "Of course." She held the door to the Edwards Cinema. No matter what happened in this life, Lido could do nothing without her sisters. That's why Mila quickly waved when Yasmin turned around at the ticket counter.

"You invited that—"

"Lido," Mila stressed, arm still interlocked with her sister. "I double dare you to show your ass for no reason tonight. Besides, you agreed that Yasmin's gonna attend the AA meetings with you. You can't speak with your sister now, but at those meetings you have to be wide open."

"Hmph, all I'm saying is, I didn't think the girl could go out after dark. At least not without Faaid." Lido grimaced as Mila pinched her. "Oh, speak of the devil."

"Yasmin's husband is going to be in a whole nother movie theater. Don't you forget what I said." Mila plastered a smile across her face. Her tone rose a few octaves as she let Lido go to hug her sister and brother-in-law.

"Thank you for inviting me, *walaashay yar*. I could never pass up an Angela Bassett film." Yasmin planted a kiss on her little sister's cheek.

"It's going to be good." With a raised eyebrow to Lido, as emphasis, Mila reached for Faaid as her two older sisters hugged.

Yasmin handed over two tickets for her sisters, and they all stepped toward the host.

"Hold up," Lido said, "I need Milk Duds, Twizzlers, something."

"The skinniest one," Yasmin shook her head.

"Who you telling? You stay slim even after the kids. I have to work hard as hell," Mila said. "Now Blake has me hiking up to the darn Hollywood sign and all, so my body isn't even trying to feel the half-ass workouts I've always done."

"How is Blake?" Yasmin asked as they stepped toward the concession stand. She and Mila stood back as Lido got into the long line.

Noticing her sister staring intently she said, "… He's good."

"Oh, Mila, tell me about him. I won't bite."

Anchored in her heels, Mila slipped her hands in her back pockets, as if exposing herself to her sister when all she wanted to do was keep mum. "I know."

They'd been doing more chatting as of recent. Yasmin had been a shoulder to lean on each time Mila and Lido attempted a new AA meeting across Southern California.

"You're glowy, you're happy, Mila. By association, I'm happy too."

Mila watched as a large bucket being filled with buttery popcorn at Lido's request. Yasmin wrapped an arm around her waist, pulling her closer. "*Walaashay yar, Waxaan ku faraxsanahay inaan idin arko* —Little sister, I'm happy to see you."

Tears burned her eyes. Yasmin kissed her cheek again telling her how happy she was for the trio to be together. And that she loved her baby sister no matter what.

"Stop crying, Mila." Yasmin smiled. But she really didn't understand. Having been at Lido's side while she detoxed and got all the horrible contaminants out of her system had been hard. There'd been no expression of gratitude on Lido's part. Blake had offered so many times the best luxurious detox spa vacations. But, no, Mila needed to be at her sister's side. Mila exhaled deeply as Yasmin rubbed her arm.

"C'mon," her eldest sister said, gingerly, "You're happy, so I gotta be happy. I'll be good. As long as I get to meet Blake… soon is preferred over later."

Mila's head bobbed once more as she smiled through tears.

"Will the two of you quit?" Lido walked past them with a big bucket of popcorn, large soda, and candy dangling from the pockets of her short chinchilla coat.

Yasmin's face twisted slightly, yet for her youngest sister's sake, she said nothing to the narcissistic Lido.

~~~

A few days later, as Mila carted her canvas Louis V luggage toward the front door, she heard the loud shuffling sounds of Lido above. She rolled her eyes. *Veronica please take her ass back home,* Mila grumbled to herself.

After a quick peck on Blake's cheek, Mila handed her duffel bag to the limousine driver.

"We gotta get the hell out of here," Mila told Blake as she got into the back of the limo.

"All right, baby, you ready for a surprise?"
~~~

"Babe, you could take me to Motel 6 down the street, I'd be good. Lido is just…"

"Where's your other sister? I know we're all supposed to get together when we return. But isn't she going to watch Lido?" Blake slipped into the limo beside her.

"No." Mila shook her head. "That psycho can watch herself." She took a deep breath then added, "Yasmin's youngest got chicken pox. To top it off, did you see the Metrolink crash on the news? Faaid will be working overtime rerouting the systems and whatever else he does. Lido acted a plum-fool this morning…"

Blake gave her the eye as she spoke. They had learned to read each other. She was attempting to explain all the reasons she should leave.

"Damn, you, Blake." She sunk deeper into the buttery leather, head falling back. "I told that diva I wouldn't fail her. But I'm not my sister's keeper. I'm being selfish."

"No," Blake said in between kissing her lips, "I like the way you're talking things out, Mila," he added, his mouth adorning the sweet taste of hers. "But…"

"I hate that word. But." She grinned as he continually bestowed smooches on her lips. "*But*, I need you to take me so very far away from here, Blake. I want that famous backrub of yours that gets better when you walk away."

They chuckled, his warm breath tickling her cheek.

"Better, Mila?" Blake arched a perfect eyebrow.

She measured with her index finger and thumb. "Just a tad. But absence makes the heart grow founder. So when you return, you blow my mind, if that's any consolation."

"Nah. Can't say that I'm placated."

As Blake leaned into her, Mila said, "Well, that's okay anyway. The massages aren't for you, they're for me. God, I can just remember the way you loved my body when we were in Tokyo. Whatever you had to run off to do, you were so intense, so aggressive afterwards."

Blake endeavored to keep his mind from Lola as he scented the sex on his woman. While Mila reminisced on the hard fuck, he recalled the strawberry blonde that took shots at his status.

"We should be able to go on vacation by the end of the week. I don't know how long chicken pox last. That trick has threatened to drink. Blake, you are so damn good to me."

His hand reached into her blouse. He began to palm her breast. "Yes, I am."

"Don't be egotistical," she bit her lip.

"Don't bite *my* lip," he said, reaching over to do the trick for her. Blake grabbed his woman by the waist and pulled her around until she was straddling him. "We are going to postpone this engagement, Mila. Albeit, my recompense will cost you immensely."

"Mmmm, so I'm damned if I do, damned if I don't?" Mila ground her pelvic bone against his cock. "Guess, I'll be brushing up on my stretching before the festivities begin?"

They had a quickie before Mila got out of the car and went back into the house of horrors.

CHAPTER 33

Grand Canyon, Arizona

THE WARM BEER had Isaac ready for any hot bed. He downed his mug of beer, then patted Blake's shoulder as they sat at the bar in the resort. "B, that ass right there," he said with a sigh, "I'm hitting that tonight."

Blake chuckled softly. That had been the usual ending of a day when they were young. He gulped down his own mug of beer and nodded toward the Latina in the tightest jeans known to mankind. "That's all you, bro. You just be ready to climb in the morning, no walking trail bullshit, but a climb."

Isaac nodded, his eyes already on his target.

"Bourbon, premium, triple," Blake told toward the bartender.

The shaggy haired man nodded, and right on time, Blake's drink was set before him. A woman with creamy white skin, dressed in a purple wrap skirt which clung to every athletic curve, claimed Isaac's seat.

Blake tipped up his drink. "See now, you got me drinking a real man's drink. Only a woman."

She sighed softly. "Glad I have that effect on you."

"Oh, boy, not only that, shit. You have me …" he physically glanced over his shoulder with a hard chuckle.

She matched his laughter, but his was contrite, the purple-eyed woman's was triumphant. "Hahaha, I make you paranoid? Well, that's exactly what happens when a female has to chase a man." Her fingers walked along the shoulder of Blake's blazer.

The bartender snuck subtle glances his way, not because he knew the tips would be good, but because the woman was such a vision. She leaned over, giving a perfect view of her perky cantaloupes. Her pink tongue glided across a pleasing bottom lip. "Blake, I'm dog-shit tired of being avoided… Your room or mine?"

~~~

"You still fooling around with that fly honey?" Isaac wedged his hand into another ridge. The sweltering sun baked his back while he pulled himself up slowly. "I'm having a problem carrying a conversation, Blake slow the fuck down."

"Bet if there were bullets flying toward your ass you'd be on one." Blake laughed, his footing digging into the grooves of the side of the Grand Canyon. He readjusted his pace for the man who grew up with him like a brother. "And yes, Mila is mine for always."

Isaac looked up.

"Bro," Blake began to admonish, "How the fuck are we going to take big-boy climbs, if you want to—"

"Nah, don't compare me to any broads. I tried to have this chat with you last night at the bar." Isaac pulled himself onto the ridge, then turned and sat back. The sight before him was breathtaking. He began to catch his breath, and his hand went to his side as he asked, "Why the fuck aren't you breathing hard?"
~~~

Blake shrugged.

"Now," Isaac panted, "Before I was rudely interrupted I was saying, Mila's a very sweet girl..."

"Bro, your statement of 'sweet' is just a code word for too good for me."

"Yeah, that's right. No doubt she's fine as hell. But how is she going to take learning about Warren's murder? I know you aren't going to tell her about the *dead* chick in Tokyo or the hacker that Lamb handled, but her fiancé. C'mon dude. B, you always keep it one hundred, even with that—what does Zenobia call your wife?"

They both paused to chuckle, reminiscing when Blake was young, dumb, and hypnotized by the scene. Blake rubbed his forearm on the stream of sweat dripping down his forehead and began to arise. "Just keep up, bro. You don't got it like I do yet, as far as climbing goes. We can chat about all that later..."

Though they'd grown up thick as thieves, Blake didn't tell Isaac about the deaths surrounding his business just because. He needed to get that shit off his chest. He hated keeping things from Mila, but this was one secret that he would have to guard. The whole situation revolved around his business, and Isaac was the only soul who wouldn't say a word.

~~~

Nine days later, a servant made arrangements for Blake and Mila to leave. Lamb had gone to retrieve Mila and her things since Blake had a few business essentials to square away. He stood in the sitting room of his glasshouse, Bluetooth glued to his ear.
~~~

"Baldwin," his assistant said through the receiver, "I've left a few portfolios on your desk for Tom's replacement. Nobody's been able to find him."

Blake took a deep breath. Ever since Todd had gone missing, there were no issues with hackers. He had no qualms with micromanagement when it came to his multi-billion-dollar company. He had yet to pick up the portfolios to review potential candidates for Tom's position.

"I'll critique the potentials when I return from—" Blake paused as a servant stood before him.

"You'll be out of the country for weeks, Baldwin, Baldwin..." The assistant hissed.

Blake addressed the maid. "Yes?"

"Miss Taylor has arrived."

His mind went to Lamb. He'd sent his most trusted cohort to ensure Mila's safety from this very person. The lady with lilac eyes! Why didn't she get the picture? Females like Cynthia fucking Taylor had a one-track mind. Her sights were locked onto him.

"Send her away," he ordered. Then back to the phone he said, "I've an entire team that I trust, these days. Since Tom's... departure, I've weeded through—"

Once again, Blake was interrupted. This time the olive-skinned, lilac eyed beauty walked into the room. Miss Taylor's stilettos resonating off the wood floor, a white blazer brought his focal point to her wide hips. "Send me away, Blake? So it has come to this?"

"Well, Cynthia, try calling sometimes, figure out if I give a damn about seeing you." Blake snatched the Bluetooth from his eardrum to jiggle it around in her face.

Cynthia Taylor's stance was menacing. "You enjoy playing me off, so we need to get a few things straight."

Blake glared at his servant, who nodded. There was an unspoken idea between the two as Cynthia began to complain. Mila was due to arrive any minute, so he had to get rid of this woman first.

"Let's go for a walk," Blake said.

"The scene is tranquil I'll give you that." Cynthia glanced outside the glass walls. "But give me a little more credit, Blake. The magazines have to be *killing* your wife these days with the way you gallivant around with that cute Somalian. You don't want *Mila*," Cynthia sighed the name, "to know about me? C'mon I saved you after the Warren mess."

Blake rubbed at the stubble across his chin.

"Your accountant was murdered. His last call was to your voicemail, and I quote: 'Blake, it appears your investments are tied up with some sort of high ranking Middle East terrorist.' You and your right hand Lamb have done a good job sweeping up the pieces. Shall I bring up that cute little mistress of Warren's? Lola? But I got the ball rolling. Besides, you frequent the Middle East for Gorges du Todra and Gay Ben Hinom..." She paused, head cocked in thought. "Amongst other mountains you've climbed or activities you've dabbled in. So who's to say you aren't such a bad guy? A terrorist."

The way she said *dabbled* made it seem like he'd been on a cannibalistic rampage every time his feet touched foreign soil.

"So, Blake. I've invested in you, way too long," Cynthia's voice dripped with emotion. "*We* need to talk."

She plopped down onto the antiquated settee, arms lingering over the headrest.

As they chatted, Blake received a text from Lamb.

I saw that fucking purple eyed hottie's Mercedes Jeep in the driveway and have Mila in your room waiting.

Blake slipped his cell phone back into his pocket.

"Cute," Cynthia shook her head. "The male species. Did your little renegade cop acquire a coloring book and crayons? Keep the little mistress somewhere safe while we chat." Cynthia's eyes roamed to the ceiling as if she knew exactly where Mila was…

~~~

Torrents of pleasure conjured a moan that weaved past Mila's parted pearly teeth, caressing her crimson-matte lips. The fucking glorious sound of it made his shaft miraculously continue to grow. Mila had that effect on him, even when he'd just parted ways with the likes of Cynthia Taylor.

"I haven't had a taste in over a week, Mila." Blake molded the tautness of her slender lower back. She was naked from ass up, the glow from the fireplace, that would otherwise be the focal point in such a grand bedroom, set fire to her beautiful ebony skin tone. One of her arms draped over the side of the chaise, a diamond tennis bracelet twinkled. As his hands roamed around, capturing and reworking the tension in her back, he said, "My beautiful Mila. Why so tense?"
~~~

Again, only a groan escaped that pleasing little mouth of hers, that always seemed to be more useful framing his cock. His hands stopped at the small of her back, looming just at the vale. Before they could push away the linen of her lower half and blaze up those beautiful mounds of ass, Mila sprang into a seated position.

One slender hand gripped the linen, not before he eyed a delightful chocolate breast. He clamped his perfect teeth, wanting to nip at her hardness. Those lush lips of hers curved into a teasing grin.

"Blake, I thought all of this," Mila waved her hand, "was for me."

"Of course."

Mila arched an eyebrow, giving life to an already flawlessly structured face. Dark marble orbs for eyes, that would otherwise be a warm ginger if happy and not in such a seductive state. She wanted it. He wanted it. So he said, "There's no such thing as me touching you," Blake looked at his large hands. They'd molded her to his perfection. *He* had molded his woman into perfection, outside and in. Outside? With his hands of course, his love, his attending to her needs. Inside? Well, his cock had fashioned her wet, inner folds into utter transcendence. He'd reworked the stunner, making Mila *his*.

"Granted, there is no you touching me without fucking me, Blake, my neck hurts." Mila's tone twined around his soul as she rubbed at her neck. The movement made the linen fall. It wouldn't do to prove her right, but Blake licked his lips when the flimsy covering allowed him a glimpse of her breast again.

Mila's eyes switched from their dark liquid lust back into warm orbs of chocolate, so Blake chose not to make a move. She'd had a hard day.

Mila picked up her glass of Pinot from the marbled floor and she leaned back with a sigh. That damn sigh gave rise to his dick, but she'd had a long day, so he complied to her need to talk.

Blake asked what he could do for her. A top row of white teeth, clamped down on her plump bottom lip as Mila ruminated. The act tensed his entire body once more. Blast, his woman had learned to acquire control. She'd gone from docile yet opinionated to headstrong and *still* so very motherfucking opinionated. These past two weeks even, she'd grown without him. The stress of taking care of her sister had made the exquisite Mila even wiser. Wisdom was the personification of beauty.

Mila moved her body, lifting one thick thigh to straddle his waist. She moved a manicured red fingernail down the taut plane of Blake's six pack.

"Let's get… married," Mila said, voice erotically tipsy.

"That would be nice," he murmured, delighting in the tender kisses that enveloped his neck as her other hand gripped the soft brown pillow of hair dusting his taut chest.

"Continue, Mila," he egged her further toward her desires while she instigated a glazing of his cock. After a while Blake was content with just the silk, wetness of her tongue gliding along his shaft.

"How about Chateau Veaux le Vicomte?" She leaned up, crossed her arms lazily over his chest. "Might as well solidify the truth."

"What truth is that?" He asked, enraptured by this gumption.

"You belong to me."

Blake's haughty chuckle sent coils of desire down her body. He clutched the hair at the nape of her neck. He was just about done with allowing her a walk along his back. "Mila, that's where you are wrong. You, my dear, are my possession."

He flipped her back around, allowing Mila to straddle him from behind. Blake leaned forward, hands grazing over the hair streaming down her back. He pushed those tresses to her shoulder, kissing a trail down her spine. Since they were seated reverse cowgirl style, he stopped at where her bra-line would meet. Then his hands moved down.

Blake's hands wove a trail down to those two large mounds that graced his lap. Mila's back arched, giving him incentive.

His fingers plunged into her asshole, sending a melodic groan into the atmosphere. Deftly, Blake took her down to the floor, on her knees. With him on his knees behind her. Mila's breath came in shards of desire. Then her exhale tinged as Blake's tongue erotically swirled and twirled in her pussy, while three fingers fucked her ass.

"Who's pussy is this?" Blake asked.

"Yours," she said, hips gyrating in his face.

Blake's tongue licked upward toward her ass, as he removed his fingers. He bit her hard on her left cheek, asking her once more.

"BLAKE, I'm yours." A sugary concoction became his goal as he explored her inner folds. He was keen to read the slight arching of her back while summoning her G spot. A hunger to lap the liquid between her thighs spurred him. There would be only this nourishing bliss until Mila forgot her request for marriage. He'd fucked up with a woman he'd grown to respect and... And... he *could never* marry her…

Finally, Mila's hands gripped the fur rug as she rode the orgasm on his face.

Her tone changed, knees and hands shaking. "Stop—"

"Don't tell me to stop," he commanded. She wanted to bask in the ambience of love. She wanted marriage, when this was not the time to ask. As her body went into a graceful arch, Blake grabbed her back up. He owned the chair, flipping her around and sinking her down on top of his cock. His woman seemed spent, but soon she'd be wide awake as he fucked her sideways…

CHAPTER 34

MILA LAY IN bed. Night engulfed the master suite of the glass house. She hadn't told him that Diane Baldwin had called. In fact, *the wife* had reached out to her on numerous occasions this past week. The calls began the day they were set to celebrate their one-year anniversary. It seemed Diane caught wind about Blake and Mila's non-departure. While Mila attended to Lido's "needs" since Yasmin dealt with a child who had the chickenpox, Diane inquired as to why Mila wasn't with *her man.*

The very moment Diane spoke after Mila said 'hello' to an unfamiliar 310-number, Mila knew it was her. Mila had thought the Los Angeles based number belonged to Veronica. Her lover's *wife's* voice strummed together like the finest silk, as if Diane had practiced and practiced and practiced how to sound seductive.

"Why aren't you island-hopping on *my husband's* yacht?" Had been Diane's very first words as Mila watched Lido purge dinner into the toilet. Lido had threatened to go back to drinking if Mila left her with Yasmin and her son. But the model had eaten like a little pig.

"Hello, Diane." Mila stepped out of the master bathroom. She'd been sleepy, and Lido had wanted to stay in the same room with her every night. Her sister was returning to an embryonic stage after acting like a toddler for all her life.

"*Diane*, hmmm. Should I appreciate you're recalling I'm Blake's wife? But you see, you and I have been so very intimate. You've licked every single inch of my husband's cock."

Mila gulped back the acrid antipathy of the woman's boldness.

"So in a sense you've eaten my pussy."

Mila's pupils almost popped. This lady was even crazier than her own sister.

"I'm supposing that I've tasted yours on occasion too. Now what should we do about that!"

The rancor of her current situation left Mila momentarily on pause. Shoulders rising slowly as Mila took a deep breath, she considered the wife's question.

"Get a divorce," the words lurched out of Mila's mouth.

"I need a drink of water," Lido shouted from the bathroom.

SLAM. Mila closed the door quickly. "Why don't you give Blake a divorce! He loves me. I love him."

"There's no question that you love him…" Diane's hard, yet captivating voice faded for a second. She had the advantage of calling, most likely rehearsing these vulgar words in her head. "It's funny. You'll be 31 in about five months. I thought Blake would choose a younger one. Prettier…"

"He chose your pasty ass, but Blake prefers my bed. So maybe you should learn a thing or two about assumptions. I'm not leaving."

That call had been on day one of ten days away from Blake. *"You are so blinded by the way he loves, Mila. Blake loves so fucking hard."* Diane had said during one of their calls. *"When Blake loves you, it is your world. The day he falls out of love with you, well, that's the day you die, Mila. I can't wait for us to be friends..."*

The words had been ominous. As if the moment Blake lost interest in Mila, the *wife*, and the *mistress* could build a partnership. Between Diane calling, holding her sister's hand or helping her purge, Mila barely survived.

She felt so dumb after asking to marry him. There'd been not one peep in the news about Blake and Diane. Over the past year, the media had run rampant each time Blake and Mila went across seas, as far as Tokyo. Diane had never called. Never showed interest. *Did Diane and her lover just have a falling out? Blake is mine.*

Now she cuddled closer to him. She decided they needed to postpone the vacation, though her body needed it. Tomorrow she'd ask Blake if they could wait a while longer. For now, she needed to present a strong front when it came to Diane Blake. The bitch must've broken up with the pool boy or whatever Blake had told her the day they first fucked. She wouldn't have slept with him otherwise. For now, she'd introduce Blake to her family. He'd already let her into his life when it came to Isaac and Zenobia. Over the past few months, she felt like she knew his Aunt Serenity even though she'd never met her. Yes, she was prepared to set the foundation for Blake being a constant in her life. Even though Diane claimed she would never extract her claws. One day, maybe not too soon, Blake would divorce Diane, and marry her...

CHAPTER 35

MILA ONCE AGAIN requested that they postpone celebrating their one-year anniversary, saying that Yasmin may need Faaid's help with the kids, especially while dealing with the grown, yet so very childish, Lido. Those were the same sacrifices Aunt Serenity made when it came to his own mother, and two extra mouths to feed.

Tonight they were to meet Mila's oldest sister's family for dinner. When he arrived at Mila's home, Lido opened the door.

"Oh, it's you…" Her voice was thick with animosity. "You're in trouble."

His eyes glowered at the woman who seemed bent on sponging up hate. He'd thought it was all the drinking at first, but now Blake realized there was something more.

"So you're cheating on my sister?"

"My relationship with Mila has nothing to do with you." And that's all he would say to her.

That gave rise to a tiny chuckle. If the shoe was on the other foot, Isaac and Zenobia would laugh it off, too. One family member is hurt, everyone takes shots. But she wasn't like Isaac or Zenobia, as the trio had each other's greatest interest at hand while younger. On the other hand, what had *he* done?

Mila descended the staircase slowly, dressed in a silk nightgown that glided across her curves. She wasn't dressed for the pending party, nor was the house clouded with any scents of the feast she'd promised to prepare. There was a magazine in her hand. On the front page there were two photos, with one of the greatest pitches ever: Love triangle? However, the triangle had been amplified. The left side was a photo of Blake and Mila through the window of Cartier's. The other was a recent photo of Blake with his wife Diane. Smack dab in the middle, was Blake with Cynthia Taylor in New York.

"One week you're giving… hold up," Mila turned the pages, "'Blake bestowed his mistress with an *engagement* ring at Cartier's.' Okay, we both know that's inaccurate. But this is you, right? The story says that we postponed our anniversary. Day one you were with a good friend—I can only assume it was Isaac from the description. You went climbing." Mila nodded. "Okay, th-that's okay, isn't it? Guy bonding time. Then you and Diane went to a gala just two days ago. That's you, no doubt getting ready to fuck *your wife* while I take care of my sister? Actually don't answer that question, even though it's clearly you in the tux—you look fine as hell, might I add. But I don't have the right to ask you about *your wife!*"

"Mila, c'mon, you're second best. You already know." Lido continued toward the living room of the house. "Oh wait a minute, third best now." Her giggle was loud, voice muffled. "*Walaashay yar*, you missed the best part!"

"Okay, Mila don't listen to that bullshit. You're so fucking important to me." Blake started up the steps. Her sister was a bitch, and clearly just inciting Mila's emotions. Then Mila mentioned what the magazine dubbed the mysterious woman with gorgeous amethyst eyes.

"No, I'm not shit; right? Just some stupid ass mistress! Another magazine dubbed the mysterious Misses Violet is the most exotic of us all. But the author doubts that you'll end up with any of us... Look, they had a behavioral psychologist provide insight." Voice hoarse from crying and screaming, Mila exclaimed, "Do you know how *stupid* you've made me? I use to like and repost comments about cheaters. One in particular comes to mind: you can't be in a relationship with a married man! You said you're separated from Diane! That's a fucking lie, isn't it?"

"I *am* separated."

She ignored the lie. "While I was helping my sister, you were fucking your wife and another slut. You know what, I can't be this stupid! I honestly can't be this fucking dumb. So you and your wife have an open relationship..."

"No, I was mountain climbing."

"Sure." She tried to throw the magazine at his face.

"Mila, listen to me, honey."

"Honey?" Those forest green orbs blazed through her heart. The *smack* echoed across the room. His chest rose and fell. Again Mila's hand raised for a strike. She wanted him to feel her wrath. To hurt as badly as she did. Instead, her forearms pressed into his body as she went weak.

Blake's arms swooped down, taking her into a hug. A bear hug.

The kind that a friend or lover gives. But in her mind, Blake wasn't her friend or anywhere close to being in love with her. A silent shudder wracked her body.

"Let me make it up to you, baby."

Her weak legs gave way as he scooped her into his arms, cradling her to a pounding, anxious heart.

Blake lay Mila down on a feather duvet, her heavy, exhausted body sinking into the heavenly cloud.

"Just leave me." A thread of will came out in a murmur.

Greedy as he was, Blake ignored her plea. He knew he should take things slowly as she brought up the contradiction of Diane cheating with "the pool boy." She didn't want to believe that his wife could cheat on him. In Mila's mind, he was too greedy for a cheating wife. All the fingers pointed to him. But he had no time to take it slow, to explain to Mila the error in her overthinking. Blake secured her gown. No bra on, her breast held the only bits of life as they sat perkily.

"I don't want you." Her words sunk deeper into his flesh than any previous hits.

"Don't deny me, Mila. I'll explain." He closed his eyes to her sobbing. Then down on his knees he went. There were no more utterances of abhorring him so he gripped firm, yet sensual thighs and slid her body toward the edge of the bed. His mouthwatering at just the sight of Mila's tight, little pussy. The creamy folds glistening, traitor to her prior words and acts of indignation.

Just as his lips were to meet the only ones that pleased him without argument, Mila struck once more. “This all I’m good for?”

The hardness of her tone was deafening.

“You fuck me first, then explain,” she inquired. “Or you fuck me then *never* actually get to the point of my enlightenment… Blake, how does this go?”

Mila’s legs clammed shut, and she sat up. “I’m bare to you, Blake. So damn bare to you, right now. Funny, how I actually considered you a walking dildo when we first met. You were supposed to be just a fuck. Perhaps once, twice, shit, you had me moaning until my lungs were raw that one night. I should have thrown away the billionaire! But even through the blur of my tears, I see that purple-eyed slut! Now instead of just sizing myself up against *your wife,* I have to compare myself to a nameless woman too?”

“Mila, right now too many thoughts are roaming through your mind.”

“Yeah… so I’m crazy then? The photos aren’t real the magazine is a fake?”

“I’m *not* cheating on you with Cynthia Taylor, shit, that’s the woman with the purple eyes.” He leaned back on his heels. They were eye level, with her seated on the edge of the bed, naked, and him on the floor.

She shook her head. “There’s a part of me, my heart, it just wants to believe every single word that comes out of that mouth. But then again, I’m biased toward that mouth.”

Their gazes collided. Blake knew she believed him about

Cynthia, even if he hadn't started to explain. It was in those chocolate brown eyes that she needed to believe him. But he wasn't able to explain at this very moment.

"And your wife, Blake have you been fucking your wife?" Mila chuckled at the ludicrousness of her question.

CHAPTER 36

IN AN INSTANT, Blake admitted to sleeping with Diane Baldwin a few times over the past year. *Shouldn't that be enough? Shouldn't that make me run?* Which was the worst situation? His wife or the exquisite purple eyed woman?

Cynthia. Taylor. Mila could google the woman at this very second, yet feel as if she still didn't know much about her. Besides, Blake blatantly denied any relations with Miss Taylor.

"So you have something to tell me, Blake?" She asked, the river full of tears had ceased to flow. Her head pounded, the after-effects of so much raw emotion for him.

He sat on the accent chair next to the bed. They both seemed to be staring into oblivion outside the balcony. A few minutes ago, she proposed that the two just part ways. Call it quits. Again, she opened her mouth to give Blake the easy way out of this circumstance.

"Mila, let's have the dinner with your family. Later, I'll explain everything to you."

She nodded as a heavy weight anchored her heart.

Everything. There was more to the story than the arbitrary article she'd picked up. She almost laughed at the look on the cash register lady's face when glancing at the magazine and then at her, when she and Lido went grocery shopping this morning.

But again, everything… *How much more can I take?*

"All you gotta do is return to your wife, or *Cynthia* or whoever the fuck you want, Blake."

His fist boomed down onto the end table, making the lamp jump. "Fuck that. Like I said, tonight, after all is said and done, you'll have the absolute truth. No more half assed attempts. There are somethings I've done, some regrets…"

"Like fuck your wife?" Mila scoffed. Round and round again, she continued to return to the same conclusion. *How have I put myself into this situation?*

She looked over at the clock. Evening descended fast. Yasmin's family was due in another hour or so. She wanted to call off the party. Was Blake Baldwin, or Brendan Walker rather, the man her mind had conjured as *the one*? Did his heartbeat coincide with hers? Was… this… love?

For a nanosecond, Warren pervaded her mind. They would've made the perfect man and wife. If he'd been Somalian, and reared in her hometown, there'd be no doubt that father would have chosen him as her husband. There'd have been no heart tug of war because Warren always heeded her as an equal.

"The rest of your family will be here soon, Mila. Should we just cater?" Blake stood from the bed and she from the chair.

Like small grains of sand, time was virtually ungraspable. She wanted to get back into Blake's arms, but the distance between the them now, she was forced to realize that she didn't trust him. Then there was that one night a few weeks back when Blake came to her home, seemingly so weighed down. Who was that Blake? And Brendan Walker. Brendan reminded her of Warren. Easygoing. Trustworthy. He was the type of man she could marry, and unlike Warren, she could fall for him…

"I'm going to check on Lido, to see if she took the initiative to start the curry sauce," Mila spoke, doubting every syllable. These past few weeks were tiring. Dealing with Lido's alcohol addiction. The calls from Diane. The magazine allowed her current status to solidify. *Mistress.*

Blake went to the master bathroom to use the restroom. So she started down the hallway, ears perked at a familiar masculine tone emanating from the entry way. Oh, God no. Not Keith.

"… Faaid invited me over. He said it was a family function this evening."

Then Lido's reply, "Well, keep your funky ass wine, Keith. My sister already has one no good bastard no need for another one."

"Is it that fucking Baldwin guy?"

"Wouldn't you like to know."

From Mila's angle as she quietly walked down the stairs, her eyes narrowed. Their interaction was a tad off. When they were around each other, the steel nails were extracted on Lido's part. The Nike's were laced to run on Keith's. Yet, Mila remembered cooking dinner for Lido and Veronica right around the time she was having issues paying the mortgage. Lido had answered the phone, there'd been some sort of exchange between the two…

At this moment, Keith's voice seemed to be filled with the same demons that plagued Lido's. "You're comfy here, Lido, with your shoes off. You go after him like you went after me, Lido?"

"Maybe... he's better." Lido seemed to dawdle on her bare heels as her back came into Mila's view.

"Damn, I'm so glad I only fucked you once."

"Hmph. I don't recall fucking you at all. Now Blake," Lido sighed the name. "He's so..."

"Now BLAKE what?" Mila shouted. Her sister's entire body convulsed as Mila descended the last step. Lido turned around. Keith even appeared shocked.

"Mila, babe," Blake's voice traveled from outside her bedroom as he started toward her. He began to mention catering...

All hell broke loose...

Lido started to explain that she'd slept with Keith when they were all in college. She'd wanted to tell her little sister that the asshole wasn't worth it. Keith shrugged, as if not deeming himself as a pawn in the least. But Mila couldn't give a fuck about the two. Her eyes bore into Blake's.

"Blake, you fucked my sister too?" Mila glanced back and forth from Lido to her boyfriend.

Lido held her head high, not saying one word. Then she sashayed her hoeing ass up the stairs. "Mila, you're having too many boy problems. That's why I stick with pussy!"

Mila's eyelid twitched as her sister's slender shape disappeared down the hall.

Blake stood before her. Instead of losing herself in that forest gaze, Mila glared at Keith. He turned around and vanished along the pathway, leaving the front door wide open. For a second, Mila closed her eyes, taking a deep breath before staring at Blake.

"Let's go back upstairs, we need to talk, Mila."

How had she put herself into this situation? Climbing the corporate ladder at a conglomerate like Hewitt, she had been ballsy. Mila regrouped, gesturing toward him.

"If you were human, not some super rich, blue-blooded billionaire, you'd know this is the fucking part where you *a-polo-gize*, Blake."

That smoldering glare of his almost popped. Blake rubbed a hand over his face. "C'mon, Mila, you aren't even receptive to anything I fucking have to say! I love you–"

"Fuck your love, Blake!" Before Mila could think, she swiped a blue milk glass vase with long stemmed lilies across the marble floor. "So when did you sleep with my sister? I saw you staring at her at that gala. Staring all hard while Lido strutted up and down the catwalk. The warning signs damn near railroaded me, yet I let you back into my heart."

His eyes stayed locked onto her, even as the glass shattered on the floor. "Shit! Just let me explain."

"Let you explain! Is that your version of 'I'm sorry,' which is a shorter phrase, I must say. Even now, Blake. Even earlier." She stuttered. "Just learning that you're cheating on me with your wife. Oh boy, I'm so sure you probably slept with Cynthia too! What the fuck is wrong with me? You know what, since you can't utter the most significant word, an apology, I don't want to hear anything you have to say. Just get out!"

"*Earlier*, Mila, I told you that we had a few issues to address." Blake's jaw clinched as Mila headed for the door. His strong, thick arm wrapped around her waist, pulling her against Blake's chest. "Wait, there's glass all over the fucking floor–"

"Let me go," Mila shouted. She wrestled out of his arms, drawing blood on the back of one of Blake's hands. Then her hand lashed out to slap him across the face.

Stock still, he stood there. The slap had reverberated against the walls, so loud, so hard. "Mila if I leave now, I won't come back."

"*Don't* come back." Her gaze stayed just to the left of his broad shoulders. Chest heaving, Mila waited, staring so hard at the gray swirls in the marble, her vision blurred. Or perhaps that was the tears.

At the crunching sound of glass, Mila concluded this was the end.

Standing in the foyer, Diane's words swarmed through her mind: *"When Blake loves you, it is your world. The day he falls out of love with you, well, that's the day you die."*

Yes, he had become her world. But forget dying over a broken heart. *This motherfucker slept with my sister, I will not let this take me down.* Mila sunk onto the stairs, head in her hands. Every fiber of her being was numb.

The front doors flew wide open when her two rowdy nephews ages 5 and 7 came rushing into the house.

"Auntie Mila," they both said as Yasmin started inside with Faaid, holding an 85 Degrees Bakery bag full of goodies. They eyed the broken glass on the floor.

"Kids, watch your step, go into the playroom please," their mother said. As the boys began in a sprint, Yasmin shouted, "And don't throw any of those pool balls off the table."

"I'll take these into the kitchen." Faaid held up the bag. He gave Yasmin a glance. "I'll get a broom too."

Yasmin sat on the stairs next to her sister, rubbing her back and hugging her tightly as Mila said not one word. Faaid finished sweeping up the glass, then mumbled about ordering pizza.

Yasmin began to hum one of Somali songstress, Hibo Nurra's songs that their mother played when the girls were little. The nostalgic melody relaxed Mila's heart. Her tears soon vanished as she began to sniffle.

Lido sauntered down the stairs in a tiny pair of jeans and a shirt, a designer duffel bag over her shoulder. "'Scuse me."

"Where the heck are you going?" Yasmin asked baffled.

"I just said *excuse* me, goodness! FYI, Mila kicked me out! As if my grown ass can't hoof it alone."

"Oh no, you're not leaving," Mila shook her head as her sister bounded down between the girls. Lido spun around, glaring. Mila stood up. "Take your things back upstairs, so *us* sisters can have a talk."

Yasmin's clouded gaze went back and forth between the two.

"Let's go." Mila took the duffel bag from Lido.

Lido grumbled, stomping back upstairs, with the oldest behind her.

"You're too old for this behavior," Yasmin said.

In the room, Yasmin asked for an update as the three took to different corners of the large bedroom. Mila stood at the sliding glass door, looking at the tranquil ocean. Lido lay across her bed, tapping her thumbs against her iPhone as if her current text conversation was of the utmost importance.

Yasmin leaned against the doorframe. "Somebody speak!"

"I'm moving back home soon," Mila blurted, eyes glued to mother nature. She could feel Lido begin to tense, while internally fighting a triumphant smile.

"Yeah, I'm leaving you." Mila turned around slowly to glare at her sister. "I'll see Yasmin on all major holidays. Faaid goes to see his family too, so Yasmin and I will always stay in touch."

"Mila…" the oldest stressed, aware of this tactic. Lido's worst fear was being alone. "For too many years, we've been at odds with each other. I take most of the blame, but we need to band together. We're sisters."

"Yes, *we* are." Mila eyeballed Yasmin.

"*All of us are sisters,*" Yasmin tried again.

Lido sucked in a breath. "Quit that. You're happy, Yasmin. This is what you do, Yas-min, you wait until everything eventually works in your favor. You got your kid sister back. *Your Walaashay yar* has been returned." Lido gave a mock smile. "I'm left out in the cold. This is how life was meant to play out for me."

A creepy chuckle took hold of Mila. "Only in this damn world does everything have to revolve around that whore! I told Clarissa, before any of my sisters about the grants I've been approved for to open up the resource center. I put all of that on hold to attend group meetings. Far and wide, Lido."

Yasmin's feet seemed to shift. This was not right. The scenario playing before them was all wrong. She and Lido would go blow-for-blow; Mila was the mediator. "Where's Blake, Mila?"

Silence…

"We're here to meet the love of your life. Let's go eat." She patted Mila's back, only to receive a cold shoulder. "Congratulations, *walaashay yar.* We chatted earlier about the resource center. Tell us the plans over dinner. Food, drinks, it will be good. Even skinny-minny Lido likes to eat," Yasmin said with a feeble grin. None of her sisters seconded her attempts. "I've had a very bad day. I had to deal with these kids this afternoon, so I would like a full belly of food and wine. We can have this sordid chat later, sisters."

The large guest room was engulfed in silence. Yasmin took a step backwards, toward the door.

"No need to chat later, Yasmin, Lido. I'm going home…" Mila finally said as the three continued their askew triangle. Come hell or high water, she would return to Ethiopia. She wanted to leave Blake for good. And she sure as hell wanted Lido to know that there'd be no more sisterly bonding.

Running away or however it was considered, she had to leave

them in her wake. But…

“Is that why Veronica broke up with you?” The question flew out of Mila’s mouth.

Lido continued to type on her cell phone. Now her left foot fidgeted incessantly.

“Veronica seemed to be trying to tell me something for a while… Was it because of… Lido, do not ignore me!” Mila started for her, but Yasmin blocked her path. Mila held up her hands in surrender, then when her eldest sister’s guard was down, she reached around and snatched up the cell phone. It went summersaulting toward the sliding glass door.

“Hey, I was scheduling a facial!” Lido shouted.

Like a blowfish, Yasmin’s cheeks puffed up as she took a deep breath. The two eldest always went toe-to-toe. She wasn’t even versed on Lido’s latest misdeeds, but she held in a plethora of disappointment, anger, and more. “A *facial*, *really*, Lido? Mila’s visibly shaken. There was some sort of altercation by the front door. You’ve been living in her home for a while now. Can we support her?”

“Hell yes.” Lido nodded, fluffing her pillow. “I’ll support her by using *her* iPhone to call AT&T! I’ll sit on the line for God knows how long so that bitch can buy me a new phone!”

Mila took out her phone. “Okay, you know what. Allow me to do everything. But by the end of the week, you need to have your bags packed. I am leaving you for good, Lido.”

“But … I’ve … just tried to leave.” Her bottom lip puckered out.

Mila rubbed the tension at the back of her neck. "I'm guessing that's all you have to say. But don't worry, I forgive you, Lido. So don't go into a nosedive believing everyone is out to hate on you. You've dug this grave. When you're ready to get out…" Mila held out a hand.

Her sister vehemently stared at the show of clemency, tears trickling down dewy skin. "I don't need your help, Mila. You're my fucking *walaashay yar*, I'm not your little ass sister! I'll never have regrets."

Mila's eyes squeezed shut. Spine rigid, she started out of the bedroom with Yasmin at her heels.

"What did she do?"

"Slept with Blake."

Her eldest sister's warm brown skin tone paled as her eyes widened. "Oh, Mila…. I… So you're returning home, then? You're *moving* back to Ethiopia? I feel like this decision was made too quickly."

"Not really, Yasmin. It's been a long time coming…"

CHAPTER 37

Addis Ababa, Ethiopia, *One week later*

The rich soil sifted into her nostrils, sending feel-good hormones to a heart that had all but stopped beating. If she closed her eyes, this was really home. Somalia, the place where her family moved from when Mila was only eight.

At the piazza she hailed a taxi, right across from Emperor Benedict's statue on his horse. Her father's practice was closer but she went to the *merkato* first. She walked down the streets lined with stores, blending in with the people. The ambience, character, and rich aromas settled her emotions. Mila negotiated for the price of a silk shawl whilc walking through.

The blistering sun had begun to set by the time Mila stepped into the doctor's office of general practitioner Ali MD. She smiled at the few families who still sat in the lobby. Memories of being a youngster and playing with other youth at her father's medical office helped settle the worry in her gut.

"*Salam Alechem, Woizrity* Mila," a soft voice greeted her.

She turned, eyes wide, to see one of her oldest Ethiopian friends, Dinha, dressed with a hijab covering her hair. It was safe to say her friend had gotten married, though Mila didn't keep up with anyone after she moved. The two bestowed three kisses to each other's cheek, and just as Mila pulled away, she tensed.

Dinha's smile began to fade. They both turned to see Doctor Ali standing at the entrance of the lobby. A mother and child were walking out with him. The woman seemed to be thanking him, yet his response faltered as he saw Mila.

There were two more families in the lobby. Her father told one they'd be next, then let Dinha know that her daughter would be seen shortly. Then he left.

~~~

She'd stayed for almost an hour waiting for her father to finish, knowing that Mr. Ali often stayed until the lobby cleared out. But jetlag had Mila deciding to head home once the sun started to go down. Her luggage was due to arrive at her parent's place in a few minutes. She'd thought she'd timed it right, but wanted to make sure she was there to explain to her mother first.

Mila arrived at their family's modest four-bedroom home just as the courier she paid to wait had arrived.

Her mother stood on the porch, face contorted in confusion, staring at the taxi and the man taking luggage from another car. Then their eyes locked onto each other. Again, Mila's heart felt something it hadn't in seven whole days. A heartbeat. A tiny sob broke from her mother's mouth as she ran down the stairs. Mila hurried past the man up the porch steps.

They worked together, putting away Mila's modest clothing. There was no talk of when father would get home or what he would
~~~

say. She just spoke of good times with Yasmin, and her mother's eyes widened at the mention of Lido's name. The dinner table was set for three when the front door opened.

Her mother told her to stay put as she went to greet her husband. Arguing began to rise. Mila leaned against the wall, listening to the words. Hand to throat, Mila heard Mrs. Ali exclaiming an old proverb, *Dhiigaaga kuma dhaqaaqo*—Does your blood not move?

"Does your blood not move..." it was a line for injustice, said on few occasions by her mom when she was but a child. Namely, the time when they fled Somalia. Mila had begun to scream for them to stop, tears streaming while watching the woman and child outside. That very moment, Mila's mom whispered those words to her father.

As always, an anxiety of the unknown began to wash over her. Instead of succumbing, her feet began to move. She stepped back into the living room.

When Mila appeared, they stopped talking. Her mother walked away, leaving father and youngest daughter alone.

"*Aabbo*—father," Mila asked her father to hear her out.

He consented on one condition…

CHAPTER 38

Six Months Later

HE WANTED TO believe that he broke her heart to save her life... *Yeah, that's fucking bullshit*, Blake thought. But it still hurt that Mila thought he'd even consider bedding Lido, her own sister. Less than three weeks prior to whatever transpired, he'd had the traveling itinerary for his and Mila's anniversary scheduled. They were to finish off in Ethiopia. He'd meet with Mila's father, chat man to man. Not even for the sake of his and Mila's relationship; but to mend a broken father-daughter relationship.

Mila had become *his* world. Her happiness was his religion. It was time for Blake to do the right things, Mila at his side. Yet the stars hadn't aligned. The love of his life hadn't reciprocated the same beliefs.

Nope. Mila accused him of fucking her sister. The hurt in her eyes was so shocking, so vivid, even now. He took the easy way out by not telling her the truth. Now it was time to wrap up one chapter of his life.

He parallel parked off Wilshire Blvd, slammed the door, and pressed his hand against the buttons of his cream-colored suit. Then Blake conformed into the humdrum of businesspersons meandering toward the cement-gray Federal Bureau of Investigations building before him. Those purple eyes narrowed as Agent Cynthia Taylor started outside. She was dressed in a navy blue business suit, the skirt stopping at her shapely calves.

They met beneath a tree.

"Well, Mr. Baldwin, I am actually happy to see you."

"Happy? You've been the prototype for the feds, rather saucy. I should have brought along Lamb."

"Yeah, right. You keep that flashlight cop away from me." She smiled, even though they both knew his right-hand man did a tad more than he should. "Let's not get sentimental since I haven't seen you in half a year. Of course, I am the stereotypical federal agent. But call me by my true name, I'm a fucking bitch. You don't get to where I am with a fucking cat between your legs. Now you ready to get down to business?"

He rubbed the stubble of his jawline. "I stay ready."

She scoffed. "That's the understatement of the century. You've been the bane of my existence ever since I caught your rich keister and *Lamb* impeding on my investigation in Tokyo. Unlike the lovely mistress Lola, who had diamond like claws, I on the other hand, didn't have time for your shenanigans."

He chuckled. Lola was linked to Warren. She'd tried to blackmail Blake since Warren had visited her on his last business trip. Warren was going to break off the sexual relationship he had going on during travel, before marriage. Lola wasn't one to be denied. However, she'd found out about the discrepancy in his business accounts, but didn't know that the numbers had been fluffed on purpose, or that a hacker had tapped his one account that was supposedly linked to terrorist funding. And with the faulty jet going down, not to mention the life insurance company's refusal to pay after the Feds got involved, Warren was murdered on purpose. Lamb had chatted Lola up… in so many different ways. Then a few months later she was murdered by one of her sugar daddies in a totally unrelated event.

"You're in the clear," Cynthia said. "Granted you've been stubborn through this entire ordeal, I even thwarted the IRS from taking a little looksee into your company, since those fuckers can get cozy."

"Appreciated." Blake began to take a step backwards, but felt like there was more between the two.

"For fuck sakes, are you going to get your lady back? Your mistress postponed most of this investigation anyway." Cynthia shook her head. As a body analysist, she knew he was still considering it. "See, I think you were smarter when younger, as Mr. Walker. You went out on the limb, did a few illegal things as a hacker in order to commence your empire."

"You know about that?" Blake chuckled remembering his college years. Though scholarships went far for prestigious universities, he had to survive. It was also how he figured out that Todd was a part of this attempt to fuck over his business, which was one of the reasons Cynthia tolerated his involvement in the federal investigation. Todd had been rotting in jail for a while now, until the head honcho had been apprehended.

"Mila has returned to Ethiopia."

Cynthia didn't seem convinced that this was the end of their chapter. "Well… yeah, but you'll think it over for a while, don't wait too late to go see her."

CHAPTER 39

IT TOOK MILA years to ask her father about the Somali mother and son. The boy had to be at least 10 at the time, because Mila had just turned 13. That is, if they'd made it. Mila had been helping sweep the office at his practice when she brought it up. It was the first time in her life that her father was at a lack for words. Mila, the one named after "People's Love" had put more thought into her sisters, her family, and a mother and child she'd never see again, then her own chance at love. That had happened all of her life, even though the years had been good to her. Making the trek from Somalia to Ethiopia dissipate to the nether regions of her cognition. Only to be remembered during tragedy, such as the death of a man who'd promised to love her a lifetime.

For six months she'd gotten into the swing of things. Every penny from the home Mila once shared with Warren was being placed brick by brick into the resource center being built in Los Angeles, on Broadway and Manchester. It was a bittersweet time, returning to California for a few weeks in order to interview potential life coaches, part-time therapist, and other facilitators for the building.

Now, Mila's bank account didn't look too funny, but due to her father's good standing, Mila received a job at Addis International

Bank. She'd learned that Lido was the reason the two younger sisters were estranged from their father. He'd never refused to speak to them again. This disrespect had prompted their father to forbid their mother to even speak with the girls in his presence. Through all her sister's treacheries, Mila kept in touch with Lido.

Then the first day of the rest of her life lingered just around the corner. Tomorrow, she'd meet the man who would be her husband. Her father's only prerequisite was a pre-arranged marriage. Her heart was no longer numb. Her soul had blossomed, albeit not as in bloom as it once was, Mila lived. A marriage of convenience would be her saving grace.

~~~

In a gold maxi dress and navy tapered blazer, Mila watched from the back seat as the taxi passed the Lion of Juda that evening. *Who am I kidding, there's no way in hell, I will be happy choosing my man. I'm wise enough to consent to my father's wishes...*

The car lurched to a stop in front of the restaurant where she'd be meeting with family and the chosen one. Staving off the slight shake of her fingers by continuously reminding herself of the mistakes in her life, Mila pulled out enough for fare. One bejeweled flat after the other, she got out.

Dancers moved to lively music on the stage as Mila went to sit with her parents. She was late. Mostly due to nerves about meeting her father's chosen, as she'd been overzealous helping at work. Yasmin, Faaid and their children were at the table.

Everyone stood as she arrived. Colorful clay tea pots and cups
~~~

were on the table, yet they'd waited for her. She apologized for her delay, sitting between her sister and mother. The sisters whispered to each other as food began to come.

"Any words of wisdom?" Mila asked under her breath as she sipped tea. Her mother rubbed her arm sympathetically. The men carried the conversation.

Before either one could speak, a warm feeling swept over Mila's skin. Someone was staring at her. Someone as familiar as the refreshing scent of rain. Neck turning slowly, Mila scanned the crowded, festive restaurant. Tingles meandering down her spine, she hastily turned forward, causing the men's conversation to hush. She stood, mumbling something along the lines of needing to be excused. Yasmin began to rise, but Mila stopped her with a hand to her shoulder.

Mila stalked toward the exit. Right outside, Blake stood on the walkway. In an instant the plethora of emotions surging through her veins broke away. She curled her arms around her chest, then instantly let go. The movement could be construed as weak. Her balled hands went back to her sides, while her gaze slithered across him. He wore a five o'clock shadow and a cream colored suit. His scent pervaded her nostrils, along with the taste of black maple bourbon.

Thick warm honey, spice and oak… his mouth was the crux of black maple bourbon; she desired the perplexity, *him,* to slide down her throat. Yet what once was mysteriously sexy now was evasive, cold. He wasn't a dark angel of desire. This motherfucker, though sexy as sin, was the devil.

"Congratulations on breaking ground on your resource center, Mila. The People's Love Project is…"

"Why are *you* here? The Simien Mountains? just passing through?" Mila slowed the rush of her words, taking on a more blasé manner. "What are you doing here?"

"I'm here to see you."

One high heel behind the other, she backed toward the door, shaking her head.

His words were measured. "May I have a few minutes of your time?"

"Nope." Mila moved to the side as the door opened and a couple came out. The festive music spilling from inside was all wrong for this moment. She turned around to step back inside, but the door swooshed close as Blake's hands grabbed her shoulders.

"Please, Mila. Just a few minutes, for the man you fell in love with?"

"*The man I fell in love with?* Hell, no. You got questions? Hell, I got them too. Please or sorry, those aren't a part of your vocabulary."

"You asked me to apologize for Lido. I *never touched her*. Nor had I ever glanced at her in any suspect way, Mila."

Again people passed by, this time from the parking lot. Instead of following the couple into the restaurant, Mila moved toward the side of the building with Blake.

"I know you didn't sleep with Lido." Mila sighed. "It took my sister a few months, but she came clean. She always does, eventually." The snake came clean about everything. Lido had dropped her clothes in front of Blake one time when he came over during her stay. He'd been cooking dinner for Mila, unaware Lido had been home, when she entered the kitchen as naked as she was the day she was born. Lido told all, saying that Blake only told her to get dressed, and that she should tell Mila of her misdeeds. This had turned out to be the reason he started only coming late at night and leaving early in the morning. Lido had ended the conversation with "*I thought you and Blake would have talked by now. Or probably at an ob/gyn appointment. It isn't my fault you weren't smart enough to get pregnant, Mila.*"

"So how can I help you, Blake? Am I to assume you craved your mistress?"

At that very moment, the dignity Mila clung to dashed away. He'd penetrated flesh and bone. Once more, her heart was in jeopardy of Blake's manipulation.

"Mila," he annunciated every syllable, green glare holding her body in a trance, "You were *never* my mistress!"

CHAPTER 40

THE PANG OF Mila's hand across his face made him wriggle his jaw. She'd tried to fucking dislocate his spine with that slap. Before she could hit him again, he took her wrists, and snatched her to his chest. "You were never my fucking mistress, Mila. I've told you that."

"Then I was even less? I was nothing to you! Nothing at all." The overactive synapses of her mind didn't allow Mila to see the truth. The truth of his love. She had it all wrong.

"You were my woman, you were my everything. Diane and I had been separated for almost three years before I met you. During those three years we didn't see each other but maybe a few times in passing. At a gala in Texas or some sort of benefactor event. Diane came from money she's always been a socialite."

"I don't give a fuck about your wife!"

"My *ex*-wife."

"Oh God," she sighed, head tilted back. "Why the fuck is he telling me this, why is this happening to me? This day is supposed to be —"

"I dated you. I've never had a mistress, never needed one. Yes, I've dated women during the three years of Diane and my separation. She was against a divorce, while I'd been trying my damndest to leave—"

"Why? Was Diane *that* money hungry that she couldn't see it was better to leave your sorry ass?"

Fire lit Blake's eyes, but he didn't react to the low blow.

"You're just a gutter snipe from St. Louis who changed his name to come up."

"That might be true, but you're wrong about Diane and me. She cheated. I was in love with her. The day I met Diane I was so fucking in love with her. She wanted a prenuptial agreement. She was rich, I was far from making my first million. Isaac, Zennie, Aunt Serenity, they never understood what I saw in her. And damnit, Diane was much more beautiful when we met, when she was real."

Mila's glance flitted toward the sky as if in disinterest. But he knew she ate every word.

"She got the prenup. We married. Half the time, she stayed busy on spa dates or using her family name to attend benefactor events while I branched out in the social media world. We were young. I was book intelligent, fuck that, street smarts when it came to the hood. But in my own fucking home, Diane had her own bank account until my company was up and coming. Then I found out she was cheating. I was done. I didn't give a fuck about money, she could leave with half, but she didn't believe that. And moreover, through her eyes, I had matched a certain status, me being a billionaire, she wasn't going to divorce me."

"Hmmm, that sounds like the psychotic Diane I spoke with."

"You don't know the half. After our lawyers spent so much time in deliberation, with my lawyers providing iron-clad proof that she could have more than her share of my company, Diane still refused. She retreated into this fantasy world, cutting here, nipping there, tinier nose, heck, she even once asked me which eye color I preferred over her gray ones."

"All right Blake, your time is up." Mila snapped. "I have to go." A crew of people stepping into the restaurant held the door open for her.

Blake's hands went into his pocket, as he waited. She really was going to walk away, giving him no benefit of the fucking doubt. Just as she began over the threshold, Blake said, "Diane had Warren murdered."

Mila spun around, stalking back over to him as the door swooshed close. "Wow, really? Are we going to take it there?"

"The day before I met you, I went back home to Diane." Blake walked toward the side of the building so they could speak in confidence. "The feds began questioning me about calls from Warren a few hours before he got onto one of my company jets. Someone was hacking into my computer system fudging numbers. That someone was Tom."

"Tom, Clarissa's ex Tom?" Mila asked.

"Diane was using Todd to fake accountant reports, while pretending to be just some hacker trying to fuck with my business. Todd didn't know Diane was also fucking someone at TSA around the same time as Warren died."

He watched as awareness crinkled Mila's eyebrows. "Warren

was apologizing while we began to plan for our wedding. He'd tell me on a few occasions that numbers weren't adding up. That the numbers… kept changing…" Then Mila's almond eyes narrowed. "So were you screwing me to see what I knew about his mu… murder?"

"Never. Though a bit rusty in my own skills, I knew the hacking was an inside job, but I trusted Warren with every aspect of my assets, Mila. So I started to see Diane once more, Lamb began to look into her frivolous activities. Then at the funeral, I fell in love at first sight."

A glossiness mirrored in Mila's eyes. He could feel her closing up. Blake took her into a tender embrace.

"I watched you at the church, tending to everyone else's needs. Being the sort of woman Aunt Serenity always taught Zeenie to be and me and Isaac to search for. And you were fucking beautiful, even through tears, you were so damn gorgeous to me. I tried to wait for Agent Cynthia Taylor to put the pieces together, but I'm not that type of fucking guy. I couldn't just let someone mess with the company I built brick by brick. My only regret was being so damn captivated by you, so hypnotized—shit, I almost took you down on so many occasions before you met me with your business prerequisites. You gotta believe, that I exerted as much control, but not enough to wait for Cynthia to complete her work."

"So you had to have me," Mila murmured, her heart beat to his chest. She felt like heaven in his arms.

"The moment I set eyes on you, I fell for you Mila. I realized I have never truly loved anyone the way I love you."

Her body wracked with sobs in his arms. "C'mon Mila, don't cry, please don't fucking cry, I hate that I've caused you pain."

"Blake, I love you." He reached down, and his lips sought the missing piece of his sanity. She didn't meet him halfway. "But it's too late, Blake."

He glared at the tears streaming down her face. Where they indeed false? Mila claimed to bare her soul to him. But all along, after Diane had fucked with his heart, he'd been truthful with Mila the entire time. Trusting her, loving her, catering to Mila's need to get over a pivotal point in her life. Blake had no fears. He'd stepped out on faith while building his business. Being calculating had been a domino effect on his status. Being a billionaire? Well, that just solidified the fact that he didn't operate on fears.

"I'm at a place in my life where family is the most important to me, Blake. I've made promises to my father. You have regrets, I do too." Her tone was etched with sorrow. "But I just promised my father that I'd—"

"Mila," an elderly man's baritone voice cut through the bittersweet moment.

CHAPTER 41

Two Months Later

HE NEVER ARRIVED. The man Mila's father had hand-selected to marry Mila had never arrived.

During the course of two months that single moment in life took siege of Mila. Every moment she spent awake, every time she lay her head down to sleep, every instance that her mind wasn't busy, she thought about how Blake ruined her chance at complacency.

Warren Jameson once held the role. He was more than capable of latching onto a certain area of her heart—the space far-and-away, nowhere near the psychosis, the lunacy of falling… falling in love.

Then Mila mended her relationship with her father. He would save her from herself, from *Blake*. The man chosen by her father left the moment he saw Mila with Blake. Had her father's choice been inside the restaurant all along? Or was he one of the patrons who'd passed by while Mila stood outside arguing with Blake?

For 67 days, Mila alternated from depression and self-made contentment. But that was only during the dark of night or when she was alone. Just like the young woman who'd climbed mountains at Hewitt Corp, Mila kept busy. People's Love Project was being furnished with donations from Target and Ikea. Mila worked 40 hours a week at the bank, and another 20 hours spent with a

Bluetooth glued to her ear.

Today she wasn't can't-eat-or-sleep in love with Blake.

As Mila stepped toward the back offices of Addis International Bank, her cell phone vibrated. She answered.

"You're gonna hate me but," Yasmin began, the worst phrase anyone can say when a person is managing a broken heart. Their relationship had gone full circle, as Lido predicted. Not that the youngest and oldest had anticipated as much. Lido was always busy with modeling, and now her claws had sunk into the sexiest Spaniard under the spotlight, a world-renowned chef. Yasmin and Mila predicted she'd tear the guy's heart out.

"What happened?" Mila paused, stopping right at the inner-office door.

"Blame it all on your nephew, he got into a skateboarding accident," Yasmin sighed. "Do you know how much I wanted to meet you in Milan? Besides I'd begged and begged Faaid for this girls' vacation."

"Yeah, I know, Yas." Mila lifted the receiver slightly releasing a heavy exhale. She whispered while walking through the back offices. "Lido also needed to see us as a supportive figure in her life. That girl has major undiagnosed problems."

"I'm heading out to mail your birthday gift, Mila. I had to cancel the plane ticket. Faaid can't care for our son like I do, my baby's leg is broken."

"All right, I'm probably going to cancel mine also. Can't I just fall asleep, then wake up next week?" Mila pressed against the bar of the backdoor. She wasn't in a hurry to turn 32, and she wasn't interested in seeing another birthday pass. Warm sunlight enveloped her as Mila stepped outside.

"Girl, what do you mean wake up next week? Your birthday is in a few days. Look." Yasmin took on an authoritarian tone. "You're my *walaashay yar*, Mila. Stop this madness. This isn't circa 2006, Mila. I refuse to go back to the role of me talking till I'm blue in the darn face, about you working so hard at *that* stressful job. All for a friggen partnership, forget this quest for a heart attack. *Let me tell you something–*"

"Damn, I thought you were already telling me how you really feel, right out the gate."

"Humph, I haven't even started. You are going to be happy if I have to get on a plane for a turnaround trip, just getting off long enough to smack you upside the head."

"Upside?" Mila scoffed, taking a seat on the bench. Again a smile graced her flawless face. Twice in one day! Then her good luck continued, as Mila gazed at a mother and daughter. The child had to be about seven. The silkiest, sun-kissed sandy brown curls, with a bright smile. Mila imagined the two heading toward the *merkato,* the daughter beseeching her mother for something sweet.

"Yes! Two months ago, you ruined it with the man who should be holding you down at this very moment. I have the feeling you haven't smiled since I've last laid eyes on you, Mila. That hurts me to my heart."

Her eyes widened as Yasmin took flight, saying she knew her

baby sister wasn't happy. It took a minute but, Mila cut in. "Wait, what are you talking about. Yasmin, now you're talking out the side of your mouth! Don't you remember my arranged marriage? Hello! The guy probably walked toward the restaurant while I was outside gallivanting—"

"With Blake! The man father wanted you to be with."

A psychotic chuckle erupted from the pit of Mila's stomach. An elderly woman walking by turned toward the odd noise, her face wrinkled. There it was, the non-mastery of her emotions. Whatever Mila once felt for Keith had been kiddy *lust*. Pure stupidity on her end. True love, the crap she was currently submerged in, sucked! She needed to stay away from Blake. His eyes still lingered in her mind, along with the moment she chose to put her family first, and walked back into the restaurant.

Mila whispered, "Are you crazy?"

"Not at all. I realize that when you were with Blake, a lot of people had a hand in your relationship. Faces you've never seen were posting screenshots of the two of you on social media, magazines, Entertainment TV."

A thick note strangled in Mila's throat.

"Blake called me a long time ago, even before Lido did that stunt in the house. Let's see, it was before that one time us girls went to the movies. Didn't you think it weird me being so friendly toward him, during our conversation? I would have at least asked a rigorous battery of questions first. Blake was very intuitive during his chat with Faaid and I."

"Faaid?"

"Yes, Mila. As is our custom, he chatted with us both. He told me that we need to be more concerned about Lido. He knew the little shit was abusing alcohol, when all you or I do is try to cover for her. At first, you know me, can't nobody tell me about my sisters. They sure as hell can't tell me about blood. But I had this feeling he was more family oriented than I could give him credit for. Anywho, we chatted a bit."

"A bit?" Mila wanted to know the specifics verbatim, but the imaginary vise-grip to her neck didn't allow it. "Family Oriented." After meeting Isaac and Zenobia, Mila knew that regardless of the timeframe the three were as thick as thieves. She felt the same warmth seeping into her abdomen as she had when Blake spoke of his Aunt Serenity.

"Yes. He wanted to know why you didn't see father, and why Wednesdays weren't a good day to call. We chatted once again when you two were supposed to go to Italy, some other fancy countries by yacht, then you were going to end up in Ethiopia. Father was waiting for the both of you. He told me that he and father had a chat. The sort of chat that he knew our dad would keep quiet about until the right time…"

Mila thought that maybe Blake told her father about the hell Diane put Blake through.

"… Blake's really considerate you know," Yasmin said. "Now, we both know from the get-go that Blake didn't mess with Lido. No disrespect to our mother, that girl was born suspect. She's foul, but for whoever stoops down to Lido's level, then we're wrong. That's just how the cookie crumbles. Now, like I just said, Mila, at the restaurant you were supposed to invite Blake in."

Those words all but blew her away. "No, that can't be true. I chose family."

"Under any other circumstances…" Yasmin's voice seemed to fade as Mila stood, readjusting the cross-strap of her purse, walking with purpose.

"What about father?" Rushing, Mila teeter-tottered around a family, mumbling a quick Ethiopian apology.

"A genius in his own right, our father probably has saved more lives than he's had conversations with anybody on this earth. That's why you were his favorite, Mila, he could be bandaging little Hakeem's arm for the umpteenth time while you talked to other ailing patients. Our father, though so very intelligent, he lacks in his ability to addrcss cmotion. Hc said nothing when the two of you came back into the restaurant, but he expected you to choose. He is a very just man, Mila. I didn't have to marry Faaid. This doesn't mean I would have went against our father's wishes, no it would have just meant that Faaid wasn't the one for me. We knew each other as children, as you and Lido also knew the men you were supposed to marry in the past. Above all, dad wanted you to be happy."

"Yas, I gotta go.".

~~~

The last twenty-four hours were a blur. After calling Blake incessantly while grabbing just enough things for a flight, Mila bit
~~~

the bullet. Lamb had answered. She'd been surprised at his offer to send one of Blake's fleet of jets for her. He stated that Blake was with "the crew" in Nepal. She'd kindly declined, purchased the next, overpriced commercial flight to the Himalayan Mountains.

On the long flight, Mila ruminated over the past. *Blake never even complained...* After all was said and done, Mila had been the lukewarm one in their relationship. Not fulling trusting, not fully loving a man whose forest green's only gazed over her with positivity. She judged Blake's ass every chance she got.

Once Mila arrived, she became a sales person's dream, buying adequate clothing and climbing gear. The bus trip to one of the Annapurna villages took her past green pastures, Buddhist villages, and even more serene sights that didn't break through her haste.

On the ride up, Mila had questioned anyone within earshot who spoke English, Somali, or Ethiopian for a voyager. One English climbing group said that they wouldn't be climbing yet, but gave her the name of one of the well-known trekkers. The gorgeous mountain view before her was nonexistent, so as suggested by the group, she passed the ascetic yogi. Her lips chattered, and every other second she sniffled. A cold chill couldn't permeate through her being; she was only focused on *him*. After about thirty minutes of traveling about the various shops, Mila found the voyager. Mila quickly made her request.

"C'mon lady, you wanna climb the Annapurna Circuit?" All she could see of the voyager were his eyes. Ice and a clean sheet of snow dusted his jacket.

"Yes, and you can take me." The group who recommended him knew of her plight, and had said he was the best.

"No, ma'am," he said as she pulled money out of her purse.

She started to shovel out cash, even though it wasn't a respectable gesture. For the first time in Mila's life, she wasn't overthinking ways to get *out* of love with Blake. The only notion roaming through her was that Blake and his crew were a day and a half ahead of her.

"Excuse me, miss…" A man held up a few pieces of crumpled cash that had flown away.

She looked toward him, unsure that it was hers. Then she took the money from him and placed it back into one of the many compartments of her snow jacket. After a quick thanks, Mila tried to follow the voyager into the bar.

"You wanna climb Annapurna?" The man who'd helped return her money asked.

Mila glanced into the establishment. Heat along with savory food warmed her face and made her stomach grumble. The voyager wouldn't budge. She turned back to the man who'd helped her. Thick neck, super-athletic build, he had to be about five-six, because she was an inch taller in her new shoes, and eye level with him.

"Yeah."

"If I may, what's the highest mountain you've climbed?"

Her chin jutted out. He was sizing her up, but this might lead to a conversation about the nameless man helping her. "La Soufriére."

"Oh. Very, very big difference, I'm not even mentioning the

elevation. So how many days have you been here?"

"Are you going to help me or not?"

He chuckled. "There's nothing I'd like better than to help. But you should know that it takes a few days to become acclimated to Annapurna's change in elevation. Therefore, you probably wanna stay down here for another two days, probably more. If you wait longer, maybe whoever you're looking for comes back down. Saves you…" his eyes twinkled, and it was so very easy to read between the lines, "the trouble."

"Trust me, I can climb anything right now. I can't wait! I have to get up there and talk to him. I have to tell him that it's been me all along who wasn't confident enough in *us.* I have to tell him that I love him, that… that he means so much to me. That, I don't doubt us anymore, and nobody can come between what we have."

There. She'd gotten it all out. But the burly man obviously didn't understand. "You should also know that there are six peaks."

"Six?" From this angle, a plethora of clouds masked her view. There was no top, the end was unfathomable at this instance. However, an imaginary concoction had spurred Mila on. Panting at the thought of scouring each peak, Mila tried to recall that one morning long ago when Blake told her about the scar to his abdomen. Had he said which summit? She repeated the number.

"Yes, Miss…"

"Miss Ali, Mila Ali." She extended her gloved hand.

"Don't even try it," A hard, yet very familiar voice said from behind her.

CHAPTER 42

BLAKE SHOOK HIS head as he watched the exchange between Mila and Jace. The ass already knew exactly who she was. As Jace extended his hand to shake Mila's, he warned, "Don't even try it."

"Fuck me." Jace looked Mila up and down while she turned. "I'm Jace by the way, surely that doesn't matter now as does me climbing this mountain with your sexy ass."

Mila stared at Blake, her chest heaving. He could read her mind as their eyes latched onto each other. The dreamiest eyes in the world that haunted him for months.

Their relationship started with her running away… Mila had spurned him after their first night together. He assumed the woman who shunned his love would be reserved for those moments where he couldn't help but think about failed challenges. Mila had been the hardest of them all. Getting through college while hustling as a hacker, marrying Diane, building a billionaire empire from the ground up—none of those tasks were as challenging as *her*.

"How did you know I was here?"

"Lamb told us to postpone our climb yesterday. Then he sent me pin-drops for the last few hours. We've been on a wild goose chase. Lamb has been using this illegal system, I invented that the law refuses to pass, it has elements of stalking." Blake shook his head.

"Wait, that doesn't even fucking matter, Mila? Why are you standing there?"

"I…" She froze. Here was the hardest part. A pivotal point in her life. Again, he read her body language. Though layers of clothing adorned the woman that once belonged to him, Mila's pupils seemed to dilate with longing. "Blake, I've spent the last 24 hours thinking about all the things Diane put you through…"

In the end, Diane had a discrete court hearing at her request. In her mind, she wasn't attempting to frame Blake for murder. She wanted to hold any one of his employee's deaths over his head in the future so they couldn't divorce. It wasn't about the money. It was the principle. He believed her. And he also believed the bitch was hovering way out in oblivion, out of her fucking mind.

"Mila, you've fought me tooth and nail. All I've ever done was try to love you in the past." Blake broke through the image of her stepping back into the restaurant with her father. She'd abandoned him.

Just like his mother, Mila left him with his heart on his sleeve.

Now they were in frigid air. This moment almost comparable to the winters in St. Louis, with his mother choosing the streets, or drugs, or even worse… pimping herself out for his father.

"Blake, baby, I was scared to give you my heart. Even still, you have become my best friend, Blake. I've told you my deepest darkest secrets, desires. You're interwoven into every day of my life, Blake. The way you put me first, the way you've always loved me…"

He wanted to tell his crew to get lost, but Blake needed to hear these words. She'd hurt him to his core. All that bullshit about not giving a shit about what anyone thought. It was true, for the masses, Blake could care less about their opinion. But with Mila Ali, any notion in her mind, any manner in which she looked at him, he *once* took all of that to heart.

Her eyes slid across all of his friends, then back on him. "Blake, can't you at least forgive me? That's all I need."

"Forgiven."

She seemed to deflate even further. "Okay, okay, I get it. It's too late. I've ruined us. Nobody on God's green earth had the capability to come between us. I just didn't trust you enough nor gave you the chance."

He spoke, each syllable calculated to perfection. "Yeah, well, I did all I could to gain your trust, given the circumstances. But don't you think the same apology could have been given by a phone call?"

"Blake, you sound as if you could give a fuck about me right now. Okay, I understand, I was stupid to come here. Even still, my mind is warped enough to believe that your voice is my favorite sound. The taste of your lips, has marinated in black maple bourbon you're always drinking. I miss that."

"Oh, you miss that?" Blake's lips hardly moved. "You're warped beliefs, eh? Let me tell you what I once believed. You and your beauty, all of you were designed to belong to me. That you were so fucking magnificently fashioned by God that only I could adorn you with jewels, with trinkets to match your beauty." He watched as Mila continued to sink before him. "But that is not the case, Miss

Ali. None of my billions can embellish what you have. I still fucking love you, actually even more than I did on day one! You're a serenity that—"

Mila leaped into his arms.

His crew began to clap and whoop.

"Yuck." Jace clapped his hands. "Which one of these two were the mushiest?"

Mila's warm body fit perfectly in Blake's arms. "Damn it, Mila. The first thing I asked was why you were just standing there. All I wanted was a hug. Now the guys will be talking shit for decades to come."

Blake held Mila at arm's length. "Now we both aren't entirely acclimated to this elevation. Let's not go into another monologue. I just need to kiss those gorgeous fucking lips…"

Author's Note:

It took sheer willpower, on my part, not to make Blake Baldwin a murderer. Whew, I just had to say that! What a perfect literary device Bad Boy Billionaire Blake Baldwin… uhhh, maybe I've gone too far and that was just corny?

Thank you so much for reading The Good Mistress! It is the beginning of my newest publication Blu Savant Press. Please review, on **Amazon**, feel free to rate on **Goodreads**. Heck, if you add a review there too I'd be grateful. Recommend it, tell a friend!

Stay tuned COVER REVAL for *Heavy Love: A BBW Destination Romance* is on the very next page! The story is set in Northern Spain.

Stay Blessed!

And last but not least, the contest to thank my readers is last, so continue scrolling…

Contact me:

For book updates and tidbits please '*like*' my

Facebook **Fan Page**

For eye candy, good company, and exclusive teasers, please join my group **Amarie Avant's Aroused**

Friend me on **Facebook**

Tweet with me

I'm not too proud to beg for reviews/ratings on … **Goodreads** LOL

HEAVY Love: A BBW Destination Romance

I have drooled all over this cover!

Just a little more about the book. I began to write wrote *HEAVY Love* even before writing the FEAR series. An abundance of emotion went into this storyline. Each time I sifted through this manuscript, I nurtured it like a child of mine. *HEAVY Love* should make you laugh, scream (in a good actress Diane Keaton kinda way), angry, or heck, consider throwing your Kindle…

Perhaps, don't through your Kindle.

This March 2016, befriend a curvy relationship therapist Angelique Curtis who just can't seem to get it right in her own relationship; and *fall in love with* a force like Franco de León. The book blurb will be posted on my **Fan Page** on Friday, February 19, 2016.